In the bright light, his eyes were the same deep shade as his shirt...

Reid looked so good, so solid, so...*Reid*. Heidi stumbled and the tote slipped down her arm, landing on the floor.

Reid tilted his head. "Are you okay?"

"Of course. I'm always good."

He sent her a knowing look.

"I just have a lot on my plate. No big deal."

"Maybe you should slow down."

So she would have more time to spend with her ridiculous romantic thoughts? *No, thank you.*

"I'll be fine. Thanks for being concerned."

"That's what friends do."

Ah, the final nail in the coffin. It was official. Reid did not have romantic feelings for her.

This is good, she told herself. Now she could move on. Get back on track. Look at Reid as her ol' buddy, not the hunky contractor who'd been causing her to daydream way too often. "You're right," she confirmed. "We are friends."

There. She'd made a public declaration...one she wouldn't take back.

Dear Reader,

I couldn't be more excited about my new series, The Golden Matchmakers Club. There's nothing more fun—or frustrating, depending on your point of view—than dealing with a group of busybodies who're sure they have all the answers to solve the love lives of the young people in town. You know laughter and high jinks are about to ensue!

Another reason I love starting a new series is because we get to meet new characters and, in this case, catch up with couples from previous books. There were so many wonderful secondary characters who needed their own stories told, so I'm thrilled that I get to make their happily-ever-afters come true.

Golden has been the backdrop for two books and will now star as the focal point of each story. My most favorite place on earth is the North Georgia mountains, the inspiration for the new books. To me, Golden is a very real place. I hope, after reading the books, you feel the same way, too.

As always, happy reading!

Tara

HEARTWARMING

Stealing Her Best Friend's Heart

—

Tara Randel

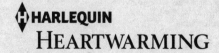

ISBN-13: 978-1-335-42636-9

Stealing Her Best Friend's Heart

Copyright © 2021 by Tara Spicer

Recycling programs for this product may not exist in your area.

This is a work of fiction. Names, characters, places and incidents are either the product of the author's imagination or are used fictitiously. Any resemblance to actual persons, living or dead, businesses, companies, events or locales is entirely coincidental.

This edition published by arrangement with Harlequin Books S.A.

For questions and comments about the quality of this book, please contact us at CustomerService@Harlequin.com.

Harlequin Enterprises ULC
22 Adelaide St. West, 40th Floor
Toronto, Ontario M5H 4E3, Canada
www.Harlequin.com

Printed in U.S.A.

Tara Randel is an award-winning *USA TODAY* bestselling author. Family values, a bit of mystery and, of course, love and romance are her favorite themes, because she believes love is the greatest gift of all. Tara lives on the west coast of Florida, where gorgeous sunsets and beautiful weather inspire the creation of heartwarming stories. This is her tenth book for Harlequin Heartwarming. Visit Tara at tararandel.com. Like her on Facebook at Tara Randel Books.

Books by Tara Randel

Harlequin Heartwarming

Meet Me at the Altar

Always the One
Trusting Her Heart
His Honor, Her Family
The Lawman's Secret Vow

Visit the Author Profile page
at Harlequin.com for more titles.

To all the wonderful Harlequin Heartwarming readers. Thank you so much for reading our books every month. We couldn't do this without you!

PROLOGUE

PERCHED IN A high-back armchair located in the formal living room of Masterson House, Gayle Ann Masterson crossed her legs. The comforting scents of lemon furniture polish and peach pie filled the air, along with the creaks and groans that came with the century-old dwelling.

Gayle Ann loved this house. Loved the stories encompassing the generations of Mastersons who had lived in the large two-story Greek revival-style home. She'd become a wife and mother under this roof, learning about love, sharing happiness and mourning loss. Grew into a strong woman, who knew her mind but never compromised her compassion for others. This was the homestead of her family, even if she had married into the lot. If the walls could talk, she wondered what they'd say. Especially once she finished with the upcoming conversation.

She smoothed a wrinkle from her pink suit

skirt, and said, "Welcome to the first meeting of the Golden Matchmakers Club."

The only other person in the room snorted. "Really, Alveda. Is that necessary?"

Alveda Richards sent Gayle Ann a dubious glance. "It's just the two of us in here."

"We have to start somewhere, don't we? Besides, I'm sure I can get Bunny Wright to join us for the next meeting. She's running out of patience with her nephews for taking their sweet time to settle down."

"Next meeting? Aren't you getting ahead of yourself?"

"No. And you should be looking for others to recruit if we want to get this club up and running."

Alveda crossed thin, aged arms over her chest. "I'm not even sure I'm in."

Gayle Ann's voice softened. "Remember, we're doing this for Heidi. She's such a lovely young lady, but she's so hesitant to get involved with anyone. I hate to see her living life all alone."

"So do I." Alveda pulled a tissue from the pocket of her worn apron and worried it in her fingers. "We've had plenty of conversations about this, but she's as stubborn as they come."

"But not opposed?"

Alveda tilted her head, thinking through her

answer before speaking. "No. Deep down, I believe she wants a lasting relationship and a family of her own."

"She did have a chaotic childhood. It wasn't until after you took her in that she finally found a place where she was safe."

"She's got moxie for sure." Pride shone in Alveda's eyes. "The way she grew up has a hold on her no matter how much she's overcome. But she's an amazing young woman."

"And," Gayle Ann said, unable to contain a grin, "I think she'd make a certain young man a wonderful partner."

Alveda rolled her eyes. "Your younger grandson?"

"Reid should be with someone too, even if he steadfastly insists on remaining single."

"I don't know." Alveda shook her head, doubt tingeing her words. "You're asking a lot by meddling in these two young'uns' lives, no matter how well-meaning."

"If we don't, who will?"

A pleading expression crossed Alveda's lined face. "We could always leave their futures to themselves."

This time it was Gayle Ann's turn to snort. "Since they've been doing a bang-up job on their own?"

Alveda chuckled. "There is that."

A montage of images of years past formed in Gayle Ann's mind. "Remember how Heidi tried to run off every gal I flung in Reid's way during cotillion season until there was no one left but her? They were supposedly in on besting me together, but maybe subconsciously she wanted Reid for herself."

"Sounds like a convoluted excuse for interfering."

"Who better than the women who love Heidi and Reid to get them together?"

"Just because you inadvertently helped match Logan with Serena, don't let it go to your head."

Gayle Ann waved off the compliment, because she did consider her…dating assistance… a personal victory. After all, her older grandson was engaged.

"It worked," she boasted as a gentle breeze drifted into the room. The strong scent of hair spray lifted in the current, tickling her nose. She'd been to the salon this morning for her weekly wash and curl, keeping her white hair from getting out of control. Gayle Ann liked everything in its proper place, from her hair to her grandsons.

She turned serious. "Alveda, consider it. Heidi and Reid are already friends, which is a solid way to start a relationship. Under the right circumstances, if we get them to see the possibilities in each other, they might want to date. And from there…who knows?" She shrugged her shoulders and hoped she at least sounded innocent.

Alveda scratched her head. Strands of wavy gray hair escaped her bun. "That's an idea, all right," came her dry reply.

Gayle Ann frowned. "Are you always going to throw the brakes on my ideas?"

"Woman, if it wasn't for my firm hand, there's no telling what kind of hot water you'd get yourself into on a daily basis."

True.

Gayle Ann stared Alveda down. "We've known each other going on fifty years. I was an unsure newlywed when I hired you as cook at Masterson House. What did I know about hiring staff? But from the moment we met, we became fast friends."

Gayle Ann had appreciated Alveda's tell-it-like-it-is attitude. Alveda was surprised and pleased by Gayle Ann's loyalty. They'd been through it all together; from watching the Masterson children and grandchildren grow, to sharing the pain of losing their spouses, to navigating the twilight years with dignity, but never without lots of fun.

"Say I want in," Alveda said, a cagey sparkle in her eyes. "What's my position?"

"Technically, you're a cofounder."

"From one conversation over coffee when we lamented the fact that our loved ones were still single?"

"That title is as good as it gets."

"Fine," Alveda huffed.

The two had sat at the round table in the remodeled kitchen at Masterson House, wondering out loud what would become of Golden, Georgia, if more tourists didn't visit the area and those who'd been born here didn't stay. For years the Chamber of Commerce had been working to make this pristine location a premier vacation destination. In the past few years, there had been events, parades, new businesses launched and rental properties updated, all with the intent to draw vacationers and their hard-earned dollars to this beautiful part of the northern Georgia mountains.

As it happened, in one of their daily conversations, Alveda had mentioned a project Heidi was involved in while Gayle Ann had been worrying over Reid walking away from Masterson Enterprises, the family business. He needed someone to share his life with, she'd said. Someone to give him focus. Direction. Teach him that while life may not be fair, love conquered all. Gayle Ann believed Heidi was that person.

"Look," Gayle Ann went on. "If we don't try, this club will never get going. Besides, you were on board when I first came up with the idea."

"I was, but knowing Heidi, she won't be happy if we interfere in her life. You know how closed off she can be. No child should have to grow up how she did." Alveda paused. "Heidi has loosened up over the years, but if pushed?" She frowned. "It won't end well."

"Reid won't be happy either, so we have to be stealthy. We have to—" Gayle Ann waved her hand as she searched for the right explanation "—guide them…without them catching on to what we're doing."

Alveda raised an eyebrow. "Reid's not going to notice?"

"Of course, he is."

Exasperation crossed Alveda's face. "Then what's the point?"

A smile that always meant trouble ahead curved Gayle Ann's lips upward. "We just have to be sneaky, that's all."

Silence fell over the stately living room as the two sat contemplating the match. A gust of fresh air ruffled the sheer curtains hanging over the open windows. The scent of colorful flowers blooming so brightly this spring wafted into the room.

Suddenly, Gayle Ann snapped her fingers. "Logan and Serena's engagement party is coming up. Since Reid is already suspicious about me trying to marry him off, why don't I suggest he bring a date? Prepare a list of single women? That won't seem suspicious because he'll already expect it." Her mind turned and she smiled at her next thought. "Heidi has her math tutoring group at the community center and Reid is teaching woodworking there. I heard the groups meet on the same night. All we have to do is nudge him in her direction."

"I don't know." Alveda didn't look convinced. "They've always been friends. Do you think they'll fall for each other after all this time?"

Gayle Ann sat up straight, confident in her answer. "With the right motivation, I believe they will."

CHAPTER ONE

HEIDI WELCH NAVIGATED her practical silver sedan along the picturesque winding road on her way to downtown Golden. The tires hissed over asphalt still wet from the early morning rain. Spring wildflowers dotted the secluded roadside, tender leaves popped out on bare tree branches and parks were calling out to hikers and day visitors to stop and enjoy nature. She opened her window to drink in the cool, clean air. Just one of the many perks of living in such a breathtaking mountain location.

From the first time Heidi had stopped in Golden with her mother, she'd been entranced. When she'd finally declared herself free from her mother and needed a place to live, the fear and nervousness of hitchhiking to Golden had been tempered by the fact that she could imagine herself here permanently. The constant couch-surfing lifestyle mastered by her carefree and job-averse mother had taken its toll.

Her phone rang. She activated the Bluetooth.

"This is Heidi."

"And this is Alveda. You forgot your sweater."

Nothing like getting right to the point.

"No problem. I can pick it up another time."

Alveda's voice faded in and out as she talked. "You might need it."

"It's a beautiful day, so stop worrying. Besides, I'm almost at work."

In ten minutes she'd start her Monday morning by taking her place behind the counter at Blue Ridge Cottage, a stationery store on Main Street and her part-time job. Once that shift was over, she'd return to her apartment to put forth her efforts into her full-time business, her growing accounting firm. Yes, she worked a lot of hours, and yes, she intended on capitalizing on those hours to make her dreams come true. The future looked rosy, as Alveda loved to tell her, even if Heidi wasn't completely aboard that bandwagon.

The older woman spoke again but Heidi couldn't hear her. "Alveda, hold the phone to your mouth and stand still, for Pete's sake."

"Can you hear me now?" she yelled.

Heidi cringed. "Loud and clear."

"Are you almost at work?"

"Yep. Just a few minutes away."

"Hmm." A pause. "And have you driven down Hanover Lane?"

"Why would you ask?"

"From what you've told me, it's your usual route."

"Not today."

"Are you sure? You still haven't put a bid on the house."

Heidi bit her lip.

"Never mind," Alveda said. "Didn't mean to push."

Sure, she didn't.

The sun was just rising over the tree line as she zeroed in on Hanover Lane. Unable to resist Alveda's suggestion, Heidi made a sudden detour. Darn it, the woman was always right.

"We never finished talking about the party," Alveda continued as if their conversation about the house never happened.

"Serena has it under control so there's nothing to do."

Heidi flipped on her blinker and turned right, tires squealing, to cruise by the house of her dreams. *Cottage* was probably a more correct term, but after Alveda's question, she wanted to make sure the for-sale sign was still posted in the front yard as it had been for the month it had been on the market. She'd been weighing her options about buying the house and property since the sign went up, but finally worked up the nerve to call the listing agent only last week. They kept playing phone tag, but Heidi was sure once they spoke, Lisa would be thrilled by Heidi's sincere interest.

"I can't for the life of me understand why Serena didn't ask me to provide the food for her engagement party," Alveda groused, just as she had in the Masterson kitchen this morning when Heidi stopped by for breakfast.

"You're a guest."

"Don't think I can just show up and do nothing."

"Look at it as a learning experience."

Alveda huffed in response.

When the house came into view, she shivered in anticipation. "Me, a homeowner," she whispered to the empty car, then chuckled. Her mother would be so disappointed.

"What did you say?"

"Nothing, Alveda."

For a year now, she'd daily checked the local real estate listing app, keeping a lookout for the perfect place to call home. Golden had left a mark on her, even at a young age. She'd been fourteen at the time, but some things you knew deep in your soul, no matter the timing. A house would seal the deal.

"You *are* driving by that house again, aren't you?"

"What, do you have spies following me?"

"No. I just know what owning that place would mean to you."

Of all the people in her life, Alveda understood how important this commitment was to Heidi.

At first, she'd hesitated about making an offer. Because her mother had branded into her consciousness the mistake of settling down? Probably. But Alveda had encouraged her, giving Heidi the confidence to go for her dream.

Heidi blurted her misgivings. "Are you sure this is a good idea?"

"I didn't teach you to be a quitter," Alveda said, steel in her tone.

That was true.

As much as Heidi wanted a house, the idea of homeownership was daunting. Could she do it? Maintain a house? Make it into the home she'd never had growing up? She normally didn't let the little details stop her, so why now?

She'd saved up a generous down payment, thanks to years of living frugally. She'd already figured out she could afford the monthly payments. Her best friend and part-time boss at the stationery store, Serena, kept telling her the place was perfect and she should give it a go. Give it a go? Was she ready for the responsibility?

Then she thought about the matchbox apartment she'd been renting and decided, yeah, she'd give it a go. So, she'd taken a bracing breath and called the agent, first for a walk-through, then trying to reach Lisa to make an offer.

Heidi's stomach still tumbled a bit over her bold move, but she ignored it. She was ready for the one thing she'd wanted for as long as she could remember: stability. And that came in the form of owning four walls and a roof.

"You're right, as usual."

"Not right, just sure about you, Heidi."

Her heart squeezed. How on earth had she gotten so lucky to have this woman in her corner? Determined, she decided that as soon as she got to work, she'd call Lisa again. If the call went to voice mail, like it had the last two times, Heidi would march over to the office and insist they sit down and nail out the details on the spot.

Dappled sunlight filtered through the thick canopy of mature trees lining the pavement. She loved this neighborhood, how the area was well established with families whose

children roamed the streets on bicycles or re-
tirees who labored to keep the landscaping
well tended. Excitement rushed over her as
she motored down Hanover Lane—she loved
the regal name—anticipation curling in her
belly. Almost there. Halfway down the road,
she slammed on the brakes.

"Alveda, I've got to go."

"Call me later, you hear?"

"I will," Heidi answered and ended the call.
She stared at the sign, outraged, and yelled,
"You've got to be kidding me!"

Someone had slapped a sale-pending strip
across the for-sale sign.

She nearly lost all the oxygen in her lungs.
Someone had made an offer on *her* house?
Okay, technically it wasn't hers, but in her
heart she'd already decorated the interior.
Painted the faded exterior. Made improvements. Yes, there was work needed. Could that
be why she'd been dragging her feet? And look
where that had gotten her.

Reality was like a punch to the gut. Especially when she noticed an empty pickup sitting in the driveway. She narrowed her eyes.
The owner was about to get an earful.

As if on cue, a man walked out of the front
door. Dressed in a black T-shirt, worn jeans
and work boots, his impressive muscles on

display, he appeared ready to take on the total renovation of this house. Not on her watch. Shaking out of her daze, Heidi pulled the car to the curb, put the gearshift in Park and turned off the engine. In her haste to make her displeasure known, she jumped out of the car and dropped her keys. She muttered to herself as she picked them up, then sped to the interloper, ready to demand answers, then stopped short when she recognized the guy.

"Reid?"

His puzzled expression cleared as recognition dawned in his eyes. "Oh, hey, Heidi."

No wonder she hadn't recognized him at first. The Reid she knew usually wore a fancy suit and tie, all business. Now that they were closer, the familiar wide shoulders, tanned skin and green eyes lighting when he smiled reached her brain. She couldn't believe her luck, or lack thereof. Reid Masterson standing here only meant one thing, and that one thing wasn't good for her future.

"What are you doing here?" she demanded as she stormed up the inclined path to face the dream killer.

"Good morning to you too," came his wry reply.

She pointed to the sign. "Really, Reid. What gives?"

"I bought the place."

Through town gossip, she'd heard that he'd started buying and fixing up houses after leaving the family business. She hadn't seen him much since last fall when he first went into this new line of work.

The enormity of that new line of work hit her. Her heart sank with dread. "Are you flipping *this* house?" If this house was just one of the many he turned around for a profit, he was about to learn that some things were more important than money.

"That's the plan." He cocked his head to the side. "Problem?"

"Yes. I've been trying to touch base with the agent to put in an offer."

He shrugged, the snug T-shirt pulling against his broad chest. "Guess I beat you to it."

Grrr. If he wasn't an old friend…

She'd known Reid since middle school, though they'd grown apart as adults. They ran into each other at town events, said a rushed hello after their group meetings at the community center, but Reid had always had an eye for business and was destined to run Masterson Enterprises when his father stepped down. Heidi wasn't sure what had happened to alter Reid's course; all she knew was the ripple had affected her goal to buy this very property.

"Is there any way you can get out of the sale?"

A confused frown wrinkled his brow. "Why would I do that?"

"So I can buy it."

Confusion turned to incredulity. "Heidi, in case you haven't noticed, this is a perfect house to flip and sell. I can make money here."

"Yes, I have noticed. That's why I wanted to buy it."

"It's been on the market for a month. You had plenty of time to make a deal."

She had, and the fact that she'd ruined her chances made her want to kick herself all the more. Why couldn't the Realtor have answered when she called?

"This is unbelievable," she muttered.

She turned her attention to the one-story white house with faded and slightly off-kilter red shutters. Her heart pinched at the front door needing a good paint job. Actually, the entire exterior needed a fresh makeover to give the dreary structure life. Placing a hand as a shield over her eyes, she squinted as sunlight reflected off the large living room window. The number one item on her list to put any house in ownership contention was windows. Lots of them, letting in plenty of natural light. She hated the dark. This house passed the first and most important check mark for her, which was why she could see herself living here.

Puffing out a frustrated sigh, she said, "Reid, is there anything I can do to make you change your mind?"

"Sorry, Heidi. I already closed the deal. The bank cashed my down payment."

She pointed over her shoulder with her thumb. "But the sign?"

"The Realtor hasn't sent anyone to collect it."

So, that's it? She'd lost her dream?

She'd been collecting paint chips since she first walked through the house, had visited online home-decorating sites with a wish list of items to buy. Her favorite was a blue-and-white comforter set for the queen-size bed she owned, the only brand-new piece of furniture she'd ever bought. She'd pictured painting the bedroom a very light shade of blue, a relaxing color for her sanctuary, buying the bed set and adding white sheers over the windows. She'd seen a DIY video on how to turn mason jars into lamps and had already imagined she'd hang them over an old-fashioned makeup table in the corner.

Don't get her started on the kitchen upgrade.

"There are other properties for sale in Golden,"

Reid said, his expression sympathetic. "I'm sure you can find another property."

"No," she said in a quiet voice as she stared at the house situated on top of the hill. "This was the one for me."

How many days had she dreamed of living here? Sinking roots deep into the rich soil. Providing a home for Mr. Whiskers. Not that the curmudgeonly old cat cared, but she did. It was everything she'd never had growing up. She couldn't lose it now. She was so close.

"C'mon," he countered. "It's just a house."

"Maybe to you."

She wanted to get angry with him, but defeat had stolen all her energy. Had her mother been right? That homeownership was not in the cards for the Welch women?

"Heidi, I'm really sorry, but I have plans for this place."

Yeah, fix it up, sell it and move on. She understood about making money, since she was an accountant who could spot a good business plan, but not when it cost her what she desired most. Security. Safety. Permanence.

Not giving up, Heidi pulled out her phone. "How about I transfer the cost of the down payment to you and I can take over." She looked up at his stunned expression. "Do you have Venmo? PayPal?"

"Heidi, I'm not doing that."

She dropped her hand.

"Instead, why don't I give Lisa a call," Reid said, brandishing his phone. "She can get busy searching other properties for you."

"Don't bother. I… I need to regroup."

And regroup she would. On the positive side, there was always the chance that Reid would sell her the house when he was finished, but then the price was sure to rise. She'd have to recalculate all the numbers. Still, if she nailed down a few more clients…

She was already booked solid as it was. Worked too many hours a day. Living in this house was going to be the reason she slowed down and enjoyed life, even if it entailed tackling the scraggly landscaping herself. And other numerous projects too. She'd been ready to push up her sleeves and get dirty. Literally. Reid had ruined all that.

She glanced at his face. He wasn't backing down, if that don't-try-me expression was any indication. Just like Reid to dig his heels in. She shouldn't be surprised; he'd been like this forever. They'd always been friends, but there were times they'd also been intense rivals. It was all or nothing for him. Of all the people in town, why did it have to be Reid to buy the house?

So caught up in wallowing in self-pity, she almost missed the mental light bulb when it clicked over her head. She could dig her heels in just like any stubborn Masterson. Rubbing her hands together in glee, she ignored the fact that her idea might not work, but she would debate the merits after Reid gave in.

His eyes narrowed. "What's going on in that head of yours?"

Oh, yeah, he should be concerned.

"Okay, so, since you bought the place, I'm assuming you have big plans?"

"Yes. Not a total gut, but a few walls are coming down. Totally new kitchen and bathrooms. This house is pretty dated."

Which had given it the Southern charm she'd first fallen in love with.

"And you're going to sell it when you're finished?"

He sent her a what's-up-with-you? look. "Like I always do."

She squared her shoulders. "I have a proposal."

Surprise flared in his eyes, but it quickly extinguished, leaving him with an unreadable expression. "There's nothing to propose. I own the house."

"Yes, but I'm still determined to buy it."

He crossed toned arms over his chest,

stretching the already snug T-shirt. "Well, once I put it on the market."

"But then the price will shoot up." She bit her lower lip before going for it. "How about I help you with the remodel? Put in sweat equity toward the purchase of the finished product?"

He stared at her for such a long moment, she thought maybe he didn't understand what she'd asked.

Finally, he broke the tension between them. "Heidi, I have a team I work with. Subcontractors who actually know what they're doing."

Okay, her forte was numbers, not craftsmanship, but she had a passion for this house that his usual crew didn't. "Are you saying I can't hammer a nail? Paint a wall? Run errands or do odd jobs?" She'd never really done those things, but desperate times called for desperate measures.

He ran a hand over his scruffy chin, also not very Reid-like. Usually he was clean-shaven to go along with the *GQ* look. But hey, her entire world was off its axis since this shift in plans, so why wouldn't an alternate Reid exist too?

"Why not wait until I'm finished and put in an offer like most people?"

"Two reasons."

He made a hurry-up gesture with his hand. "This I gotta hear."

"One, like I said, the cost will go up after you make improvements."

"Yes, and if I barter you for your work, I won't make a profit."

She paused, trying to come up with a counter-argument.

"Face it," Reid continued, "if you bought the house as is, you'd have some projects to do to make the place more habitable."

"Which brings me to my second point. If I was remodeling with you, I'd have a say in colors and textures and any major design changes. I can't do that after the fact."

He regarded her with his savvy gaze, his green eyes probing. She shifted, not liking anyone sizing her up, but she held her ground.

"Who's to say your suggestions are feasible?"

"We won't know unless we try."

"You're making this hard on me, Heidi."

"My intentions, exactly." She grinned.

WHY, REID SILENTLY questioned the universe as he stared at the persistent woman standing in front of him. The brilliant sunlight picked out highlights in her ash-brown hair, her amber eyes glittered with intensity. Heidi at her fiery best. Her bold outfit of a bright red dress and black ankle boots fit her personality.

He swallowed a groan. All he wanted to do was flip this house and make a profit. Move on to the next project without any problems. He'd had enough conflict when he'd worked for his father, so working on his own had been nice. Peaceful even. Until Heidi had turned up, determined to throw a wrench in his plans.

With a sigh, he ran a hand over his thick hair. He didn't need a partner, even one as perky as Heidi. He worked mostly alone for a reason and intended on keeping it that way.

Your brother was supposed to take my place.

His father's words echoed in his head. Reid tried to shake them off, but as usual, the words clattered around his brain. No matter how many times his brother, Logan, told their father he wasn't interested in running Masterson Enterprises, a real estate and commercial construction company, their father pushed. Why, when he had a son who wanted to run the family business? Had wanted it since the first time his dad had brought him to the office.

"This is something you have to see through. You can't just do it a day or two and then claim it's not working for you," he told her.

"It seems to be working for you."

If only.

Reid remembered the day he'd thought of as

his destiny as clearly as if it happened yesterday. His father had asked him to come downtown. At eight years old, Reid had dressed in the suit his mother had bought him for Easter Sunday service, made sure his shoes were shined and managed a halfway decent knot in his tie. Not the clip-on kind, the real deal. Even then he'd had a thing for professional business attire.

"This is vastly different from the stationery store or bookkeeping."

Heidi refused to budge.

He sighed. The most important lesson he'd learned in the intervening years was that dreams didn't always come true. Heidi needed to get the memo too.

"Heidi, I appreciate your enthusiasm, but this isn't a good plan."

Her lower lip jutted out in a way that warned Reid she was nothing but trouble. "Why not?"

Wow, she was tenacious. "I told you. I have a crew."

"So sign me up."

"So you can work when, in between clients or shifts at the store?"

"Okay, that may be problematic, but I can sort it out."

Birds chirped overhead as Reid watched her animated face. The fire lighting her soul reminded him that he hadn't been passionate about anything for a long time now. Not since the day he'd gotten that first glimpse of his father's massive desk in the huge private office. Reid had been hooked from that moment on. He'd planned his future so that he'd end up taking over that office one day.

How he wished he could find his way to that simple time again.

Shaking off his disappointment, he focused on the problem at hand. "I hate to say it, but you'd most likely be in the way."

Heidi jammed her hands on her hips, the skirt of her dress twirling around her tanned legs. "Reid Masterson, you will not throw the inexperience card at me. Not after the times I kept your grandmother from matching you up with those society girls at her fancy parties."

Figured she'd bring that up.

"You enjoyed messing with her plans as much as I did," he countered.

"But I didn't have to help you."

True, she hadn't, but at the time, he was thankful she did.

Reid didn't know much about her childhood, just that she'd shown up on Alveda's doorstep, a small cottage located on the vast expanse of the Masterson property, when they were in middle school. The details were never revealed, and he respected her enough not to push. He'd gotten to know her because Heidi hung around the kitchen in Masterson House, where he grew up. They'd been friends, then accomplices concerning his grandmother, during their shared summers. During the school year, academic adversaries. After he'd gone away to college, they'd only crossed paths every now and again.

"Now that your brother is engaged," Heidi said, "you know your grandmother will have her sights set on you."

He ground his molars. "Please don't remind me." It was the truth, but he'd figure out how to dodge that bullet, right after he convinced Heidi that he didn't need help with the renovation of this house. "You'll have to come up with something better than once interfering with Grandmother's plans."

He watched Heidi and could imagine the wheels in her head turning quickly. Scary and impressive. "What about the night you and your dad had that big argument? You were ready to do something stupid until I stopped you."

She was really going there?

Yes, it had been a terrible fight. His dad had been all over him about striking out in the championship baseball game. His error had caused Golden High School the state title. That night, both had said things they couldn't take back. Reid had stormed from the house, only to literally run into Heidi on the driveway when she'd been leaving the kitchen. He was hurt, furious, not thinking straight, and she knew it. Seeing him in that state, she wrestled his keys from him and told him if he was going to do something life altering, she'd be the one behind the wheel. He'd never know if her intervention had stopped him from making a fatal mistake, like getting in a wreck on the twisty mountain roads, but he did owe her for possibly saving his life.

When he didn't speak, she said, "Sorry. I shouldn't have brought that up."

"No, you shouldn't have."

They stood in awkward silence for a drawn-out moment before Heidi got back on track.

"I'm a fast learner," she threw in as a final salvo.

She was. Actually, he wondered if she'd ever had her IQ tested because she was extremely smart. Beat him at every scholarly event at school, and he was no slouch.

Intelligence aside, and the fact that he did owe her, he couldn't get her hopes up. "Fast learner doesn't mean you can handle tools. When was the last time you used a hammer?"

She got that steely glint in her eyes, the one that showed up when challenged. "I built a bed for Mr. Whiskers."

He tried to hide the twitch of a smile. Heidi didn't have one ounce of whimsy in her body, yet she'd adopted a cat named Mr. Whiskers.

"And how did that project come out?" he asked, pretty sure of her answer.

She murmured, "After I removed the nail to detach the piece of wood from my living room floor, things got better."

He rubbed his temple. "How about a wrench?"

"I handed one to Mr. Donaldson once when he fixed my sink."

At least she knew what it looked like.

"You're forgetting," she countered. "I joined in to paint that mascot mural on the side of the high school."

"Yeah, because someone drew the design beforehand and you filled it in like a paint-by-number."

"Hey! I did a good job. And knowing what's at stake here, I'll be the best painter you've ever hired."

He had to admit, she had gotten into that school project, putting in the most hours of anyone.

"Granted I have a few things to learn," she went on, "but who better to show me the ropes than you? You teach those kids down at the community center. Just think of me as one of your students."

He set his jaw. "Heidi, I'm running a business."

"How about an intern then?"

"In a profession you don't have any desire to work in?"

She pulled her shoulders up to her ears and held her hands out at her sides.

Give me patience.

"Reid, I'm serious here."

He looked past her to the house. It wasn't anything grand or fancy. It was dated, worn and needed a lot of attention. The structure sort of sagged under his critical eye, but he knew once he was finished with the final touches, it would appeal to a serious buyer.

Then he peered down the street. The neighborhood was full of decent, hardworking people. A place to raise a family, if you wanted that sort of thing. Not that Heidi had ever confided that *she* wanted the whole family thing. So why was she trying so hard to talk him into sweat equity?

To him, a house represented profit, a business transaction. Once he finished a project, he contacted the listing agent and stepped aside until he received a check for the asking price. Then he moved on, never putting any personal stake in a project. Getting personal meant getting hurt and he avoided that at all costs.

Heidi kept talking. "Look, I promise not to get in the way. I'll do as I'm told. Be a team player."

To that claim, he groaned.

"As much of a team player as possible," she revised with a sheepish look, which boded ill for him.

"And what if you don't like a certain design choice?"

"I'll politely ask what you're doing, then give you my point of view."

Great. "What if you disagree with the color scheme."

"I'll gently guide you in the right direction."

He hid the hint of a smile. "What if we can't come to terms on a selling price?"

"That's what Realtors are for."

"You have all the answers, don't you?"

She lifted one shoulder, her golden earrings flashing in the sunlight. "I pride myself on being quick on my feet."

That much he remembered. When she moved in with Alveda, she'd worked in the kitchen whenever needed. At school, she'd tutored students in math and although she was second string on the volleyball team, she'd cheered for her team from the bench at every game. If there was need, she was there, no matter how she argued that she'd rather be alone.

"This won't be easy," he warned, using a stern tone in hopes of scaring her off.

"Nothing worth having ever is."

This time he allowed a genuine smile, despite the renewed pain her words brought. "Let me guess. Alveda?"

Heidi nodded, smiling back at him. "She does have a wealth of wisdom she's willing to share."

When they were kids, Reid and Logan had spent hours in the kitchen watching Alveda bake their favorite pies while doling out life advice that he still, to this day, used on a regular basis. Alveda and Grandmother had been instrumental in encouraging the brothers down the straight and narrow path, at least until they hit puberty and then all bets were off.

"She is one of a kind," Reid mused. "Grandmother too."

His mother loved him, but had always catered to his father's whims. Until the truth came out and the family had nearly been destroyed.

The secrets had been about Logan's birth,

and hadn't directly affected Reid, but they'd created collateral damage. His father still wanted Logan in the business. But Logan was a PI and happy in his line of work. Yet Reid had given it his all and it wasn't enough. Finally, he'd wondered why he'd ever bothered trying in the first place and walked away.

He missed Masterson Enterprises every waking hour of every day.

He wasn't mad at Logan. Despite everything, he and his brother maintained a close relationship. But his father? Let's just say they'd never see eye to eye, so Reid had done the only logical thing he could think of to mask the pain. He'd moved on.

"You're a businessman." Heidi interrupted his thoughts as she continued to lay out her case. "You understand that in the course of a transaction, you make decisions that facilitate a future sale. I'm a good bet on buying this house down the road. Why not get me on board now?"

Yes, he did know about business. Finance had been his major in college, but he'd grown up around Masterson Enterprises. Knew his way around a company. Making a deal was in his DNA. The question was, could he come up with a deal that would satisfy them both?

He couldn't ignore her eager face. She was

practically standing on her tiptoes as she awaited his answer. Could he let her down? The friend who had indeed kept him away from the girls his grandmother had tried to match him up with? The friend who had sat with him quietly by the lake more than once after he'd had another go-around with his father? His time-to-time rival? Deep inside, he knew he couldn't say no.

But he was also going to regret this move.

"I'll draw up a cost analysis for the project. I can't agree that I'll sell it to you for what I paid, but I will credit your work effort."

"That's fair."

"There will be rules," he said.

She held up a hand. "I promise to mostly follow them."

He restrained another groan. "When we're on the job, I'm the boss."

She nodded, not saying a word, but he wasn't convinced.

"This is business only, agreed?"

"Of course."

He hesitated for a second, then reached out his hand to her. "You have a deal."

She vigorously shook his hand, her face sunny and full of excitement. He closed his eyes and counted to ten before meeting her satisfied gaze. Remembered that look shining in her eyes from summers past, the one that had twinkled when she thought she'd won and then all kinds of trouble broke loose.

"You won't regret this," she said.

CHAPTER TWO

REID FORCED HIS expression to go blank. No way could Heidi see that he had misgivings only seconds into sealing the deal.

"So, now what?" she asked, looking down at their clasped hands. A funny expression crossed her face and she quickly let go. Reid didn't know why, but her pulling away from his touch, like it burned her, bothered him.

He took a step back and dismissed his reaction. "We only just made the agreement."

Squaring her shoulders, she announced, "I'm ready whenever you are."

"Hold your horses. First I want to draw up some paperwork documenting our deal."

Her mouth fell open. "You don't trust me?"

"It's in both our interests."

Since this was his first foray into hiring an intern—if you could call Heidi that—Reid decided to err on the side of prudence.

"Okay. Then what?"

"I've got the keys. I need to go over the

structure again and add to my initial projections before starting."

"Didn't you already do all that?"

"I made a preliminary plan, yes. Now I need details."

"Just tell me when and I'll be here to point you in the right direction."

His qualms did not dissipate. "Is working together going to be a problem?"

By the way her eyebrows rose, he figured she was smart enough to know she'd pushed him enough for one day. "Nope."

"Do you promise?"

A spunky grin he rather liked curved her lips. "Like a pinkie swear?"

"Like a…" he muttered, running a hand over his hair. "Heidi, we have a job to do."

"Right." Then she saluted him.

This was not the Heidi he remembered hanging out with when they were kids.

Back then, she'd always held herself at a distance, like she was figuring out how to fit in to a situation. It wasn't until she'd lived in Golden for a few years that her sense of humor started to shine, along with her competitive streak. They'd had plenty of laughs, he recalled, but she'd made sure to never reveal her inner self or secrets. At least that aspect of her life appeared to be the same.

"I need to get to the store," she stated, glancing at the house with a small smile. Not sure he wanted to know what was going on inside that head of hers, he decided he was better off in the dark. "You have my cell number. Call me with your...our schedule."

What have I gotten myself into?

When she turned to walk to her car, he stopped her. "Heidi."

She swung back, her thick hair swirling around her shoulders. She sent him a soft smile and the vicinity around his heart pinged. He went still. What was that about?

One of her eyebrows rose.

Shaking off the weird sensation, he said, "I appreciate your enthusiasm, but please don't go overboard."

The joy from moments before faded from her face. "I won't. I'm just happy you're including me."

Now he felt like a bully. "Keep in mind that this is a construction zone. Safety comes first and I intend to keep it that way."

"Whatever you say, boss."

With that cheeky comment she hurried to her car. Before climbing in, she waved at the SUV pulling into the driveway. She started up her car and disappeared down the road.

"What're you two up to?" his brother, Logan,

asked as he rounded the hood of his vehicle to join Reid.

"Did you ever notice that Heidi has a way of talking herself right into the middle of something she has no business meddling in?"

Logan grinned. "I remember that being mentioned a time or two when we were growing up."

Reid shook his head. "I'm not entirely sure how it happened."

"What happened?"

"She talked me into letting her exchange her help with the remodel for first dibs on the house when it goes on the market."

"I didn't know you were taking on accountant slash shop employees for your crew."

"I wasn't until ten minutes ago." He pictured her smiling face. The twinge in his chest reminded him that he'd relented too easily.

Logan stopped beside him and glanced at the house. "Doesn't seem like too big of a project."

"It's not, compared to others I've tackled." He had an experienced crew and he did much of the hands-on work himself. What could Heidi give him that he didn't already have?

Reid waited for his brother to tell him why he was here, but Logan remained silent. By the serious look on his brother's face, this wasn't a casual drive-by. "Want to go inside?"

"Sure."

The two made their way up the path to the front steps.

"The outside will get a new paint job," Reid explained as they walked. "I'm going to remove these steps and add a wide porch."

"You have a good eye."

"Thanks." He opened the door and they stepped inside. A faint musty smell of disuse lingered in the air. "The place has been closed up for a while."

Logan walked around, taking it all in, puffs of dust rising as his boots echoed on the hardwood floor.

"We'll restore the floors and paint." Then Reid pointed to a wall. "Take that down so there's an open living room and kitchen."

Still pacing, Logan nodded.

"Okay, you didn't come here to find out how I plan on bringing this house to life."

"No. I didn't." He shot Reid an amused look. "Serena and I haven't received an answer from you about attending our engagement party."

"I thought it was a given. Of course, I'm coming."

He kept walking. "That's what I told Serena."

"So, this visit is only a reminder?"

"More like a heads-up."

A trickle of unease skittered over him.

"I spoke to Grandmother this morning. She invited me over for coffee."

Reid didn't like where this conversation was heading. "Why are you giving me your personal schedule?"

"You're deflecting."

"If this is concerning Grandmother, it can't be good." For him, anyway, if Logan's wry smile was any indication. "Just tell me."

"She discussed providing you with a list of single women, any of whom she feels would be a suitable date for you to bring to the party."

Reid's mouth fell open. He quickly regained his composure and asked, "What is she doing, inviting random women to your celebration?"

His brother chuckled. "I wouldn't put it past her, but no, they're legitimate friends of the family."

"You ruined being single by falling in love with the woman Grandmother picked for you," Reid griped. He didn't begrudge his brother's happiness, but now all the pressure fell directly on him.

"Funny how that happened." Logan didn't look the least bit sorry about that turn of events.

Even though Reid didn't want to be part of

his grandmother's machinations, he needed to know what he was up against. "What did you tell her?"

"That you could find your own date."

Relief washed over him. "Thanks."

Logan slapped him on the back. "That's what big brothers do."

By the pained expression on Logan's face, there had to be more. "What?"

"She's up to something. I can smell it."

There was that warning alarm again. "She's always up to something. What's different now?"

"I can't put my finger on it. When Alveda came into the dining room with a fresh pot of coffee, they exchanged this weird look."

"They've always been thick as thieves."

"Yeah, but this time was more…sneaky."

All this was too much. He pointed to the room they were standing in and said, "Logan, I don't have time to worry about Grandmother's schemes. I'm starting a new project and need all my attention here."

His brother shrugged. "Just wanted to let you know she'd be calling you to discuss the potential dating pool."

Great. He had enough on his plate without trying to outsmart his grandmother, who, despite her prying, he loved dearly.

Logan's grin faded. "There's more."

Reid groaned. Could this day get any more crowded? "You're the bearer of bad news this morning, aren't you?"

"Mother came in at the tail end of the conversation."

"Please tell me she didn't have a list of her own. A man can only take so many glowing reports about the women in the Ladies Guild."

"No. She mentioned that Dad was going to initiate a conversation with you at the party."

His gut clenched. It had been months since he'd talked to his father. After their last argument when Reid had stormed out of the office, neither had sought the other out. What could his father want now? And why couldn't he call Reid instead of cornering him at a party?

"Dad is nothing if not tenacious," Reid grumbled.

"That's why I wanted to warn you."

"I get it."

His brother's expression turned sympathetic. "Reid, I know how much Masterson Enterprises means to you. I wish you and Dad could find some common ground."

"You know better than anyone how unreasonable he can be," Reid said, jamming his hands in his pockets.

"I do. And no matter how much he wants it

or how many times he pushes, I will never be a part of the family business."

"I thought he gave up bugging you."

"Me too. Once we hashed out the past, I assumed he'd leave me to my PI business. Even though I left Atlanta, I'm busy. It's like ever since you walked away, he wants one of us in the office. Problem is, he's asking the wrong son."

Pain lanced through Reid's chest. "And we both know he won't ask me to return anytime soon."

"He might."

Reid knew that ship had sailed. Arthur Masterson was inflexible and would never go back on something he'd said. Reid tried to protect himself, but his father's actions still hurt.

Wearily, he said, "No, he'll demand you do it. Lay on the guilt. Make promises he won't keep. The usual."

"You don't have to worry, I'm not falling for his tactics," Logan said, ever loyal.

Reid nodded. When the truth of Logan's parentage came out just as he was ready to go away to college, there had been years of tension between Logan and their father. Reid's mother was not Logan's biological mother. When Logan stumbled upon this secret, it had created major problems personally and professionally. Reid had managed to navigate the conflict pretty well, but when Logan had come home last fall for a case, he and their father had finally had a long overdue talk and were able to come to a truce. Thinking things would be so much better in the Masterson family going forward, Reid had donned his rose-colored glasses, secure in his place in the family business. Until his father ramped up his campaign to get Logan on board and basically overlooked all that Reid had done in the interim to grow the company's revenue and reputation.

It wasn't until he came to grips with the knowledge that his dad was never going to accept that his second son actually had the skills and desire to make the company more prosperous, that Reid finally left and never looked back.

Whatever his grandmother had cooked up was bad, but having an unwanted conversation with his father was worse.

The whole ordeal stank and he didn't want to talk about it.

"I should hire you to dig up whatever Grandmother is up to," he said, changing the subject.

"Don't think I didn't see what you did there."

Ignore the sting? Yeah, he was self-protective like that.

"You have a heads-up," Logan said. "Now you can do what you need to about the party."

"Send my regrets?"

"Serena would never allow it."

And Reid would never do that to his future sister-in-law. He genuinely liked Serena, and Logan was happy, so he'd paste a smile on his face when he showed up at the event.

"Here's an idea," Logan suggested. "Why not ask Heidi to come to the party with you? She'll be there anyway."

"Heidi?" He hadn't thought of that. Not after the way her unexpected visit this morning had gotten away from him. "We're friends."

"So?"

Did he really have to explain? "I'm supposed to discourage Grandmother. Coming with Heidi will only stir her up."

"Not necessarily. You two have been friends for a long time. Grandmother might not think of you two as a couple."

"I suppose." He'd always liked her. Plus, she'd looked so pretty earlier, standing in the sunlight with her hands on her hips as she read him the riot act. He almost smiled at the vision. "Besides, Alveda knows Heidi best. I'm sure she wouldn't encourage Grandmother."

Logan shot him a pitying look. "It's like you don't know them at all."

His brother had a point.

"I'll think about it. No point dragging Heidi into the dating drama when I'll already have to deal with her assisting me with this house."

"It'll be like old times, like when she got you out of those cotillion dates."

There was that. "Or beat me out as valedictorian in high school."

"You two did manage to hold a good grudge."

"We did, but she doesn't deserve to be caught in Grandmother's scheming." No one did, even if it would serve Heidi right for hijacking his renovation. "It'll be enough that we're working together. She basically told me she doesn't trust my interior design instincts."

Logan chuckled. "I'd love to be a fly on the wall."

"You could stop by and actually help."

"Nah. Had my fill of remodels. You did work on the cottage we're going to move into and didn't charge me a fortune to make Serena's dream come true."

"That would mean you owe me."

"Consider the warning that Grandmother is up to something as repayment, so we're even."

Reid shrugged. "Fair enough."

"I need to run. I have a client meeting in Atlanta."

"I thought you were working up here now?"

"I still need to be there a few times a month."

"Then I suppose I'll see you at the party."

His brother's sentimental grin returned. "Can't wait."

Easy for him to say. Logan was over the moon in love. Reid, on the other hand, wasn't sure what his future held.

"At least you have something to look forward to," Reid griped to the empty room as his brother strode away.

Instead of focusing on the job, he walked to the wide French doors. The stunning backyard view was worth the price of the property alone. From this vantage point, he could see the highest point of the mountains in the distance. Oaks, pine and a scattering of shrubs filled in the space past the property line. He'd hiked these mountains often as a kid, trailing behind Logan and their motley crew of friends, searching for one adventure after another.

He loved Golden. Had planned on living out his life here. But now? He wasn't sure. If his father was really going to approach him at Logan and Serena's party with who knew what kind of demands, Reid wasn't sure he wouldn't lose his patience. His father never listened to him, so what could he possibly want with Reid now?

Swallowing hard, an unpleasant thought hit him. Maybe he should leave town? Strike out somewhere new. Create a life he could be proud of without what-ifs constantly swirling in his head.

But what about family? his inner voice taunted. *Grandmother is getting up there in years and Mother would be devastated if you left. And now Logan is back and you've reconnected. So, what's your next move?*

A wave of sadness nearly drowned him. Logan would understand whatever decision Reid made. His brother had walked away from family once. Gone into the military before starting his own firm. He was a self-made man and Reid wanted the same opportunity. To stand on his own. Be proud of what he'd accomplished.

He turned, surveying the empty house. He couldn't deny that he found a sense of worth in flipping houses, but it wasn't his dream job. At some point he had to make a solid decision and honor it.

Getting to the job at hand, he grabbed his leather binder and zippered it open. He'd already started notes on a legal pad but now needed a more precise list. He pulled out his measuring tape and started taking exact measurements to add to the blueprint he was working from. He paused in the kitchen, picturing how cozy it would be once he replaced cabinets and appliances. Envisioned Heidi feeding her cat, dancing around the kitchen in her bare feet, belting out a country song.

He blinked. *Where did that come from?*

Bemused, he refocused on the demo and decided the eighties wallpaper was the first thing to go. Then he moved on to the bathrooms. By the time he'd finished, he had a layout of how to make this house inviting and sell for a good buck, without an uninvited image of how Heidi would make this house a home.

If his friend had anything to say about it, he might not walk away with much of a profit. Was what she'd done for him that long-ago night worth it?

He pictured her smile again. The one that had crept into his thoughts and refused to leave. "Right," he muttered under his breath and strode from the house to carry on with his day.

"You're late," her boss called out as Heidi hurried through the front door of the shop.

"Sorry!"

"It's not like running late is a firing offense. If that was the case, we would have parted ways a long time ago."

"Ha ha." Heidi stopped at the counter. "That's what makes you a good friend and boss. You're willing to overlook a tardy minute or two."

Shaking her head, because they both knew it was more like many minutes, not two, Serena grinned. "Friends first."

"Always."

Heidi glanced around the store. A couple of women were browsing and pointing out items to each other, but otherwise it was quiet. "Doesn't look like I missed anything."

"It's slow." Serena's blueberry-colored eyes sparkled. As usual she dressed in signature blue, the color scheme of Blue Ridge Cottage, a specialty greeting card and stationery store located on Main Street. "What's your excuse this time? Did you get lost in a column of numbers on a spreadsheet? Are you revising a business plan for a client?" Serena snapped her fingers. "I've got it. Mr. Whiskers escaped again."

"None of the above. Although that wily cat of mine did make a run for the door when I was about to leave. Do you think he hates living with me?"

"The way you spoil him? Nah. He just likes keeping you on your toes. Letting you know who's really in charge."

"That explanation makes more sense. Sometimes he looks like he's plotting my demise." Heidi shivered. "Although who he thinks will feed him if I'm gone is beyond me."

"I still find it hard to believe you took in an animal."

Serena had coaxed Heidi to the local animal rescue's monthly event called the Tail Wagging Bonanza in Gold Dust Park one Saturday. The coalition had been looking for possible pet owners to adopt animals for their forever home. Heidi had no intention of falling for a furry critter, but when she came upon Mr. Whiskers, she'd stopped short. From the droll expression on his face, she'd determined he had the same no-nonsense outlook on life as she did.

She shrugged. "What can I say. Our gazes met and it was destiny."

"I'm just happy you have a roommate."

"You're still mad that I wouldn't room with you?"

"It would have been nice," Serena said, "but then Carrie showed up, so it was moot anyway. And now that Logan and I are getting married, our place will be ready to move into soon."

She got out her phone and scrolled through the tons of pictures she'd taken of the place as Reid and Logan had restored the cottage that Gayle Ann had given to her grandson and Serena as a wedding present. "Have I shown you the newest pictures? Logan fixed up one of the bedrooms for me to use as an art studio. Isn't he the best?"

A dreamy expression crossed Serena's pretty face. Could her friend get any sappier from being in love? Since Heidi had never suffered that malady—dating meant vulnerability and her heart wasn't up for that—she didn't have an answer.

Serena snapped out of her daydream. "Hey, speaking about moving, any chance you want to take over my bedroom in the apartment? The location is perfect because it's right upstairs, so you wouldn't have an excuse to show up late anymore." She wiggled her eyebrows. "Like how I worked that in?"

"You're talented that way."

"And it's bigger than your apartment," Serena went on, ignoring Heidi's sarcasm. "Even if you'd have to share it with Carrie."

The excitement from earlier rushed over Heidi. "Thanks, but I have another plan in motion."

"Really?" Serena glanced at her friend and a

smile spread across her face. "You finally got a hold of Lisa to put an offer on the house?"

"Not exactly."

Serena's brows drew together. "A different place then?"

"Nope. Still the house on Hanover."

Serena crossed her arms over her chest. "Heidi, what's going on?"

"It sold. The house on Hanover sold."

She gave Heidi the once-over. "Then why do you look so happy?"

"Reid bought it."

"Okay, I'm still missing something here."

Heidi clapped her hands. "I'm going to help him flip it so he can sell it to me all fixed up."

Serena dropped her arms. "I'm confused."

Heidi explained driving by the house, about seeing the sale-pending sign, confronting Reid and talking him into being an intern.

"He's really on board with you hammering and nailing stuff? Considering you don't know the first thing about construction?"

"Why does everyone have a problem with that minor detail?"

Serena burst out laughing. "I do admire your confidence."

Heidi waved the point away. She was too pumped to let anyone get her down. "That's all for show."

"I think—" Serena was cut off when the phone rang. Holding up a finger, she went to the counter to take the call.

Heidi went to the storage room to drop off her purse and put her lunch in the mini refrigerator. She placed a hand over her stomach and blew out a breath. Now that she'd been told twice that she had no idea what she was doing, she wondered if Reid and Serena were right? Could she really be of any help when she didn't have a clue about what a remodel entailed? She'd searched enough information to have a theoretical idea of how it was done. Practically, could it be that hard?

Then she pictured Reid's handsome face. How he wasn't the least bit convinced she could pull this off. What had she gotten herself into?

"Don't panic," she admonished herself. "You *will* do this. And prove Reid wrong." Honestly, if she didn't encourage herself, who would?

Okay, Alveda did. Serena. Mrs. M., as they all called Gayle Ann Masterson—they were all on her side. Even though she'd lived in Golden since she was fourteen, she still went about things solo. Drove Alveda crazy to no end, but some deep-seated traits couldn't be changed.

She understood Reid's desire to be independent, because that was her own personal mantra. She admired that about him. Almost felt guilty for horning in on his project, but couldn't deny the little of flash of competition that sweetened the deal. She preferred to think of it as moxie, but even if a lack of it was more the truth, it would not keep her from owning a home.

After a positive nod for her internal pep talk, she headed back to the sales floor ready to start her shift.

Serena hung up as Heidi returned. "Listen, I have some details to take care of before the engagement party. Mind manning the store alone for an hour or so?"

"Sure." She tilted her head, tucking her hair behind her ear before it slipped over her cheek. "Need any help with the party?"

"No. So far it's under control. I can't believe it's next weekend. I have to check in with the caterer and florist to make sure everything is ready and it's easier to do that face-to-face."

"You know Alveda is unhappy you didn't ask her to cook for this shindig."

Serena's face dropped. "She does so much. I want her to be a guest, not work all night."

"Which is her way of celebrating, but I get

it. I worry she does too much. You'd think at her age she'd want to retire or something."

Serena giggled. "Could you see her and Mrs. M. on a cruise?"

"It would be mayhem."

"Exactly. But the stories they'd tell…"

Heidi shook her head. "Well, those two aren't going anywhere, so let's focus on your big night."

Serena stared at the diamond ring securely placed on her finger, the rock glittering under the fluorescent lights.

"Show-off," Heidi teased, wondering where the tiny squeeze of jealousy came from.

Serena clasped her hands together and placed them over her heart. "I never thought I'd see this day," she whispered, tears in her eyes.

"Hey, you both deserve it." Heidi swallowed hard, appreciating her friend's joy and good fortune. Not everyone fell in love. Or fulfilled a longtime dream.

Wiping her eyes, Serena laughed. "Look at me, all weepy when I should be dancing in the street."

"No need to go that far."

"Right, that's not your thing. We'll save the dancing for the wedding reception."

"Good call."

Serena reached under the counter for her purse. "I shouldn't be long."

"But aren't you meeting Mrs. M.?"

"Yes."

"Then most likely I won't see you until after lunch."

Serena raised an eyebrow.

"You know she'll talk you into eating at that new bistro."

"A Touch of Tabby is a pretty wonderful place."

"Enjoy," Heidi said as Serena crossed to the door.

"Want me to pick up lunch for you?" her boss asked before leaving.

"No, I brought my own."

"It wouldn't kill you to splurge every once in a while." She offered a quick smile and left.

Heidi didn't splurge. Not when she was saving up for her house.

She poured a cup of coffee and pulled up the store's revenue spreadsheet on the computer, conveniently located on the sales counter. If Blue Ridge Cottage stayed quiet, she might get a bit of business done.

Serena was one of her accounting clients, along with many of the store owners in downtown Golden. She loved the connection to the community she'd created by serving the businesspeople she'd come to know and respect. At first, she was afraid they wouldn't think she was up to the job, since most of them knew she'd shown up back in town unexpectedly and on her own when she was just a teen. To her surprise, one by one, they'd hired her and she was grateful to each and every person.

Numbers were her comfort zone. They didn't let you down. They made sense in a sometimes chaotic world.

The door opened and a woman walked in, taking in the shop as if deciding where to start browsing.

"Good morning," Heidi greeted her. "Can I help you find anything?"

"Just looking for a gift," the woman replied.

"If you need assistance, just let me know."

Returning to the spreadsheet, Heidi thought about her first few clients. Once she'd become financially solid, thanks to them, she'd thrived. She'd started off visiting each location to get any paperwork she needed, then worked from home. Her apartment was not cutting it in terms of the space needed for the growth of her business, and she hoped that once she bought her own place, she'd create a dedicated home office.

So much was riding on that house.

The door opened again, snagging her attention. Heidi called out a hello to a group of women entering the store. They waved, clearly caught up in an ongoing conversation. Placing her elbows on the counter, she dropped her chin into her upraised hands.

She was thankful to Reid for giving in. He hadn't liked her bargaining chip, made obvious by the flash of hurt in his green eyes. Bringing up that night was low, made worse by the fact that she was desperate. She couldn't lose this house.

But when he'd smiled again, a genuine smile that glowed from deep inside, it made her chest tighten. He didn't share it often, especially since the falling-out with his father. She'd missed it, because she missed her up-for-any-adventure friend. The one she got into mischief with one minute, followed by a heated debate over the merits of said risky decision the next. If anything, could their time together be a way of bringing the old Reid back? Even if her strange awareness of him was anything but friendly?

Shaking off the vision of Reid strolling out of *her* house like he owned the world, she tried to tamp down her frustration. He hadn't known she was serious about that property. But if he had, would he still have bought the house? She'd never know now, but at least he was letting her work alongside him, albeit reluctantly.

Would inserting herself in the middle of Reid's project affect his livelihood, ultimately destroying their friendship? She bit down on her lower lip, pondering that thought before brushing it away. She had to take the risk.

Heidi sent him a quick text, reminding him to let her know when she could start. She had her schedule to rearrange, after all.

"Excuse me," the first customer who'd come into the store said as she approached the counter. "Do you have another box of this stationery? I'd like to buy two."

The memo pads featured a beautiful drawing of Golden Lake from the vantage point of Pine Tree Overlook. Serena was a talented artist, her original designs on stationery, cards and other paper products making up the bulk of their inventory. Heidi couldn't draw a stick man to save her life, but she admired Serena's ease with her colored pencils and watercolors.

"Sure. Let me get one from the back."

Her phone dinged as she hurried to fetch the customer's request. Grabbing it as she passed the counter, she swiped the screen to see that Reid had answered her text. Excitement curled in her belly as she opened it.

Excitement about the house or Reid?

Heidi went still. Reid was her friend. Always had been. Yeah, she couldn't help but notice his broad shoulders today. And his moss-green eyes seemed especially bright, his gaze switching from indulgence to humor as he kept up with her conversation. She'd always thought he was handsome, but what was so unique about today? Was it because he was helping her achieve her plan to get her house?

Shaking off her silliness, she read his answer.

Tomorrow morning at six.

"Yes," she said out loud with a fist pump to the air, startling a woman browsing the wall of greeting cards.

"Sorry. Good news," she explained.

The woman nodded and continued picking up a card here and there to read while Heidi continued on her mission. After bringing the requested box of stationery to the pleased customer, Heidi typed a return message to Reid.

See you then, boss.

Then added a saluting emoji face, sure to annoy him.

She'd just put down the phone when the

door opened and a teenage girl strode in as if she owned the place. Heidi frowned, acknowledging that a whirlwind had just arrived.

CHAPTER THREE

"MIA, WHAT'RE YOU doing here?" Heidi asked the leggy teen with long, curly blond hair as she zigzagged around customers to reach the counter.

A puzzled look crossed the girl's face. "You said if I needed help to tell you."

"Yes, at our group meeting at the community center." Heidi glanced at the wall clock. "It's only eleven. Shouldn't you be in school?"

The girl shrugged, swinging her designer leather backpack onto the counter with a thud. How the girl managed to look so effortlessly stylish in a pair of denim shorts and off-the-shoulder peasant shirt was beyond her. Heidi worked hard to pull off a decent wardrobe and still never came that close to trendy.

"I skipped out before lunch."

Heidi pinched the bridge of her nose. "That doesn't sound good."

Mia shrugged. "I have a test later and I need your help."

"We went over the material just last night over the phone."

The teen's fingers stalled over the zipper enclosure of the backpack. "But I'm nervous," she said, her anxious expression touching Heidi's heart.

When Heidi had agreed to facilitate a math tutoring class at the community center, she hadn't expected all the teen drama that went with it. Tears, frustration and derision were just a few of the attitudes she dealt with on a weekly basis. Had she been this melodramatic when she was that age? Heidi didn't think so, not after the childhood she'd experienced. Because of that, it was sometimes hard for her to relate to these kids, but for all the town of Golden had given her, she had the deep-seated desire to give back. Math happened to be Heidi's strong suit, so when Mrs. Arnold had asked her to sign on as a tutor, she hadn't hesitated.

Until she actually had to interact with students who didn't have a clear understanding of mathematical concepts. And for some reason, Mia had decided Heidi was *the* person to solve all her problems.

Focusing on the teen, Heidi asked, "Did you study the worksheet I made up for you?"

"Yes." Mia frowned as she extracted a notebook from her bag. "Are you sure all those equations are important to study?"

"Do you want to go to college?"

Mia wrapped a finger around a strand of curls and twirled. "Not really. I want my car back."

One of the reasons Mia had ended up in Heidi's group to begin with. She had to lift her failing grade in order to get the keys to her sporty BMW.

Heidi rephrased. "Your parents want you to go to college, so you need to pass."

"But Algebra II? I barely made it out of Algebra I alive."

Heidi hid a grin. Same story for most of the kids she tutored. "Mia, you're capable."

The girl bit her lower lip. "Not in math."

No, unfortunately not in math. They'd spent hours going over the same concepts until they were both ready to pull their hair out. But, as Alveda pointed out, she hadn't taught Heidi to quit, so she'd stuck it out with Mia, hoping one of these days the formulas would click.

Heidi pushed her sleeves up. "All the more reason to work harder."

Mia's shoulders sank. "I want to be a cosmetologist to the stars, not a rocket scientist."

"Didn't your folks say this was the last math class you had to take?"

"Yeah, but it's ruining my life." Mia fluffed her hair over her shoulders. "Math is dumb."

The same old rhetoric. *Math is dumb. I won't use it in real life. Can't you just take the test for me?*

Heidi gestured toward the backpack. "Show me where you're tripping up."

Mia opened a notebook full of squiggles that had nothing to do with numbers and letters and pointed to the worksheet. "Why doesn't this make sense?"

It was one of the more complicated equations. Could Heidi come up with a way to explain it so Mia would retain the principle?

"I wish I was a senior," Mia muttered. "Then I'd be off to Hollywood this summer."

"Senior year is the best. Don't rush it."

Mia rolled her eyes. "Please. I've already been to prom twice. What's left to accomplish?"

Heidi stared at her.

"What?" the teen asked in an affronted tone.

Shaking her head, Heidi said, "I don't know how to answer that question."

Mia rested her elbows on the counter. "I promise if you help me figure this out, I'll give you tickets to the school play. We're doing *Beauty and the Beast* this year and I get to do all the makeup!"

The arts were not in Heidi's wheelhouse, except for the year she painted the mural, but when she spied the passion in Mia's eyes, she understood why getting through math wasn't as important as it should be to the girl. Hey, if Heidi could help Mia pass with a solid C, she'd consider it an accomplishment.

"I appreciate the offer, but I'll help you *and* buy my own ticket to support the school." Heidi grabbed a pencil and worked out the problem again, slowly and in a way she hoped Mia would retain. From the blank expression in Mia's eyes, Heidi was worried about the outcome of the test.

Throwing down her pencil after trying to figure out an equation, Mia looked close to tears. "This is useless. It's like a black hole."

A customer chose that moment to bring items to the counter to check out.

"Mia, why don't you take a seat at the activity table and I'll join you in a minute."

Collecting her things, Mia muttered, "Fine," in a tiny voice before moving away.

"Looks like you have your hands full," the woman said with a sunny smile as Heidi rang up the sale.

"One of the students I tutor."

The woman chuckled. "My daughter hated all things math. It seems like her high school

years were a litany of us ruining her life because we made her learn a skill."

Heidi grinned. "I hear that all the time.
Thankfully the kids keep coming back."

As the customer handed Heidi her card, she
asked, "Do you have children?"

Heidi paused, not expecting that question.
Sure, she thought about a family, but shied
away from imagining what it would look
like. There was no chance she'd allow a child
to grow up the way she had. That's why she
needed a house before thinking that far into
the future.

She finished the transaction, then placed a
half dozen cards and stationery boxes in the
bag. "Not yet," she said with a smile.

The woman took the bag Heidi held out to
her. "It's a special time. I highly recommend
it."

A loud sigh carried over from the table Serena used for her calligraphy and greeting card
classes. Heidi and the customer exchanged
glances before chuckling.

As the group of women left the store, Heidi
strode toward the table. Suddenly, she came
up with an idea that might help. She pulled a
chair close to Mia's and sat. "Do you act in
any of the plays at school?"

Mia wiggled the pencil between her fingers. "I did, but now I work backstage."

"So, you've memorized lines?"

Curiosity glittered in Mia's eyes. "Yeah, why?"

Heidi held up the worksheet. "Look at this problem as a line in a play. If you can close your eyes and picture it, it will help you when you take the test."

"You mean like when we ran through our parts?"

"Yes."

Doubt wrinkled Mia's forehead. "Are you sure? That sounds too easy."

Heidi held out her hands. "I can't think of a better way for you to focus on the material."

Mia stared at the notebook, then at Heidi. "I can try."

Heidi placed a hand over Mia's. "That's all I ask, Mia." Heidi pointed to the girl's head. "It's in there, I'm sure of it."

"At least someone is," Mia muttered as they went over the subject material a final time.

As Mia closed the notebook and stuffed it in the backpack, Heidi asked, "I thought Todd was helping you?"

A pink sheen brightened Mia's cheeks. "He was, but he has his own problems to worry about."

The blush was a sure sign that Mia had a thing for her classmate.

"Like what?"

Mia stood. "Getting Mr. Masterson to sign off on his woodworking project."

At the mention of Reid's name, that twinge of excitement from earlier tickled her insides. Her cheeks heated. Good grief, she was as bad as Mia. *It's about the house*, she assured herself.

The groups she and Reid worked with at the community center met on the same night. She'd seen Mia and Todd hanging around afterward on a few occasions, but usually she and Reid hurried off. Why didn't they ever hang out like they used to? she wondered. That would change once she started working on the house with him. While she was happy to rekindle her friendship with Reid, she was a tad concerned that her current awareness of the man might make things awkward between them.

"What's Todd making?" Heidi asked, gathering up the extra pencils from the table.

"A birdhouse." Mia giggled. "It's truly awful."

Heidi thought about the cat bed she'd attempted to make for Mr. Whiskers and flinched. "We can't all be creative."

Mia hesitated, then said, "I'd help him but he won't let me."

Sounded familiar.

"You can work with tools?" Heidi asked.

"A little bit. My uncle used to let me hang around when he was building stuff."

Heidi found herself jealous. She had to prove to Reid that she wasn't clueless when it came to construction.

"If you want to branch out from cosmetology, maybe you can build stage sets too."

Mia's eyes went wide. "How did you know?"

"Know what?"

"I'm already working on sets for the play."

Heidi chuckled. "I didn't. It was just an idea."

"A good one." Mia slung on her backpack. "And another reason I don't need math."

Heidi held up a finger to stop Mia before she escaped. "Really? Do you measure and cut?"

Mia nodded.

"Put together pieces of wood at different angles to build a prop?"

Mia frowned like she didn't get Heidi's point.

Heidi grinned. "That, my friend, is math."

Mia rolled her eyes again with such teen disdain that Heidi decided Mia must have the strongest facial muscles ever.

As Mia moved to the door, Heidi called out, "You have my number. Text me with your grade if you get it before our next group meeting."

"Thanks, Heidi."

"Anytime." She met the girl's unsure gaze. "I mean it."

Heidi knew the importance of someone caring about you, mostly because she'd grown up completely the opposite. Alveda had stepped up, interrupting her own quiet life when Heidi needed her the most. She'd never forget what a lifeline the older woman's sacrifice had meant to her.

And Reid? Having his friendship, no questions asked, when she'd been so withdrawn and raw, had also given her faith. She didn't want to jeopardize their friendship by exploring this puzzling attraction she was struggling with.

The teen stopped and looked as though she was going to say something else, then waved and took off.

"Just another day in Golden," Heidi said. The store phone rang and she took an order for one of Serena's personalized products.

She'd just hung up when the back door slammed. Before long, Serena's roommate

Carrie materialized, holding an open laptop in her hands. She glanced around the store.

"Where's Serena?"

"Off taking care of details for the engagement party."

"Let me guess. With Mrs. M.?"

"Yep. What's up?"

"I wanted her to read my résumé." A frown marred Carrie's forehead. "I've been over it a dozen times and I'm seeing double."

Heidi hesitated. She and Carrie had become friends since Carrie landed in town, but they weren't as tight as Carrie and Serena. "I can take a look if you want?"

Her face lit up. "Really? You wouldn't mind?"

At the positive response, Heidi nodded. "Not at all."

Carrie handed her the laptop. "I can man the desk while you read."

"It's been quiet." Heidi placed the laptop on the counter. "Serena has a class this afternoon, so with the extra traffic things should pick up then."

Tossing her honey blond hair over her shoulder, Carrie bit her thumbnail. "This isn't the first résumé I've put together."

Heidi looked up. "But?"

"I don't know. It just feels important."

"You're really going to stay in Golden?"

"For now."

Given the uncertainty in Carrie's tone, Heidi didn't question her. She understood keeping one's business to oneself.

Ten minutes later, she'd finished reading. "I only made a few notes," she told Carrie, "It's clear you know how to hook an employer."

"Phew. After the debacle at my last job, my confidence took a major hit."

"Any business would be happy to have you," Heidi said, and meant it. Then she thought about this morning, how she'd talked Reid into letting her join the house project and bit back a grin. He was clearly not thrilled that she was on board, but he hadn't said no. Not that she'd given him a chance. But the range of emotions on his handsome face had been fun to watch, not to mention they went a long way in lifting her spirits. And if she were being honest, they also made her heart beat a little faster, which made her question, why? Reid had been her friend forever. Working with him was going to be fraught with potential problems if she didn't get a handle on these feelings.

Carrie's voice broke into her conflicted thoughts.

"Thanks, Heidi." Carrie perused the notes,

then closed the laptop. "So, have you gotten a gift for Serena and Logan?"

Relieved by the reprieve, Heidi pulled herself together. "No. Though the party is next weekend, and I'm running out of time."

"Me too. Serena doesn't want anything but we can't show up empty-handed."

Heidi tapped a finger against her chin. "I keep thinking a fancy picture frame, but that's boring."

"It's more than I've got." Carrie grimaced. "But one perk of the party is that I finally get inside Masterson House."

Heidi grinned. "Curious?"

"Like everyone else in town who hasn't been there."

"It is a pretty amazing house."

"That's right—you grew up there."

This was when things got tricky, since she didn't talk about her childhood. "Kind of."

"So, it's no big deal to you. Going to a party there, I mean."

Glad Carrie hadn't asked about the past, Heidi replied, "It will be. Usually when I visit these days, it's to see Alveda."

"Serena is thrilled about having the party there, and Logan seems happy to agree to anything she wants, so it should be a great time."

"And the Masterson family is happy Logan

is staying in town, so they're on board with the wedding plans."

"How about Reid?" Carrie asked. "I haven't seen him around."

The last time they'd all hung out together was last fall when they'd volunteered during Oktoberfest. "He's flipping houses."

"Huh. I thought he liked working in an office."

So did Heidi, especially since his new profession had messed up her plans. It bothered her that he'd walked away from a job he loved, and that his expression closed when mention of Masterson Enterprises came up. She didn't want to pry, even though he kept his feelings closer to the vest than she did. The fun-loving Reid of their youth seemed to have disappeared, replaced by a more serious man. Still, he'd agreed to her sweat equity proposition and it still gave her a chance to fulfill her dream.

Hanover Lane, here I come.

Soon Serena returned to get ready for her calligraphy class. It meant Heidi had time to stop by a client's business to check her facts for a tax prep job. She'd just reached her car when her phone rang.

"Hello," she said, holding the cell phone between her cheek and shoulder as she juggled her belongings.

"Heidi, can you hear me?"

"Yes, Alveda."

The woman had difficulty figuring out her phone.

"Can you stop by? I need to discuss something with you."

"Sure. What time?"

"I'm right in the middle of preparing dinner. How about seven."

"I'll be there." Heidi took a breath. "Are you okay?"

"Why wouldn't I be okay?" came Alveda's pat answer, reassuring Heidi. "Nothing's wrong with me."

"I didn't…" Heidi knew better than to question the older woman. If possible, Alveda was more stubborn than Heidi. She worried about Alveda just like she would her own grandmother, if she had one.

"I'll save you some pie."

"Then you know I'll be there."

Alveda laughed and ended the call.

Heidi had just enough time to get home and finish the accounting job she'd started yesterday, make dinner, feed Mr. Whiskers and change before heading to Masterson House. For someone who generally kept to herself, she wondered when she'd become such a social butterfly.

Her mind shifted to Reid and she wondered if they'd run into each other at the House. He'd moved out, but Alveda had mentioned that he still stopped by from time to time. As she got into the car, anticipation bubbled through her. "Get moving," she muttered to herself, unsuccessfully pushing aside the hope of running into Reid. Seeing him in this new light was definitely going to be a challenge.

REID CHECKED TO make sure there was no classic Cadillac in the vicinity before parking on the gravel drive beside Masterson House. When his grandmother asked him to come over, she'd assured him that his father would be gone, but plans could change. One thing about his grandmother, she never set up "chance" meetings between him and his father. She knew that was a relationship breaker for Reid and would never cross that line. She loved him enough to respect his wishes, unlike the man he'd once looked up to.

He leaped up the steps to the wide veranda, his shoes pounding on the old pinewood. How many times had he raced across this space when he was a kid, laughing and playing without a care in the world? Too many to count. There were lots of good memories of getting into mischief with Logan. Heidi too, when

they were older, as long as she wasn't poking into his business. He'd loved growing up in this place.

A night bird cried out from a nearby tree, interrupting his thoughts. It was a warm night, serenely quiet this far away from town. He reached for the ornate handle of the hand-carved front door, disillusionment and resentment washing over him. Instead of ringing the bell, which would have been customary since he didn't live here anymore, he let himself in, coming face-to-face with his grandmother in the foyer.

"I thought I heard a car."

"Hello, Grandmother," he said, closing the door behind him and kissing her soft cheek. Her floral perfume, the same scent she'd worn for as long as he could remember, made him feel at home.

She reached up to cup his face in her weathered fingers. "You're okay?"

"I'm good."

She briskly nodded. "Then let's get down to business." She pivoted on her heel and strode to the living room. Resigned to whatever his grandmother's business entailed, Reid followed.

"Take a seat, young man."

"Yes, ma'am."

Grandmother chose her favorite armchair to settle in. He took the couch. Getting comfortable, he said, "Lay it on me, Grandmother."

"You're awfully cheeky tonight."

He shrugged, mentally preparing for this meeting. His grandmother was transparent when it came to what she wanted.

"First of all, I'd like to thank you for the azalea bush you gave me for my birthday. I had it planted by the steps and it's starting to bloom."

"I know how much you enjoy your flowers."

All his life, Grandmother had been busy tending to plants on the grounds. She'd enlisted his help often, letting him dig up the soil to plant new bulbs or paying him well to weed her precious flower beds.

"I do." She folded her hands in her lap. "Just one way to make Masterson House less daunting to visitors. Homier."

He crossed one leg over the other. After work, he'd changed into khakis and a button-down shirt. "I don't think homey fits this place."

"Grand? Majestic? Severe?" Grandmother waved her hand. "It's home to me."

"And you've always made it a remarkable place for everyone else."

She smiled, her lined skin glowing in the

soft lighting. The evening sky might have faded from streaks of pink to purple and finally black, but the glow of his grandmother's love enveloped him.

"Tell me what you've been up to?" Grandmother asked.

"I bought that house I told you about. The one on Hanover Lane." He paused, an image of Heidi filling his mind. Her big smile had made him rethink working on the project alone. It was like she was a magical fairy, tricking him into going along with her scheme. But she was certainly a flesh and blood woman and there really were no tricks.

All afternoon he'd thought about her motivation for wanting the house. Bits and pieces he'd heard over the years about her unconventional upbringing had to be the reason why she was so adamant about buying the house. Otherwise, why bring up the night that had caused him so much pain? Heidi wasn't cruel, but he understood how past events could shape a person. Wasn't he still dealing with those issues himself? So, yeah, he'd give her a chance at her dream. Maybe along the way he could figure out what to do about his.

He cleared his throat. "This job will be a little different than the others."

Interest glowed in Grandmother's eyes. "In what way?"

"I have an intern."

Grandmother frowned. "I don't understand."

He chuckled. "I didn't either until it was foisted upon me."

"Is it anyone I know? Ernie Keene's grandson?"

"No. It's Heidi."

Grandmother blinked. "Our Heidi?"

"Yes. It seems she missed out on buying this house, so she talked me into letting her help with the renovation and in exchange I'll sell it to her after I make the upgrades."

His grandmother beamed. "Reid, that's wonderful."

"I kind of think it'll be added work."

"How can that be?" Grandmother huffed away his concerns. "I'm sure she'll be a valuable intern."

"Really? Have you ever seen her build anything?"

"Well, no," Grandmother conceded.

"How can I say this nicely?" He shook his head. "She doesn't know the first thing about construction."

"She'll learn."

"Which will cost me more time and money."

"It's Heidi—it'll be fine," his grandmother said in a positive tone.

Would it? Add in his new fascination for Heidi and he'd painted himself into a corner. If this project went south, what would that mean for their friendship?

"Now, on to other business." Grandmother got that shifty look in her eyes. "Logan's engagement party is fast upon us."

"Don't worry. I'll bring a gift."

"It's not a gift I'm worried about. It's about a date. For you."

He closed his eyes and rubbed his eyelids. Took a breath and steadfastly met her gaze.

"Are you worried that I don't have a date? Or that I do and it's not who you want it to be?"

She pursed her lips in disapproval, then said, "Reid, I only want the best for you."

"And that means a woman in my life?"

"Look how besotted your brother is."

"I'm happy for Logan, but I'm not looking."

"Exactly. That's why I took the liberty of printing out a list of potential dates."

His eyes went wide and he choked. "You did what?" He hadn't thought she'd go that far, but Logan had warned him.

"I can't leave something this important up to you," she said in an annoyed tone.

"Grandmother, I'm more than capable of asking a woman to the party."

"Have you asked anyone?"

He uncrossed his leg. Shifted in his seat. "Not yet."

"The party is just over a week away."

"I still have time."

"Not if you want said woman to have time to prepare." His grandmother took a piece of paper from the end table beside her and passed it over.

When he took it, a list of names in very neat rows met his gaze. *This can't be happening.*

"It is, indeed, young man."

He'd said that out loud? "Grandmother, this is crossing the line, not to mention insulting."

"Didn't I just have a birthday?"

He frowned. "Yes, but what's that got to do with anything?"

"I'm not getting any younger. I want to see you happy. Married. Preferably with a great-grandchild I can hug before I'm ancient."

He blew out a breath and dropped the paper on the cushion beside him. "I'll find my own date."

Grandmother pointed at the page. "But those women are friends of the family."

Exactly why he wouldn't date them. They were part of the family history and therefore a reminder of what he'd lost by leaving Masterson Enterprises.

She continued to sell the idea. "They are kind, well-educated and have good jobs."

Still wasn't happening.

"Can you come up with a better list of candidates?"

He cringed. "Candidates?"

"Dates. I mean dates."

Sure, she did.

He rose. "I promise to bring a date to Logan's party," he said, ready to hightail it out of there before his head began to throb.

"Now, Reid, just think—"

The echo of footsteps came from the direction of the kitchen. Alveda entered, her face lighting up when she spotted him. "Reid, I didn't know you were stopping by."

He gave her a quick kiss on the cheek.

"I smell peaches."

"You always had a good nose." Alveda grinned. "There's a fresh peach pie in the kitchen with your name on it."

"You don't have to tell me twice."

He started to leave when his grandmother said, "Young man, we aren't finished."

"We are." He stopped, placed his hand on Grandmother's shoulder and squeezed. "I love you, but I can find my own date."

She opened her mouth to argue, he was sure, but he squeezed again and then strode down the hallway.

Silence fell over the room.

"Well?" Alveda whispered.

"Our plan worked. He's headed to Heidi, or rather, his destiny now." Gayle Ann gave a firm nod.

Alveda shook her head, a worried expression crossing her face. "I'm not sure I like these sneaky tactics."

"I know my grandson. He doesn't want to be told who to date. He'll ask someone simply to bait me or prove he's in control of his own future."

Alveda narrowed her eyes. "Isn't he?"

Gayle Ann crossed her arms. "Not if I have any say in the matter."

"What if this backfires? What if by pushing Reid and Heidi together we damage their friendship?"

"Or we make it stronger."

Alveda sighed, a clear sign she was done arguing. "You're sure about this?"

Leaning back in her chair, Gayle Ann grinned. "What could possibly go wrong?"

CHAPTER FOUR

HEIDI HAD JUST cut a large wedge of Alveda's amazing peach pie, inhaling the fruity goodness, when the swinging door to the kitchen opened. She nearly dropped the pie server. Reid's tall figure appeared in the doorway. He stopped for a split second, then resumed his trek illuminated only by the light over the sink.

"Wow. Twice in one day," she said, placing her piece of pie on a dessert plate.

"Who said Golden isn't a small town?"

Be cool, she ordered herself. "You're here for pie too?"

"Just stopped by to visit my grandmother, but Alveda caught me before I left and sent me in here." He opened the cabinet door above her head to remove another plate. He was so close she could feel his body heat. She held her breath, waiting for him to move away so he wouldn't catch on to her inner panic.

He didn't.

Handing the plate to her, he said, "Please cut me a piece."

She slid her plate over to him. "Take this one. You look like you need it more than me."

He grimaced. "That obvious?"

"Afraid so."

He examined the plate, then asked, "Ice cream?"

"In the freezer."

When he moved to the massive appliance and opened the big slide-out compartment, she let out a long breath. He rummaged around in the freezer and removed a quart. "Vanilla?"

"Works for me."

He shut the compartment with his knee and carried the carton to the counter. Heidi sliced another piece and placed it on the empty plate. Reid grabbed forks and spoons from the utensil drawer, and soon they were seated at the round table, smothering their pie with ice cream.

Reid took the first bite and groaned. A shiver ran over Heidi at the sound, but she dutifully ignored it.

"I swear that woman has never made a bad pie in her entire life." He took another forkful and closed his eyes.

Heidi tasted hers and agreed, savoring the burst of sweet fruit along with the flaky pastry.

"She's got some kind of magic touch that no one will ever be able to replicate."

"Has she taught you her secret?"

"No. We bake together from time to time, but I can't come anywhere close to her magic."

"Too bad she didn't go pro." He dug in for another forkful. "She could have her own dessert dynasty by now."

Heidi pushed a piece of crust into the melting ice cream. "It wouldn't be about the fame or money for her. She'd be happy that we're all happy enjoying her dessert."

A rare smile lit his face. "Well, she's made me extremely happy."

On impulse she asked, "Because you weren't?"

He took another mouthful and chewed. While she waited for an answer, Heidi dipped her fork in the mound of ice cream for another taste.

"Grandmother is interfering again."

Heidi laughed. "What now?"

"She presented me with a list of potential dates to ask to Logan and Serena's engagement party."

Heidi's hand stilled as she brought the fork to her mouth. "Are you serious? I thought she stopped doing that?"

"Me too. But now that Logan is engaged,

she expects me to follow suit." His face pinched into a panicked look. "Wait, she's not sick again, is she?"

"No," Heidi assured him. Mrs. M. had had a health scare a while back, but she was now as fit and ornery as ever. "Alveda would have told me."

He blew out a breath. "Good, because last time was tense."

"Your grandmother is a survivor."

"She is." He scooped up a bite before dropping his fork with a clatter. "Why are you here?"

"Alveda wanted to talk, so she asked if I'd stop by."

He wiped his mouth, which had Heidi noticing his lips.

"To set you up on a date too?"

She snorted, glad his silly question took her attention from how good he looked. "Please. Alveda knows better."

"Maybe she can explain boundaries to Grandmother."

Heidi chuckled. "I'd love to be a fly on the wall for that conversation."

They ate in silence until their plates were empty.

"So, I have to ask," Heidi said. "Who'd your grandmother put on the list?"

He rattled off a few names.

"She needs a new roster. Some of those names are left over from high school."

"She's nothing if not consistent."

Heidi rested her elbows on the table. "What're you going to do?"

"Find my own date."

Heidi chuckled. "Good for you."

He smiled again and the room seemed to brighten. She swallowed hard, taken aback by her reaction to him. Good grief, what was in this pie? Or the air, since this wasn't the first time today she'd thought of Reid as being… attractive.

"I wish she'd focus on Logan and Serena and leave me out of it," he complained, blissfully unaware of her racing thoughts.

"Your grandmother is an equal opportunity meddler."

"True." He shook his head. "Let's change the subject."

She certainly understood that tactic. Had taken it more than a time or two herself. "Okay. What are we doing tomorrow?"

"Knocking down a wall, so it'll be pretty gritty."

She wrinkled her nose.

He pointed his fork at her. "Hey, you wanted this. It's all part of sweat equity."

"I get it." She glanced at his button-down shirt and pressed slacks, giving him the once-over. "Now, there's the Reid I know."

He shrugged.

"I have to say, the tool belt threw me off. Seems like you replaced your briefcase with one."

"Funny."

"Just observant."

He nodded at her flower-print blouse and jeans. "Make sure you wear something you don't mind getting dirty tomorrow."

"Got it, boss."

"Yeah, the boss thing has to stop."

"You're no fun."

"So I've been told."

Heidi stood to collect the plates and silverware to carry to the sink. She ran the water and squeezed dish soap over the dishes and cutlery. Reid grabbed a towel and waited for her to wash and place the items in the draining rack.

"I'm kind of surprised to see you here," Heidi said, hoping she wasn't venturing into murky waters. "Alveda said you don't come around much anymore."

"I stay away when my father is here."

Guilt over using his estrangement with his

father to secure the house remodel job niggled at her. "She said he had a function tonight."

Reid shrugged as if he didn't care, but the stress lines around his eyes told Heidi otherwise.

Finally, she just spit it out. "Look, Reid, I'm sorry I brought up that night as a way of making you give in."

He didn't look at her. Waited for her to hand him a wet plate. "Goes to show how determined you are."

"It wasn't really about getting my way." She stopped. Waved her hand. In the process, water and bubbles shot into the air between them. "Okay, maybe a little bit. I shouldn't have brought up something so painful when I know you don't like talking about it."

"That night is over. In the past."

"Is it though?"

When he mulishly kept his mouth shut, she went on. "Look, that night you were… I don't know…out of control. I'd seen you in the aftermath of an argument with your dad before, but this time was different. You scared me."

He reared back. "Like I'd hurt you?"

"No! More like I wasn't sure what you'd do." She rinsed off another plate. "I knew there was a team party and the guys were bringing alcohol. It's not like you hadn't partied before. In fact, you were kind of making a habit of it. I was afraid you'd do something dumb like get drunk and then try to drive home. Let's face it—you were a bit of a race car driver when you zipped around the mountain roads."

He ran a hand over his face. "You were at the other parties where I drank too much. I didn't and wouldn't have done it again."

"Are you sure?" She chanced a glance his way. "At those other parties you were having fun. Blowing off steam. But that night, I couldn't take the risk that in your dark mood, you'd drink and drive and maybe wreck the car. Or hurt an innocent bystander." She bit her lower lip, then said, "I couldn't let anything happen to you. You had so much to look forward to. College. Taking on the family business. I had to stop you."

He shot her a tight smile. "I appreciate it, so can we quit rehashing the past?"

"See, that's the problem. You never want to talk about stuff."

Both dark eyebrows rose. "And you're any better?"

She grimaced as his words hit their mark. "No. Not really."

"Heidi, in all the time I've known you, I haven't really heard your story. Why you ended up on Alveda's doorstep. Why you refuse to talk about your past. What was so horrible that you ran away?"

The very question she didn't like to discuss or analyze. She procrastinated now by slowly washing and rinsing the utensils. "Why does it matter? I've been in Golden for a long time."

Reid took the silverware, dried it and put it away. "Because you can't call me out on the past, push me into letting you onto the jobsite because I owe you, then give me nothing in return."

He was right. Alveda didn't really know the entire story either. If she did, she would have hunted down Heidi's mother and given her what for.

Suddenly the dim lighting that should have made this conversation intimate and romantic—if they hadn't gone down this road—made her restless. She dried her hands, then crossed the room to flip the wall switch, trying to control the pounding in her chest.

"So, that's it," Reid said, a frown wrinkling his forehead. "We're done?"

"No." She rubbed her hands up and down her arms, as if the motion could calm her racing heart. "Sorry. It was just a little too dark in here."

He raised an eyebrow.

"I…" Why was it so hard to talk about this?

With Reid, of all people? He'd been her closest friend growing up.

Reid pushed away from the counter, tossing the towel aside. "If you can't be honest, then there's nothing to say."

"No, wait." She reached out to touch his arm, then stopped in midair, afraid to make contact with him. "It's not easy for me to talk about my childhood."

He waited for her. In his gaze, she read patience, and decided, yes, it was time to unburden herself, at least to tell some of her past.

"My mother was a kind of free spirit. We moved from place to place, sleeping on people's couches or in spare rooms. My mom would meet folks and hang with them for a while, but then we'd be off again." Her arm swung in an arc to encompass the room. "You grew up in this beautiful house. I never had anything close to this."

"You thought I wouldn't understand?"

She flinched. "You have a grandmother who adores you. Your mom is really nice, and you and your brother are tight. Sure, you have issues with your dad, but that's nothing like never knowing where you were going to sleep, or whether you'd have food." She traced the seam of the wood flooring with the tip of her shoe, not wanting to see the expression in his eyes when she told him about her upbringing. "I don't have a lot of pleasant memories from my childhood."

Thankfully he didn't ask any additional questions. His expression was blank.

After a few moments, Reid opened the cabinet and lifted the plates to place inside. His shirt pulled taut over his muscles. Heidi was confused. Why was she suddenly noticing muscles or how the color of his eyes changed with his mood? Or had she always done so, but had never realized it before?

She decided to blame the noticing on the cozy kitchen and close proximity to him. Or maybe it was because they were doing something so homey together. Either way, she had to remember that their friendship came first.

She watched Reid close the cupboard door and fold his arms across his broad chest. *Scratch that, just plain old chest*. His gaze captured hers and darn if his green eyes didn't hold secrets she'd love to uncover.

"Why is that house on Hanover so important to you?" he asked in the quiet space between them.

She stilled. Would he get her reasoning, the desire to have one place to call her own?

She went with, "I think, for me, anyway, after turning thirty it's time to settle down."

He barked out a laugh. "You're basing your decision on your age?"

She shrugged. It was as good a reason as any.

"I'm not buying it."

"Why not?"

He met her gaze and held it. Shivers broke out over her skin. Because she was caught in his very attentive sights or because he was seeing inside the real Heidi?

"The disappointment I saw on your face when you discovered I'd already purchased the property was much more personal than your age."

Busted. She leaned against the counter beside him, their shoulders brushing. His body heat and the scent of his cologne made her heart go haywire and she had to focus on what she was saying.

"You know how being involved at Masterson Enterprises is like winning the lottery for you?" she asked. "My lottery is that house."

He shrugged. "How do you know I want to go back there? Maybe I'm happy away from the hassles of the family business."

She sent him a sideways look that said, *I've got your number.* "Please. You used to eat, sleep and breathe Masterson Enterprises. It's all you ever talked about. I don't know what happened to make you leave, but it's very clear you miss it."

He offered a wry smile. "We're a fine pair."

She laughed. They were, both with pasts they'd rather not talk about.

Reid hadn't experienced a childhood like hers. Heidi had dragged around her meager belongings from town to town as her mother… Well, she wasn't sure what her mother did. Not hold a job, that's for sure. Reid had a true family at least.

"I'm not an expert on families," she went on to say, "but it seems to me that if you two sat down, you and your dad could talk out your problems."

Reid pushed away. "You're right about the second point. You don't know anything about my relationship with my father."

His words stung. "I didn't mean to…" She ran a hand through her hair. "I thought maybe…"

"Please stay out of it. I know my family better than you do and trust me when I tell you there's no going back."

She was about to apologize, but Reid moved off. "I need to get going," he said, and he left the kitchen without a backward glance.

Heidi sagged against the counter. "You stepped into that one," she muttered to the quiet room. Who said confession was good for the soul? Obviously, Reid disagreed.

She wouldn't make that mistake again.

JUST AS GAYLE ANN was reaching for the switch to turn off the living room lights, she heard the sound of a car starting up. She hurried to the window and brushed aside the curtains in time to see headlights. Was that Reid leaving already? She'd purposely kept scarce so that he and Heidi could visit as they shared slices of Alveda's pie. Had their conversation been a success?

Footsteps. She turned, the satin fabric slipping from her fingers. Alveda looked resigned. "Heidi's on her way home. She didn't want to talk about it, but when she said goodbye, I could tell she wasn't herself and was holding something back."

"Oh, dear."

"Sure you want to carry on with this scheme of ours?"

"More than ever."

Alveda tsked, but nodded. Gayle Ann would have to come up with their next step. She'd come too far to have her entire plan unravel now.

AT THE SOUND of someone entering the house on Hanover the following morning, Reid tensed. The renovation plans were spread out on the kitchen counter. He'd arrived early to review them, making mental notes of what needed to be accomplished today.

Heidi peered from around the corner as if taking the temperature of the room before she entered.

"Good morning," she chirped in a cheery tone.

Reid focused on the plans. He was ticked at his behavior last night and hadn't slept well.

She stepped into the kitchen and handed him one of the two coffee cups she was holding. "Peace offering."

He took one and gave her a quick apologetic nod. After their previous conversation, he was still raw, but that was no excuse for being moody toward Heidi. She'd only acted like a concerned friend. And it had given him a brief glimpse into her childhood, which he considered a rare gift. "Sorry for being so short last night."

"I went too far. Sometimes I do that." Her attention bounced around the room but didn't meet his gaze. "I shouldn't have pushed. It was nice that we were having a moment."

"Which I ruined."

She faced him. "Why don't we pretend it never happened?"

He saw hope reflected in her eyes and felt worse. He took a sip, savoring the burst of caffeine. He could do this. "Truce it is."

He watched the tension drain from her, then her perkiness ratcheted up a notch.

"So, what's on the agenda this morning?" she asked.

"First, look over the document I drew up. If you agree with the conditions, sign off and we'll get started."

He appreciated that she took her time reading the agreement instead of just signing on the spot. It showed she was taking this seriously.

Once she gripped the pen and added her signature, she asked, "Now what?"

Pointing to the sledgehammer in the corner with his free hand, he said, "Demo."

Her eyebrows angled over wide eyes. "Which you're doing, right?"

He set his cup on the counter. As the general contractor on this job, he had a part to play in everything related to this project. "You want to be part of the team?"

"Yes."

"Then you have to know the first rule of construction. Demo is a big day. To be honest, we all love it."

Now her gaze turned puzzled. "I don't understand."

He tipped his chin to the wall separating the kitchen and living room. "Needs to come down."

"And?"

From a bag on the counter he handed her goggles, a mask and heavy gloves. She'd taken his advice, dressing in worn jeans, a baggy T-shirt and sneakers. While the clothing was out of character for her, somehow she made the outfit look trendy as well as work friendly. He found it appealing. Then frowned at the thought.

Last night's conversation in the quiet kitchen, where they'd revealed times in their lives they actually didn't want to revisit, was bad enough. Regarding Heidi much more closely than he normally would had to stop.

Setting her cup next to his, Heidi donned the protective gear without asking any more questions. He picked up the hammer and held it out to her. "Take a swing."

"When I said intern, I meant running errands. Cleaning up stuff. Not destruction."

He grinned, looking forward to how this would play out. "Every intern usually looks forward to demo day. Haven't you ever watched those DIY shows?"

She had, so she slowly moved across the room, shook out her arms and rolled her neck. "Hand it over," came her muffled demand.

He passed the hammer to her. Once she had a hold and he let go, the hammer nearly slipped out of her fingers. She caught it before it hit the floor.

"This is heavier than I expected."

"Needs to be if you want to break through drywall."

She blinked rapidly and stepped up to the wall. Then she lifted the hammer, pulled back to swing, only to miss the wall completely, and Reid, by mere inches. He jumped out of the way. The hammer continued its arc to the floor, almost taking Heidi with it.

"Sorry!" she cried as she quickly regained her balance.

"Next time take better aim." He suppressed a chuckle. "At the wall, not me."

She rolled her eyes and tried again, making a small dent in the plaster.

"Yes!" she yelled, fist pumping the air.

She continued to take efficient swings, but soon got to the point where she had to finesse her moves to reach higher. Even though Heidi gave it her all, Reid wanted the wall down sometime today. After placing a mask over his mouth and nose, he slipped on his gloves and claimed the hammer from her.

"Watch and learn." He took a great whack at the spot, removing a heavy chunk of drywall near the ceiling. He repeated the process three more times until there was a large enough area cleared away.

He lowered the hammer. "What do you think?"

"That I should have made this deal after spending a month at the gym." She pinched her biceps. "I need more muscle mass."

"You look good just the way you are."

She flushed at his compliment.

Reid's mask hid a smile and he nodded at what was left of the wall. "Want to finish up?"

"Are you kidding? This is better than therapy."

She lifted the hammer and took a more direct swing. This time she managed to expand the hole and several pieces of drywall flew off. When she faced him, he could tell she was smiling by how her eyes sparkled.

"I'm getting the hang of it."

"You sure are."

With a whoop, she swung again, making a mess and laughing the entire time. Reid couldn't remember when he'd had this much fun on a project.

Once he was sure that Heidi had a handle on things, he started removing the old cabinets from the walls in the kitchen.

An hour later, her swings were getting clumsy. "Let me take over," he said.

"No way. I can do this."

And she did.

Before long, she'd finished, and a haze of debris hung in the air. Reid pointed to the door. She nodded and followed him to the front porch. Once outside they both removed their protective gear.

"Okay, that was officially cool," Heidi said, her complexion red from exertion.

"Now you see why demo day is so awesome." Reid breathed in the fresh mountain air. The misty shadows of morning were giving way to streaks of watery sunlight. He loved this time of day, when everything was fresh and new, and possibilities and opportunities lay ahead.

He'd always been an early riser, ready to get moving and greet the day. Having Heidi join him this morning made him appreciate the special moment all the more.

A smile still lingered on her sweet face. When she reached up to tug a strand of hair from her damp cheek, he noticed broken fingernails earned while swinging the sledgehammer so determinedly. A shadow of fatigue fringed her eyes. She'd never voice her weariness, not even hint at it—because this was Heidi—but she'd worked as hard as any crew member he'd ever had.

She closed her eyes and tilted her head back, as if appreciating the heat from the sun filtering through the tree branches. Her hair, pulled into a ponytail, swung back and forth across her shoulders. When she lifted her eyelids, their gazes collided and he found himself rooted to the spot. The connection continued and he couldn't have moved even if he'd wanted to. But she blinked and the magic suddenly ended, leaving him wanting more.

More? Of being with Heidi? He wondered what she'd slipped inside the coffee to make him wax poetic.

"What happens next?" she asked, breaking the odd tension between them.

"Now you get to do intern things."

"Like?"

He pushed open the door and pointed inside. "See that square of canvas?"

"Yes."

"Load all the debris from the wall on it and we'll slide it out to the dumpster."

"You got it, boss."

"We can make a few trips," he offered.

Obvious relief swept over her.

"Don't forget to put your gear on," he called to her retreating back.

"Yes, boss." Her reply floated through the air and he couldn't stop another smile.

While she tackled the debris with her usual fierce determination, Reid finished knocking down the rest of the wall, removing the pink insulation hanging from the studs. He tossed it on the canvas as Heidi added loose pieces of drywall to the mess.

"What's next?" Heidi asked as she straightened up.

"I finish off the edges. We'll fix it up so you won't know there was ever a wall here."

She slipped off her mask. "I'm impressed. I never really thought about all the effort that goes into remodeling a house." She wrinkled her nose. "Or the messy clutter."

"All part of the first phase. My team will be here soon and we'll tear out the rest of the kitchen cabinets and appliances. Once you clean up that'll mean the worst of the destruction will be over for this house."

She placed her hands on her hips. "When *I* clean up?"

"Intern."

"Right."

He chuckled, then took pity on her. "One

more load to the dumpster and then you can take off if you want."

"No way, I'm going to pull my weight. I rescheduled the morning so I could be here."

Impressed by her dedication, he admired how she persevered, although exhaustion was soon evident on her face.

"I'll have you out of here before noon," he promised as he heard truck doors slam outside.

Heidi groaned. "The crew?"

"Right on time."

"More loud banging and crashing."

"It's the only way to get the job done."

She squared her shoulders. "If it means getting this house, then I'm all in." She continued collecting scraps of the old wall.

What would happen if she couldn't afford the place when the reno was finished? This was just a deal, like every other deal he'd been involved in, right? After Heidi had explained why she'd used the owe-me card, he had to admit, he was pulling for her to get this place.

The crew piled inside and before long chaos started. Heidi laughed and helped the guys. Well, sort of helped. She accidentally dropped the sledgehammer on Joe's foot when she moved beside him, making him hop away with terror in his eyes. When she tried to drag the canvas to the front door to get to the dumpster, she nearly came into contact with the kitchen sink that Mike had tossed her way. She yelled, which made him yell right back, until she wagged a finger at him and he blushed.

Ernie, the oldest of the crew, asked her to hand him a crowbar, and when she begged to use it, he relented. Reid cringed when she misunderstood the instructions and used the tool on the wrong wall, adding another item to what they'd have to fix.

Reid strode across the room and gently removed the crowbar from her hands.

"Hey! I was helping Ernie."

Ernie frowned and moved away.

"You know what," Reid said. "My guys have a rhythm. How about we let them at it so we finish this job on time."

"You really don't want me handling tools?" she asked, a hint of hurt there.

"I really don't."

"Fine. Your loss." She shrugged. "But I'm warning you, I'll have someone teach me how to use them before this project is over."

Sassy reply given, she sauntered into the living room. Ernie's grandson, Phil, stood in the corner swiping through his phone. When Heidi sweetly asked him to give her a hand to dump the canvas, he seemed confused, but put away his phone. Before he knew it, she was bossing him around. Reid respected her tenacity.

Reid admittedly hadn't been keen on hiring the young man but wanted to give the kid a chance because he'd known Ernie for a long time. So far, the twentysomething seemed to be good at one thing—pushing his work off on someone else. Reid would give him instructions, only to find Ernie doing the task. If the kid kept this up, Reid would have no choice but to fire him. His attention reverted back to Heidi as it always seemed to these last few days.

Ernie stood beside him. "What are you thinking?"

"It's a long story."

The older man met his gaze. "You must really like her."

"It's not like that."

Ernie rubbed his head, white hair jutting here and there. "Right. I'll remember that the next time she asks to use a tool."

Joe, muscular and tan from hours spent in the woods, piped up. "I didn't know it was bring-your-girlfriend-to-work day."

"It's not—"

"Is it?" Mike, tall and thin, clearly missed the joke. "Because Josie has a ton of upper-body strength and could empty this kitchen out in no time."

"No girlfriends," Reid said, then grimaced. "Not that Heidi is my girlfriend."

"Right," Ernie said, slapping him on the shoulder. "You keep tellin' yourself that."

Reid dropped his head back and stared at the ceiling, wondering how he'd lost control of the situation. Maybe he should take Mike's advice and hire Josie to balance out the team.

He moved to the opening in the wall and watched Heidi sweet-talk Joe into letting her use his crowbar to remove the baseboard so they could refinish the wood floor. And Joe was smiling at her. Smiling. The guy who never cracked a smile, even when Ernie told a downright funny joke. And soon he found himself smiling, like it was contagious. How did she do it?

Heidi beamed at Joe, then got back to her task. The determined expression on her face proved her commitment. If she could focus on her goal, was it possible he could do the same? They hadn't talked in depth about him returning to Masterson Enterprises last night, but watching her today as she tried to tear down the wall, he wondered what it would take for him to break down the wall between him and his father. But what if he tried and was shot down again. Could he survive another emotional hit?

The answer was simple. No.

Heidi coming back into his life had him hoping again, and he wasn't sure he liked it.

CHAPTER FIVE

BETWEEN DOING WHAT she could at the house on Hanover and trying to squeeze more work hours into her day, Heidi arrived at the community center Tuesday night with only minutes to spare before her tutoring group met. Her shoulders ached from the demo, her legs sore from hauling debris to the dumpster and, let's face it, she was just plain tired. If she could have called off the session tonight, she would have, but the kids were getting close to the end of the school year and needed the guidance for finals.

Mia greeted her as soon as she walked through the door. "Heidi. I got a B on the Algebra test."

Despite being weary, the news brought an instant smile to Heidi's face. "That's wonderful. I knew you could do it."

The teen grinned. "I'm closer to getting my car keys."

"And the satisfaction of making a good grade doesn't matter?"

"I'm closer to my keys," Mia repeated. "My. Keys."

"Okay, I get it."

Heidi dropped off her tote bag and purse. She scanned the room. Not as many students tonight, and the ones who were there were slouched in their chairs. To be honest, she would have liked to have stayed home too. But no, she honored her commitments. To Serena's store. Her clients. The house remodel. She summoned whatever energy she had left.

Heidi straightened and had the students get out their homework to review. The hour passed with the usual roadblocks. Mia, excited about her test grade, chatted the entire time. The high school's baseball pitcher only had the upcoming championship on his mind. And the others, varying from those truly struggling and those who didn't care about school at all, merely went through the motions. Heidi's mind was elsewhere, as well.

On broad shoulders and deep green eyes. Strong arms and glances that made her toes curl.

Beyond that was the fact that she felt she could depend on Reid, unlike some in her past. He'd kept his part of their deal, instead of paying lip service. Hadn't he given her the space to complete her tasks at the house without butting in to get her to do it his way? Sure, her being there created extra work for him, but he'd been patient. Maybe even a little impressed if his smiles were any indication. And those smiles…wow. To see one aimed at her was a major motivator.

"Okay, everyone," she said to the preoccupied students, hoping to instill a little motivation, "Only thirty more minutes and we'll call it a night."

Once they'd gone over the material for the final test, it didn't take long for the kids to rush out. Only Mia remained to pack up her notebook and pencil at turtle-like speed, her attention focused on the doorway. She applied some lip gloss.

"Everything okay, Mia?"

The girl jumped. "Yeah, I uh…"

"Waiting for Todd?"

"No." Her cheeks went pink. "Why would you think that?"

Heidi hid a smile. "Just a guess."

"I'm not in a hurry, that's all."

Right. Heidi wasn't buying it. She stood at her weathered desk and collected her stuff.

Mia wandered over to stand beside her. "Can I ask you something?"

"Shoot."

"Did you ever ask a guy to prom?" Mia all but whispered.

"No. In fact, I never went to prom."

Not because she didn't want to. It was a case of no one asking her and Heidi never working up the courage to ask the one guy who would have made the night fun. Reid.

He'd been popular and never had to worry about getting a date. She'd envied him for that. Or had she envied the girls he'd asked out? Or the other girls who may have asked the guys?

Mia's eyes went wide. "That's like…sad."

Yeah, it was. Or so she'd thought at the time. "I didn't mind."

Looking back, would she have done anything differently? Probably not. All of the difficulties she'd endured along the journey had made her stronger than she'd ever imagined she could be. The curveballs life had thrown her way had made her appreciate what she had now, no matter the struggle. Didn't adversity develop character? She hoped so.

So, no, the memory didn't sting so much anymore. Life went on and high school traditions didn't seem important in the grand scheme of things. Not when she had a grasp on the future in the form of a lasting home.

Curious, Heidi eyed Mia. "Is there a reason why you're asking?"

Mia looked away, then back at Heidi. "I've gone to prom before, but my dates always asked me first."

"No one's asked you this time?"

Mia tried to pull off an air of nonchalance. "Yeah, but I'm not interested."

"And the boy you want to go with?"

Her bright countenance faded. "He's not interested in going, I think."

Heidi could easily sense Mia's insecurity, and relate, but still, it wasn't a great feeling.

"Then take a chance," Heidi said, a bit surprised by her bold suggestion. "Lots of girls ask boys out. What could it hurt?"

Plenty, Heidi realized after she'd posed the question.

Should she take her own advice?

After she'd spoken to Reid at Masterson House, the idea of asking him to attend his brother's engagement party had stayed front and center in her mind. It made sense, really. They'd both be there, so why not go together? Yet every time she attempted to bring it up, he'd give her a long look that took her breath away and she'd chicken out. Her excuse for asking was that she wanted to help Reid by getting his grandmother off his back, but at the same time, she wanted to know if this interest in Reid was only one-sided. What better means to find out?

"You're right," Mia said. "I can ask him. At least then I'll know where I stand."

"That's very grown-up of you."

Mia shrugged. "And if he says no, then I can tell one of the other guys I'll go with him."

The door across the hallway opened and the sound of voices filtered into the air. Mia looked over her shoulder, seeing the kids file out, she ran to get her backpack to meet the others.

"Bye," she yelled and dashed out the door.

Heidi watched as Mia singled out Todd and started a conversation. So, yeah, Mia had her eye on Todd.

Heidi had to admire Mia. The girl went after what she wanted. Why shouldn't Heidi do the same?

Her mind spun in circles and the wild notion that had kept her awake bombarded her again. Reid was in the room across the hallway. She could march right over, suggest they go to the party together like it was no big thing.

She cringed. Fear of rejection kept her from moving. Sure, they were friends. Showed up at the same events even. Why would this one be any different?

Because you want to go with him as a date, not friends.

Yep, that was her dilemma.

Don't be such a chicken.

Okay, refocus. She could make another deal with him, although this time she didn't have a bargaining chip. It would be Heidi, putting herself out there when she had no reason to think Reid would ever be interested in her in a romantic way.

But he could be, and if you don't ask, you'll never know.

"Be quiet," she muttered to herself. She didn't believe it was her imagination, the gentle smiles Reid sent her way or the heat that seemed to ramp up when they brushed arms while doing a task. Surely, he'd felt the zing when they removed the mirror from the bathroom wall, crowded into a small space, bumping into each other while at the same time trying to keep their distance.

But what if she was wrong?

She heard Alveda's voice in her head. *I didn't teach you to be a quitter.*

Okay. It was now or never.

She walked to the doorway, smoothing the creases wrinkling her skirt and tugging the denim jacket tighter over her silky tank top. Her low heels echoed on the cement floor.

Then she crossed the hallway. Then she went into Reid's room where she…stopped.

His back was to her. His muscles pulled against the forest-green Henley shirt he wore. His jeans fit exactly right, and his boots looked a little less beat-up than the ones he normally wore on the jobsite. She was so captured by the sight of him that it took a moment for her to realize he was on the phone.

"I know it's last minute, Ains, but time got away from me. I promise, it'll be a fun night if you agree to come to my brother's party with me."

It took Heidi several moments to comprehend that Reid was asking the person on the other end of the phone to the engagement party.

"You remember Logan. He came to visit during our last semester at college."

An old college girlfriend?

His shoulders relaxed. "That's great, Ainsley. I'll pick you up around six on Saturday."

Heidi's face heated. Well, if she had any questions about Reid being attracted to her, that conversation cleared them up. Slowly tiptoeing away so Reid would never know she was there, Heidi made for a hasty exit. But Reid chose that exact moment to catch her trying to escape with her dignity intact.

"Heidi, I didn't see you there."

She swallowed hard, giving herself time to go for unaffected instead of mortified. She turned.

"Sorry. When I noticed you were on the phone, I tried to leave so I wouldn't disturb you."

"No problem. I'm finished." He tossed the phone on the long table where some tools and half-constructed projects were scattered across the surface. "Just making plans for the party."

"Oh. Good."

He started putting tools away in a metal box, but then paused. "Something up?"

"No. Just thought I'd come by and say hi." *Lame.*

"Like we didn't see each other enough at the jobsite today?"

"True." She forced a laugh. "I'll let you get home—"

"Wait. I have good news."

She raised an eyebrow.

"I got a date for the party."

Tamping down the twinge of jealousy, she managed a teasing tone she didn't feel. "So, you did indeed thwart your grandmother after all."

"I did. Ainsley is someone Grandmother

would fix me up with herself, so she can't complain."

"Well then, you should be pleased."

"I am." He grinned. "You'll like Ainsley."

Would she? "An old college friend?"

"Yeah. She lives down near Atlanta, so we don't bump into each other often."

Heidi was impressed by the fact that her voice sounded normal. "It's nice you've maintained a connection with her."

"It's been a while, but my family already knows her. I brought her home to visit when we were attending Clemson."

Heidi had been away at college herself, so she'd never met Reid's friends if they came home with him on long weekends.

"That's great that it all worked out." She made a point of checking her watch. "I'll see you Saturday," she said, giving him a little wave as she left the room.

Once she was safely back in her own room, Heidi closed her eyes. What had she been thinking? If this didn't prove that she and Reid were only meant to be friends, she didn't know what else did. She had to get him out of her system, because letting this attraction grow would only make her miserable.

She stuffed papers into her tote, then slung the bag over her shoulder. Silently flinched at the achy muscles. As she fished for her car keys in her purse, she heard the door across the hall close. Not wanting to walk out of the building with Reid, she procrastinated in order to give him a head start. Once it was quiet, she turned to leave, only to find Reid leaning against the doorjamb. In the bright light, his eyes were the same deep shade as his hunter-green shirt. He looked so good, so solid, so... Reid. It hurt.

She stumbled and the tote slipped down her arm, landing on the floor. Two small cans rolled out and she got down on her knees to retrieve them.

Reid hurried over, placing his toolbox on a table before he joined her.

"You okay?"

"You just startled me. I thought I was alone."

Reid reached for the can. Held it up and smiled. "Cat food?"

"I stopped by Masterson House earlier. Alveda gave them to me. She's always buying toys or food for Mr. Whiskers."

"I need to meet that lucky guy."

Reid at her apartment? She nearly choked. Yeah, that wasn't going to happen.

"Usually she makes his food from scratch and sends it home with me. He's picky, so I try to bribe him with fresh chicken, fish..."

Why was she going on about her cat?

Once she had her belongings inside the tote, she rose. Reid took hold of her arm to steady her. Actually, it was his casual touch that set her off-balance, but that seemed to be a regular reaction these days.

"Thanks."

He tilted his head. "Are you okay?"

"Of course. I'm always good."

He sent her a knowing look.

"I have a lot on my plate just now. No biggie."

"Maybe you should slow down."

So she had more time to spend with her ridiculous thoughts? No, thank you.

"I'll be fine. Thanks for being concerned."

"That's what friends do."

Ah, right. It was official. Reid did not have romantic feelings for her.

This was good, she told herself. Now she could move on. Get back on track. Look at Reid as her old buddy, not the hunky contractor who had a starring role in her daydreams.

"I'm glad you said that," she confirmed. "We are friends."

There. She'd made a public declaration she wouldn't take back.

Reid looked at her with a funny expression but shrugged. He opened his mouth, but just then, his phone dinged. He pulled the cell from his pocket.

"It's Logan," he said.

Saved by a text.

"He wants me to meet him at Smitty's Pub."

"Then you should probably get going."

He picked up the toolbox. "Want to come with? It's a nice night and we could walk over together."

Smitty's, the local hangout for Golden residents, was four blocks away. While it would indeed be a beautiful night to enjoy, the idea of spending more time with Reid made her antsy.

"I'm going to head home."

Reid nodded. Waited.

"Is there something else?" she asked.

"Just waiting so we can walk out together."

Ever the gentleman, he wasn't going to let her go to the parking lot alone. Not wanting to make a scene or have him continue to ask what was wrong with her, she walked along beside him.

This whole friends-only act would be hard to maintain.

SOMETHING WAS UP with Heidi. She was uptight and barely talked on the way to the parking lot. She'd been nonstop chatty since he'd agreed to let her work at the house reno, so why the near silent treatment tonight?

The evening had grown chilly. It was early April after all, but a long way from the cold winter they'd just endured. Spring had always been Reid's favorite time of year, and this one was shaping up to be stellar. He needed to carve out a few hours from his schedule to go hiking or out on the lake in the family boat. Maybe the gang could get together and make a day of it. He was busy but could always make time for a much-needed break.

He glanced at Heidi. She loved going for hikes up to Pine Tree Overlook. They could pack a lunch, stop somewhere along the trail, just the two of them…

"Warbler?" she asked.

He shook his head as the picnic scene in his head dissipated like smoke. "What?"

"The bird making noise above us. It sounds like a warbler."

"You remember?"

"Sure. You taught me."

Because his grandfather had taught him.

Josiah Masterson had been an important figure in Reid's life as he grew up. Whenever things got dicey at home, Pops would search Reid out and they'd go off to the woods on an adventure. The older man had been an avid bird-watcher, showing Reid everything he knew. Reid, in turn, shared his knowledge with Heidi when they'd go hiking often during the summer. His friends would have probably razzed him over his ornithology interest, but Heidi was game to learn all his granddad had taught him.

Pops had faithfully gone to the Masterson Enterprises office every day until he retired, although his heart had been devoted to the great outdoors.

"My granddad left quite a legacy."

"You also learned to use your woodworking tools from him."

She remembered that too?

Reid nodded. "It always amazed me how his woodwork was so detailed and precise."

"Is that why you got your general contractor's license? Because of your granddad?"

"He always told me to have another avenue to fall back on in case finance didn't work out for me."

"I really didn't think much about it at first, but then I put two-and-two together. Between Masterson's commercial construction and you flipping houses, you'd need a license."

"I took the contractors' test right out of college." A bitter laugh slipped out. "Ticked off my dad."

They'd had an argument about it, highlighting one in their long list of differences. His father didn't think Reid needed the license as long as his father had connections to contractors. But Reid had been committed to the family business and getting the license was another way to make a solid contribution to the company. It had been a vow he'd promised Pops, because his grandfather had wanted Reid to be able to stand on his own two feet, have multiple skills, something his father never understood. Pops didn't say much, but he saw everything.

Heidi lightly touched his arm. "I never got to meet him, but I'm positive he'd be proud of you."

Reid swallowed hard. His grandfather had meant a lot to him, and when he'd died right before Heidi came to town, it had knocked Reid off his axis. How many times did he wish Pops was here to give him advice or play hooky and go fishing for an afternoon?

Leave it to Heidi to sense his mood and try to make him feel better.

"Your grandmother must miss him too," Heidi said. "She never remarried."

"Said she couldn't pretend she'd ever love anyone else." They stopped by Heidi's car. "Although, sometimes I think she gets lonely."

"Your grandmother?" Heidi laughed. "With all the activities she's involved in? I imagine her rising at dawn to map out her conquests for the day, then falling into bed at night after she's meddled in enough people's business or made sure she had her say in town events. I wish I had half her energy."

At that picture, Reid chuckled. "She is constantly on the go, but sometimes she gets this... I don't know...lost look in her eyes when she doesn't think anyone will notice."

Heidi pressed the key fob to unlock her sedan. "I suppose that's what having a great love is all about."

Was it? Reid didn't know. He'd never fallen so completely in love that he couldn't imagine life without that other person.

Once she had the door open, Heidi glanced at him. "So, thanks for escorting me to my car. Your duty is done."

"It's not a duty. I like making sure you're okay."

Her eyes went wide. "Is that why you tried to run me off from the more detailed jobs at the demo?"

He placed a hand on his chest. "You've found me out."

"Honestly, you need to give me a chance."

"Like when you were dragging the sink out

of the bathroom and tripped, nearly landing facedown on the floor? Or when I had to explain to you and Phil about job safety?"

"This is all new to me, Reid. Give me time and I'll run circles around you."

He laughed. From experience he knew if given the chance, Heidi would one-up him. That's why he always tried to stay a step ahead.

She tossed her bags inside. "Since you don't need my help at the house for the rest of the week, I'll see you at the party."

They were at the stage of the remodel where the team would finish up the demo and then bring in new drywall, wood and other materials to start the next phase. There was electrical work to be done, as well as additional plumbing. He had to admit, he'd miss her sunny face greeting him in the morning.

"Be safe," he said as she slid into the driver's seat. He had a grip on the top of the door and once she was settled, he closed it. She sent him a wave and he nodded, then tossed his toolbox into the truck bed and began walking to Smitty's to meet Logan.

He slowed down at the end of the block, waiting for Heidi to drive by on her route home. A few minutes passed and he couldn't ignore the feeling that something was wrong.

He retraced his steps, discovering her car in the same spot. Concerned, he walked over and rapped on the window.

She almost jumped, her surprise evident when her gaze met his. She rolled down the window.

"You scared the life out of me again. Twice in one night."

"Sorry. When you didn't pass by, I came to check on you."

"The car won't start."

He opened the door. "Pop the hood. Maybe it's something obvious."

She did as he suggested and exited the car. As she brushed by him, Reid inhaled her floral scent. He froze for a split second, then went to take a look at the engine. Lately, it seemed like every time he was in confined spaces with Heidi, his attention zoomed to her and not the job at hand. All his focus would shift to her pretty amber eyes or the smile that made his chest hitch. If this kept up, he'd need his own refresher on job safety whenever Heidi was around.

"Do you think it's the battery?" she asked.

"Or the starter." He closed the hood and joined her.

She blew out a breath. "I've been meaning

to bring the car in for maintenance, but time got away from me."

"This late, the auto garage is closed."

Heidi searched around the car's dim interior and produced her phone. She rested her free hand on the door frame. Her fingers brushed his and he felt that buzz of awareness he'd been craving lately.

"What are you doing?" he asked, focusing on her moving fingers instead of his reaction to his friend.

"Calling a tow truck. If I can get the car to the shop tonight, maybe Mark can look at it first thing in the morning."

Reid took his phone from his pocket. "Let me text him. Mark owes me a favor, so I should get you first on the list tomorrow."

She grinned. "See how this owing thing comes in handy?"

He sent the message. "Done."

Heidi's phone rang and she answered it. A moment later, she said to him, "Someone will be here within the hour. They'll text me when they're on the way."

"That long?" Reid looked up and down the nearly deserted street. The business district of Golden closed early until the summer crowds showed up.

"Yep." She waved him off. "Go on to Smitty's. I'll wait in my car."

"No way. Come with me until the driver contacts you and I'll walk you back."

"You're supposed to be meeting Logan."

Why was she pushing him to go alone? "If I didn't know better, I'd think you're giving me the brush-off."

"I don't want to be the reason you miss spending time with your brother."

"If I did meet him and he found out I'd left you alone, he wouldn't be happy, and neither would I, so you're stuck with me." Her stand-offish look shouldn't bother him, but it did. "Besides, you'll need a lift home."

"I can call a ride share."

Okay, enough was enough. "Heidi, what gives? Are you upset with me about something?"

She was chewing her lower lip, like she did when she was uncertain. "What do you mean?"

"You didn't want to walk to the car. You don't want me to wait with you or drive you home later."

"You know I hate depending on people, Reid."

Why did he feel like her excuse was just

that, an excuse? Frustration made his tone sharp. "I'm not leaving you."

"Fine," came her equally short response as she reached into the car for her purse. "Let's go."

It was only four blocks to Smitty's, but it felt like the longest walk of his life. Outside the bar, he tried again and asked, "What's up?"

"Why does something have to be up? My car won't start and tonight the kids couldn't concentrate. You were busy finding a date—"

"Is that what this is about? That I have a date?"

"Don't be silly. I'm glad you found someone to go with you to the party."

This was why Reid didn't get sucked into relationships. Half the time he didn't understand what was going on.

"But you'd tell me, right?"

She rolled her eyes and opened the door. Laughter and loud music spilled out, effectively ending their conversation.

As soon as they entered Smitty's, the amazing scent of pub food enveloped them. Heidi hightailed it across the room to a group of people including Serena and Carrie. Clearly something was bothering her, but was it him or something else? He hadn't done anything wrong—in fact, he'd gone out of his way to let her work at the jobsite, so it didn't make sense.

He was staring at her when his brother sidled up beside him. "Took your time getting here."

"Heidi's car wouldn't start so I stayed with her while she called a tow truck."

Following the direction of Reid's focus, Logan asked, "What's so interesting?"

"Nothing."

"Really? Tell that to your face."

Annoyed, Reid met his brother's amused gaze. "What?"

"I know you aren't interested in Serena or Carrie, so that leaves your pensive expression focused on Heidi."

"Things between us are off tonight."

Logan nodded.

"Usually she can't stop talking."

"Maybe she doesn't have anything to say."

"That never happens."

Logan shrugged. "First time for everything."

His brother's comment bugged him. He didn't like it that Heidi was tense and tonight she seemed overly stressed.

He looked over at his tormentor. "Why are we here?"

"I can't have a beer with my brother?"

Reid stared at him.

"If you're going to take my head off..."

Reid ran a hand over the back of his neck. "Sorry."

Logan paused. "This thing with Heidi is really bothering you?"

It was. More than it should and he couldn't figure out why. Instead of supplying his brother with more fodder to give him grief, Reid said, "Long day."

Logan laughed. "Right."

"So, what? You're going to give me a hard time all night?"

"I don't have to. I think Heidi's already done the job."

Reid searched for her. She was laughing at something a friend said, the highlights in her brown hair shiny under the lights, a smile brightening her face. It bothered him that she hadn't smiled at him like that tonight, and it seemed she was in a better mood with anyone but him.

Did she mean it when she said she wasn't upset about him taking a date to the party? She'd seemed like her old self before he gave her the news. And why should it bother him? Then it dawned on him. Maybe she didn't have a date of her own.

"I'm dense," he muttered under his breath.

Of course, Logan heard his brother, chuckling despite the loud music. "Of the two of us, I've always thought so."

Reid elbowed him. "Do you know if Heidi has a date for your engagement party?"

Logan lifted a shoulder. "She doesn't normally fill me in on her social calendar."

"I was on the phone with Ainsley earlier and she overheard. She might be upset with me because of that."

"Why? It's not like you two have a thing going on."

Reid frowned.

"Wait. Do you two have a thing going on?"

"No," Reid rushed to say. They were friends. First and foremost. At least he thought they were. Could he have missed the memo? If he was honest, the idea of them together was... nice.

"Oh, no," Logan said.

Shaking off his thoughts, Reid looked at his brother.

A slow grin spread over Logan's lips. "Dude, I recognize that expression. You're in trouble."

Reid sought out Heidi again and his chest went tight.

He repeated his brother's amused words. "You're right. I'm in so much trouble."

CHAPTER SIX

"WHY CAN'T I find a dress?" Heidi complained as she browsed through the rack of high-end designs. The colors all blended together in one bright splotch as she listlessly pretended to go through the motions of shopping.

"You aren't trying hard enough," Serena teased.

Heidi shot her friend an annoyed look. They'd taken their lunch hour to find Heidi a dress for the upcoming engagement party while another part-time employee at Blue Ridge Cottage filled in. Carrie had to run an errand, then she'd be joining them at Tessa's, Golden's fancy clothing store.

"I suppose you already have a dress," Heidi complained.

"Got it a few days after Logan proposed. I knew I'd be busy with my dad getting remarried. Now that his big day is over, I can concentrate on my own wedding." Serena pushed the hangers slowly along the rack, the scrape of metal on metal grating Heidi's nerves. "But

I should have a backup." She glanced at Heidi, panic on her face. "I should have a backup, right?"

"What on earth for? Do you like the dress you picked out?"

"Yes. It's lovely."

"Then quit worrying and help me."

Serena crossed her arms. "The party is three days away. Why haven't you bought a dress yet?"

"I meant to. Then I picked up two new clients and—"

"Heidi?"

She looked over the rack at her friend, hearing the censure in her voice.

"I thought we talked about this."

"We did, but I can't turn down work."

Serena blew out a breath. "You're spreading yourself too thin."

"Maybe, but now my car needs to be repaired, so I have to work overtime."

Mentioning the car made her think about the uncomfortable ride home with Reid last night. They barely spoke and there was a strained atmosphere in the truck. Once he got to her apartment building, she'd jumped out with a brusque "thanks" and rushed inside. Mr. Whiskers demanded food, then, noticing her mood as she got ready for bed, nudged his nose against her leg. She scooped him up, taking solace in the steady sound of his purring.

At least this male returned her feelings for him.

"You probably have more money squirreled away than Carrie and me put together," Serena said, unaware of Heidi's inner turmoil.

Serena might be right. Heidi refused to repeat her past, so sure, she worked too much, but she was financially stable. All other areas of her life were up in the air.

"As soon as the house remodel is finished, I'll have some extra time in the day."

"Which you'd better use to relax. When was the last time you went hiking?"

Her favorite pastime. "Um… Just before Christmas?"

"That was four months ago."

"Really?" The weeks had flown by.

"Are you taking a vacation this year?"

"Can't. House to buy. Wedding attendant." Heidi gasped. "I'm still in the wedding, right?"

"Yes. That would never change."

"Then think of all the duties I'll have. First, making sure this engagement party goes off without a hitch—"

"You think there'll be a hitch?" Serena paled. "I don't have any more secrets."

When Serena had come to town, she'd been

hiding some heavy secrets. Logan had smoked them out and everything broke loose, but in the end, they'd fallen in love and nothing could destroy that. Heidi wished for the same one day.

"Sorry, poor word choice on my part." Heidi took a breath and counted using her fingers. "As I was saying, there's the bridal shower, shopping for your wedding dress, the bachelorette party, making sure you get to the altar on time…"

"Oh, I won't be late."

Heidi laughed. "What was I thinking?"

"That you need to find a dress." Serena gave a cheer and clapped her hands. "Back to it."

They returned to the hunt. Heidi selected three styles to try on. Serena picked two more. Just before she went to the fitting room to try them all on, Carrie, Serena's roommate, rushed into the store, her cheeks red as if she'd run the entire way from her appointment.

"I did it," she said, breathless, fanning her face with her hand. "The interview at the Chamber of Commerce went great. Now I have to wait on the board's decision."

Serena hugged her friend. "They'll hire you, I have no doubt. Then you'll be in Golden permanently."

Carrie looked a bit shocked. "I suppose."

"Don't change your mind now," Serena said with a smile.

"I won't. I need a break and Golden is the best place to regroup."

Serena slung an arm over Heidi's shoulders. "Because we're here."

Carrie chuckled. "Yes, because you're both here."

Heidi slid out from under Serena's arm, always a little self-conscious when others showed her affection. Her mother had been far from cuddly. Heidi's raggedy stuffed bear came to mind. Boy, had Heidi squeezed the stuffing out of that thing, especially when it was dark. She'd had a difficult time parting with her best childhood friend, but once she moved in with Alveda, she hadn't needed the bear any longer.

Serena shooed her into the dressing room. "Let's get a move on before we need to return to the shop."

Heidi went into a fitting room and closed the door, still able to hear Serena questioning Carrie about her own dress. "You two are the worst bridesmaids."

Heidi grinned because, despite the words, she heard the genuine affection in Serena's tone.

The first two dresses weren't right. The third was possible and by the time Heidi got to the fifth, she liked the final choice the best. Opening the door, she stepped out to find Serena and Carrie seated by the mirror. Carrie had a dress folded over her arm.

Heidi's mouth dropped open. "Don't tell me you found one so quickly."

"Actually, I stopped by here a few days ago and chose my outfit." She nodded at Serena. "Just wanted to make my roommate here suffer."

"Mission accomplished," Serena said, laughing, then she studied Heidi from head to toe. "I like it."

Heidi turned around to look in the mirror. The shimmery sheath-style dress hugged her curves. "Is it too tight?"

"No, that's the style," Carrie said. Heidi took her word for it, since Carrie had lived in Manhattan for years and had more fashion sense in her little finger than Heidi had in her entire body.

"I like the color," Serena said. "Apricot looks good with your skin tone."

Heidi tilted her head back and forth. Her brown hair looked darker and the amber flecks in her eyes popped. She had to admit, this dress was spectacular.

"Do you have shoes to go with?" Carrie asked.

"I think so. They're a nude heel."

"Perfect."

Heidi twisted to get a view of the back, then faced her friends. "Okay. I'm going with this one."

Serena clasped her hands over her heart. "Finally."

Heidi removed the dress and returned it to the hanger. She rejoined her friends, who were regarding her with amused expressions. Heidi looked down, making sure she'd put her clothes on correctly. "Am I missing something?"

"No," Serena said. "We were just chatting about dates and realized you don't have one for the engagement party."

Heidi glanced at Carrie. "When did you find a date?"

"Last night. I asked Jamey."

Heidi blinked. Jamey owned Smitty's Pub. He was fun loving and as big as a bear, with a long beard to match.

"Why didn't I think of asking him?" Heidi frowned.

"Because you've been too busy with Reid."

She tried to look innocent. "He has a date."

"Uh-huh, but you wish it was you," Carrie crowed with a satisfied grin.

Panic made her knees tremble. *How did they know?* "Why would you say that?"

"Because you kept sneaking glances at him at the pub last night."

"No, I didn't."

"Don't even," Serena said. "Carrie and I both saw it."

She dropped her head. *Had Reid noticed?* Heidi's feelings for him had been increasing; she'd been careful to act unaffected, but last night had been rough after finding out he'd asked another woman to the party.

"Seriously, when did this start?" Serena settled into her chair.

Heidi groaned. "Nothing has started. There is nothing."

Carrie laughed. "Girl, you've had your eye on him for a long time."

"Wha…how…" Heidi stuttered.

Both of her friends laughed.

No point in covering up any longer. Not with her friends, who could apparently read her emotions better than she could. "I thought I was doing a good job not letting it show."

"Nope," came Serena's perky reply.

"Does Reid know?" Carrie asked.

"Not a clue. He only thinks of me as a friend." Which hurt because, yes, she had been trying, and failing, to ignore her attraction for Reid for some time now.

Serena considered her remark. "Well, you have known each other for years."

"And nothing has ever come of it. That's the very reason why it'll never be anything more than friendship."

"But you want it to? Become more, that is."

Heidi bit her lip. Couldn't deny the longing building inside her heart. "There's no point."

"How do you know?" Carrie challenged. "Maybe he has hidden feelings for you too."

"If he does, he sure has done a better job hiding them," Heidi scoffed, the hurt welling again.

"So, make him notice you. That dress will do it."

Heidi stared at the dress in her hands. Could she turn Reid's head? Make him wonder what if? Maybe pursue her?

"Stupid tool belt," she muttered.

"Did you say something about a belt?" Carrie asked, then chuckled.

Why did the image of him in his work clothes sporting that darn belt make Heidi's blood race? "Just ignore me."

Serena moved beside her. "Falling in love is scary, but so worth it."

"But you know Logan loves you."

"I didn't at first. It took time."

"How many more years do I need before he notices me?"

"See, this is why I don't get serious," Carrie said. "Too much angst."

Serena lightly poked her friend's arm. "Not helping."

"She's right," Heidi said. "I don't want to lose Reid. If all we can ever be is friends, that's okay with me."

Neither Carrie nor Serena seemed convinced.

Heidi went to the counter to pay for her dress. She ran her fingers over the gossamer fabric, picturing Reid's face when he saw her for the first time, dressed to the nines…while he was with another woman.

Her hopes sank.

No. Friendship would have to be the extent of things between them. Her heart couldn't take anything more.

GAYLE ANN MASTERSON'S smile had disappeared an hour ago. Reid was not going along with her plan. Every time he went anywhere near Heidi, the girl made sure to move to the opposite side of the living room. What was going on between them?

Making her way through the crowd of

guests, Gayle Ann found Alveda filling a plate at the hors d'oeuvres table and tugged her aside. They'd both dressed in their finest, Gayle Ann in a flattering powder blue dress, Alveda in a floral wrap, her hair in a soft flowing style instead of her usual tight bun.

"What is wrong with those two?" Gayle Ann asked in a low voice so as not to be overheard.

"Your guess is as good as mine."

"Did you talk to Heidi before the party?"

"No. We kept missing each other." Alveda looked out across the wide room, then took a bite of a stuffed mushroom. "Now this is just downright good."

"Alveda," Gayle Ann huffed.

"I think Heidi's avoiding me."

"Whatever for?"

"Beats me." Alveda shrugged and tried a spicy stuffed pepper that smelled so savory, it made Gayle Ann's stomach growl.

"You could act a little more concerned," Gayle Ann told her friend.

Alveda grinned. "Why? Because your grand scheme is going haywire?"

"It's not haywire, only a bit off the rails."

"Admit it. You can't stand that Reid bested you."

True. Reid seemed to have the upper hand

here tonight, and it was getting to her. He'd been the attentive beau, introducing his date to the guests and making sure she had a drink or food. "Ainsley is a lovely young woman, but we need to stick to the original plan—getting Reid and Heidi together."

"Heidi doesn't look like she wants his company."

Gayle Ann had been quick to notice that. Before she could say another word, a tall, distinguished man with thick silver hair and mustache joined them. "You two aren't very good at being discreet."

Judge Harrison Carmichael, an old family friend. He and Gayle Ann's late husband had been members of the Golden Bird Watcher's Society. Since retiring, the man popped up at the most inopportune moments.

Gayle Ann straightened her shoulders. "What are you going on about, Harry?"

"I've been watching you two. If I'm right—and after many years in the courtroom, I believe I am—you two have your sights set on getting Reid and Heidi together."

He always was much too perceptive.

"You don't know what you're talking about."

"He does," Alveda cut in.

Harry smiled. "Thank you, Alveda."

"And on that note, I'm going to try more

of this delicious food." She glanced at Gayle Ann, a twinkle in her eyes. "If I'd have known how good this catering company was, I'd have stopped volunteering to cook for parties a long time ago."

Once her cohort was gone, Gayle Ann faced Harry. "You think you're so smart."

"I do." He grinned and she had to admit, he was far too handsome for his own good. "But I fear you're too obvious."

"Reid doesn't have a clue."

"Maybe not about Heidi, but he knows you're up to something."

"Which is why I encouraged him to find his own date for tonight's event if you must know. But, in the end, he won't be happy unless he's with Heidi."

The judge peered at the guests. "You're right about someone being unhappy, but it's not Reid."

Gayle Ann caught sight of Heidi again. She was wearing a becoming dress, her hair in a fancy updo, her jewelry glittering in the soft light. Yet she hovered on the sidelines like a wallflower at a Regency ball.

"This isn't going according to plan," Gayle Ann muttered under her breath.

"Perhaps a suggestion?"

At this stage of the game, she'd take Harry's

advice, no matter how reluctantly. "What are you thinking?"

"Send them on matching errands."

Gayle Ann thought it through. His proposal made sense.

"You may be retired, Judge, but your mind is still as sharp as a tack."

"Which is why I want in."

She jerked back. "Excuse me?"

"Your matchmaking club."

Her hand flew to her chest. "How on earth—"

"Bunny Wright mentioned it."

"Blabbermouth," Gayle Ann groused. "It's supposed to be hush-hush. By invite only."

"I'm inviting myself."

"Why on earth would you be interested?"

"A man can only play so much golf. I need a hobby. Something to keep my mind busy."

Gayle Ann had to admit, having a male perspective would be a huge advantage. And if Harry's astute legal rulings over the years were any indication, he would be a strong ally.

"Fine. You're in."

He rubbed his hands together. "Where do we start?"

"That errand you mentioned?"

The annoying man just grinned.

Reid hadn't had a chance to talk to Heidi all night. Since he'd arrived, he'd been introducing Ainsley to the other guests and catching up with friends. Ainsley had kept her hand in the crook of his arm the entire time, holding tight, even if he needed to veer away to get them drinks or something to eat. He really wanted a few minutes alone. The thought immediately made him feel guilty. He'd asked Ainsley for the very purpose of showing his grandmother that he could find a date and the crafty woman hadn't batted an eye.

His date fit right in with this crowd, but to his dismay, his grandmother hadn't made an attempt to throw him an I-told-you-so glance, and it disappointed him. Then he got a glimpse of Heidi. He'd nearly choked as he was taking a drink from his water glass the first time she came into view.

From across the room, their gazes met and held for a split second before she moved out of sight. After that, she seemed to steer clear of him. They hadn't spoken since he drove her home the night her car died. On the drive over here, he'd wondered if they'd have a chance to talk. Clear the air. But by the way they were pretending not to notice each other, the uncomfortable tension that had filled his truck cab was still simmering between them.

With merely a glimpse of Heidi here and there, wearing that stunning dress, he tried to focus on his date, but it wasn't working.

Heidi was standing in the shadows, looking lost, and it bothered him. Every shred of decency in Reid screamed to go to her, but he hesitated. Heidi had never been comfortable in gatherings with lots of people. It had been like this since she came to Golden. But she didn't make a fuss about it, instead simply preferring to be in a smaller group setting. He had to admire her resolve. This party was for her friend, and Heidi put her personal issues aside and attended anyway. He wished he had a tenth of her strength.

Especially when he spied his father making his way over to him. "Ainsley, will you excuse me for a moment?"

"Um, sure," she said, already scoping out the room like she was searching for someone else to attach herself to. Just when Reid thought he might avoid his father, the man stopped in front of him.

"Reid."

A beat.

"Dad."

Silence.

The older man let out a melodramatic sigh.

"You're going to make this difficult, aren't you?"

"Actually, I'm not."

Surprise flashed in his father's eyes. "Good. A situation has arisen at the office. Logan has kept his silly promise not to be involved in the company, so I'd like you to handle it. It has to do with one of the accounts you managed."

"I don't work there anymore."

"You've made your point. Come back to the company and we'll pretend none of the unpleasantness transpired."

"It's not that easy."

"Sure, it is. The files I want you to look over are on your desk."

"Dad, I can't just walk away from my new responsibilities. I have deadlines. A crew." Heidi's hopes for the Hanover house.

"Appoint someone else foreman. Your talents are wasted in home renovations."

Just like his father to expect Reid to ditch his obligations so he could serve his dad. "And they're appreciated at Masterson Enterprises?"

"You're a Masterson. That says it all."

It really didn't. "Can you promise to let me work without interference?"

"Reid, I've run this company for a long time. If it looks like you need to be given some…direction, I have to speak up."

"Then the answer is no. I won't come back to the office."

"Reid—"

He cut his father off. "There's nothing more to say. Now if you'll excuse me, I have people to visit."

His father stammered over Reid's insistence. Taking advantage of the moment, Reid weaved through the crowd and ended up in the dining room beside the food table. He took a few cleansing breaths before noticing his grandmother looking over the sumptuous spread, a frown wrinkling her forehead.

"Everything okay, Grandmother?"

"I could have sworn I gave the caterer my best chafing dish for the Swedish meatballs. Where is it?"

Reid looked at the table. "Maybe they forgot."

Grandmother placed her hand on his arm. "I wanted it out tonight especially. We have so few family traditions anymore."

"Do you want me to go find out what happened?"

She glanced up at him, thanks reflected in her eyes. "Would you mind?"

"Not at all. Where should I go?"

His grandmother tapped a finger against her chin. "I thought I put it on the counter in the kitchen, but perhaps I forgot to take it out of the pantry."

"I'll check."

Grandmother stood on tiptoe to kiss his cheek. "You are a special boy."

Reid accepted her compliment with a chuckle and took off on the errand, glad to leave the crowd in case his father decided to corner him again.

The kitchen was busy, staff preparing dishes to replenish the empty platters in the dining room. He found the woman who owned the company, but she didn't know anything about Grandmother's chafing dish. He crossed the room, noticing the pantry door partially open. He stepped inside, stopping short when he glimpsed Heidi, standing on her toes as she searched through a shelf.

"Heidi?"

She spun around, the surprise on her face quickly erased. "Reid. Hi."

"What are you looking for?"

"Alveda's secret seasoning. She asked me to get it for her. You?"

"A dish Grandmother wanted."

"Which one?"

"A chafing dish?"

Heidi looked around and reached out to take a silver dish from another shelf. "Here you go."

"Thanks."

She nodded and resumed her hunt.

"So, are you having a good time?" He was curious.

"Sure," she said over her shoulder. "You know, lots of people…"

"You're okay?"

"I will be once I find Alveda's shaker. Why on earth did she hide it?"

"Because it's a secret?"

Heidi laughed, which made Reid happy to his bones.

"Oh, here we go." Pushing some condiments around, Heidi held the bottle up like a priceless treasure.

"It's a good thing those women have us."

"True. Alveda is enjoying herself so much, I didn't have the heart to tell her she didn't need to fix someone else's cooking."

Reid chuckled. "It is a nice party. Logan and Serena can't stop smiling."

"Exactly like a couple at their engagement party should be." She sent him a smile and moved toward the door. Her floral perfume jangled his senses as she brushed past. He wished he wasn't holding the dish so he could reach out and stop her, but she moved on like there hadn't been any underlying friction between them.

"I should get back, um… Grandmother will be waiting."

They left the confines of the pantry, Heidi disappearing to deliver the requested item. Reid brought the dish to one of the servers and asked that the meatballs be transferred to it, then rejoined the party. His grandmother was holding a serious conversation with a woman he recognized as a teller at the local bank. Grandmother glanced up, saw him and sent him a mischievous smile.

When Reid noticed his father making a beeline for him, he turned on his heel and fled back to the kitchen, holding the door for a server carrying a tray.

A movement near the back door caught his eye. Heidi, holding something in her hands, glanced sideways as if checking to see if anyone noticed her, before slipping outside. Always up for solving a mystery, Reid followed.

Stars sparkled in the indigo sky. Small lights glowed around the perimeter of the patio for atmosphere in case any guests wandered out this way. More twinkling lights lined the branches of the trees above. The scent of damp earth perfumed the air. At the edge of the brick patio he spied Heidi, crouched down, speaking softly. A cat moved into his line of vision, rubbing up against her leg as she scratched its head. He moved toward her, his footsteps making Heidi look over her shoulder.

"Why am I not surprised?" he called out to her.

She stood, her face in the shadows of the twinkle lights. Her you-caught-me expression made him want to laugh.

"One of the barn kittens." She held out a container. "Alveda said the mama had a litter a while ago." Heidi looked around and said in a conspiratorial tone, "Don't tell anyone, but she's been feeding the family."

He stepped closer, enjoying the sparkle in Heidi's eyes. She looked much more at ease out here than in the crowded living room.

"So, you decided to duck out of the party to take care of your new friend?"

"Actually, I was coming outside to sit and enjoy the quiet, when I saw this little guy. He looked up at me with those huge eyes and I couldn't resist." The cat zigzagged between her legs. She set down the food container, which the kitten pounced on, and she brushed her hands off. "What's your reason for escaping?"

"Maybe I wanted to enjoy the cool night air." And talk about why things were strained between them.

She frowned. "Try again."

Her words shut that idea down. "That obvious?"

She shrugged. "Lots of family and guests. I suppose someone got to you."

"My father."

She nodded but didn't pry. He appreciated it.

"And Grandmother. Even though I came to the party with a date, I caught her talking to a woman who works at the bank. She had her matchmaking face on."

"Sheesh. I thought you and I were competitive. She takes the prize."

The cat meowed and Heidi bent down to pick him up. She rubbed her nose against the dark-striped kitty, and Reid was consumed with envy.

"When did you become such an animal lover?" he asked.

Heidi lifted her chin toward the dark property beyond. "Remember when you used to meet me in the barn before we went hiking? I always snuck in early to feed the cats."

"My grandmother thought we had a charitable trespasser."

"Nope. Just me."

Unable to resist, he walked over, giving the cat a good head rub. Their fingers tangled for an electric moment and he heard Heidi's sharp intake of breath before she backed away.

Her words were rushed when she said, "Reid, you should really give your grandmother a break. She loves you."

So, she was also affected by his touch. Good to know.

"I know she loves me, but it doesn't translate into running my life."

"How long will you continue playing this game?"

"For as long as it takes for her to get the message."

Heidi rubbed her cheek against the kitten's silky fur. Envy washed through Reid. He wanted to brush his fingers against her cheek, imagining she'd angle her face toward his palm.

"She'll wait you out," Heidi said, her voice unsteady.

"Sure, but I'm onto her tactics."

The cat bumped his head against Heidi's chin. She chuckled, the joyous sound floating into the night. "I, for one, can't wait to see who wins."

"Should we make a bet?"

She narrowed her eyes at him. "Reid, why would I lose my hard-earned money when it's clear who the victor will be."

"Oh, really? And who would that be?"

The cat chose that moment to jump out of

her arms. He circled Heidi again, then ran to the grassy area where the edge of light turned into darkness, sitting down to lick a paw. Reid joined Heidi to watch, so close he could feel her slight shiver. The cat looked at them, his eyes glowing. Heidi made a move toward him, but as soon as she took a step, the cat ran off.

"That's the thanks I get?" she muttered after the animal.

"We could follow," he suggested.

Her eyes went wide and she shook her head. "No. Um, I heard Alveda say that the electricity is being redone in the barn. It'll be too dark."

"You always were a scaredy-cat when it came to that stuff."

Her eyebrow rose, which meant he was annoying her, just like he'd intended.

"Really? A cat pun?"

He shrugged.

The low ebb of laugher and voices, of plates and silverware being handled in the kitchen, drifted from the house. "We should go inside. Serena and your brother will wonder where we went."

He didn't want to go in. He wanted to walk to the barn with this woman to see if they could re-create the magic from when they were kids. When they didn't have any cares or worries about what other people thought. So, he pushed more. "C'mon, it'll be like old times. Running off while my grandmother's plot fails."

"Reid, no. I promised Serena I'd make sure the party ran smoothly."

"Everything went off perfectly." He stepped over the line of light into the darkness, holding out his hand. "How about I dare you? That used to work."

Her gaze ran over the sky and she shivered, wrapping her arms around her waist. Though the stars had made an appearance, the moon was shrouded behind thick clouds. "Not tonight."

Why was she so skittish?

Their eyes met and they both went still, locked in the moment. Seems he'd discovered the answer. Her expression went soft and, man, did he want to kiss her. She didn't move a fraction, so he leaned closer. Took a chance and placed his hands on her shoulders. She let out a soft sigh and her breath caressed his face. His gaze fell to her lips and once again the urge to brush his mouth over hers took precedence. It didn't matter where they were or that they'd had this weird tension between them. No, the opportunity presented itself and he wasn't one to throw away a gift.

But the questions in Heidi's eyes made him pause. Made him remember another woman waited inside for him. In the moment, Heidi had made him forget.

"What are we doing?" she whispered. "This is…"

"Not what friends do?"

Her eyes startled and she tucked a loose strand of hair into her fancy style with trembling fingers. Disappointment surged through Reid. Could this growing attraction he'd almost acted on be why she seemed so unlike herself? The romantic ambience certainly explained his desire to run off into the night with Heidi while the party was still going full force.

"Reid?" came a voice from the door. "There you are. I've been looking all over for you."

Heidi went stiff. Reid swung around. Did they both look guilty?

Pulling himself together, he said, "Sorry, Ainsley. My friend had a cat emergency and I was helping her out."

"A cat emergency?"

Heidi waved. "Hi. I'm Heidi. And yes, a hungry kitten qualifies as an emergency."

"Oh." Ainsley frowned and looked at Reid.

"So," Heidi said in a brisk tone. "Emergency over. Time to mingle some more." She shot him a look. Before she disappeared into the house she said under her breath, "Point made. Thanks, *friend.*"

When Heidi was gone, Ainsley asked, "Is she okay?"

"Yeah." Although Reid wasn't sure about himself. "Let's get back to the party."

He stopped at the door and turned, gazing into the dark night, wondering what would have happened if Heidi had taken his dare.

Too bad she hadn't because he'd really wanted to find out.

CHAPTER SEVEN

SEATED AT A bistro table on the sidewalk outside Sit A Spell Coffee Shop, Heidi watched Reid carry on a conversation with the very nice woman who worked at the bank. The sun shone brightly, enough that Heidi had to don sunglasses to shield against the glare. The temperature hovered in the midseventies. Tourists took advantage of the appealing spring day to meander in and out of the charming shops lining Main Street.

Taking a sip of her coffee, Heidi winced. It was still hot enough to burn her tongue.

This was the fourth time—not that she was counting—she'd come across Reid and a "date" in the last week. Since the engagement party, Mrs. M. had upped her attempt to find Reid "a considerate woman to settle down with," as she put it. Except Mrs. M. was going a bit overboard, resulting in Reid seeking out his own dates just to annoy his grandmother.

This was a game neither of them was going to win, but it was also painful to watch.

After her almost kiss with Reid under the stars, Heidi wondered if she'd been giving off signals that made Reid look at her as more than a friend. She didn't know for sure, but she couldn't deny that she'd wanted to be the focus of his attention. That she wanted to give in to her attraction for Reid.

And then came a wake-up call in the form of Reid's date showing up. So, yeah, despite his interest that night, Reid wasn't there yet. If he ever would be. So, no kissing.

If she wanted to maintain a friendship with Reid, which was paramount, she couldn't let silly things like feelings and emotions and longing get in her way. She had a goal, the house. She needed to act accordingly.

Friends only.

No romantic attachments.

She was a strong woman, the driver of her own destiny. No messy entanglements would give her what she really needed—security. Safety. Love would come eventually, she hoped, but not now. There was too much at stake.

She had to keep her focus.

Keep telling yourself that.

"Shut up," she muttered under her breath.

Even though Mrs. M. had pulled out all the stops since the engagement party to find Reid a match, Heidi had to admit she was relieved the wily older woman hadn't considered her as a potential dating candidate for her grandson.

The thought gave her pause. Why hadn't Mrs. M. considered her? Probably because everyone knew she and Reid were just friends. If Mrs. M. received the update that Heidi's feelings had changed, she wondered if she'd be in the dating crosshairs.

It shouldn't really bother her that Reid was determined to outdo Mrs. M. with his frantic dating, but really, she knew her friend well enough to tell he wasn't interested in any of the women he was hanging out with. Whether his own choice or Mrs. M.'s.

Her *friend.*

Heidi stifled a groan. Yes, she'd found it romantic to be alone under the stars with Reid. Her heart had raced when he'd moved in for what she'd hoped was their first kiss. She'd wanted more than anything to close that gap and feel the touch of his lips on hers. But hadn't she decided that could never happen? That he'd shown her they were friends only by asking another woman to the party? But the night and the moment had been perfect. Had Reid been so caught up in the ambience that he'd thrown caution to the wind like she wanted to?

Thankfully, she'd come to her senses, because a split second later his date had found them. What if they had been caught kissing? What a disaster that would have been. So, no, Reid had to stay in the friend zone. No more wishing on a shooting star for her.

Too bad, her heart mocked.

Reid finally broke away from the woman and hustled over to Heidi, a storm raging in his green eyes. She tried not to notice how rumpled his usually neat hair looked, as if he'd run a hand through it a dozen times.

"Another strikeout?" she asked.

"She was nice, but we're too different."

"This is the fourth woman who hasn't measured up."

"I know, and I feel bad."

"Why not admit defeat and go out with one of your grandmother's picks?"

"Actually, I'm going to have a long talk with her. I can't do this anymore. Trying to date to prove a point and work on two houses? There's not enough time in the day."

He'd bought another property, this one needing more interior work than the Hanover house.

"This is exactly why I ask Alveda to mind her own business. At least she listens." Heidi pushed the additional coffee she'd ordered for

Reid across the table more than ready to avoid conversation about his dating woes. "Why don't we change the subject?"

"Please." He sent her a grateful smile. "What did you have in mind?"

"I could help you on your new project."

His hand, holding the cup, paused halfway to his mouth. "One, I have enough of your *help*, thank you." He took a sip. "Two, this new location is going to call for a lot of specialized finishing work."

"Which means what, exactly?"

"Highly trained carpentry skills. Which is why I hired Josie, Mike's girlfriend. She's really talented."

"Which I lack. Got it." She tapped a finger on the table. "But I have a solution for my lack of woodworking skills."

"For the love of…"

"Reid, your crabby self is showing."

"That's because the people in my life are making that life difficult."

How sweet. She was having an effect on the man who was inching his way deeper into her heart.

Taking another sip of her coffee, she waited him out because, of course, he was going to ask.

Eventually, he gave in. "Your solution?"

Victory. She sat on her free hand so as not to throw a high five.

"I read in the community center flyer that you and Josh Freeman are running another how-to seminar for beginning woodworking tomorrow."

Reid and Josh were old friends. She'd also discovered that he'd hired Josh as a master craftsman for a number of his high-end house flips.

"That's right. We devote the entire day to a project. It's—" His eyes went wide as he finally realized her intent. "No way, Heidi."

"Why not? I'm a beginner and I want to learn a new skill."

He closed his eyes and Heidi swore he was counting to ten in his head.

"I noticed a bunch of high school girls have signed up. I want to show them that we women can do anything we put our minds to."

"I admire that, but does it have to be now?"

"When I move into my house, I'm going to need to do odd jobs. Learning how to use tools, therefore making me more independent, suits me."

"You could always call me."

Wouldn't she love that? To call Reid any-time of the day or night and know he'd show up for her? Still... It would be more like misery than assistance.

"Independence," she repeated, firm in her stance. At his probing expression, she turned her grin into a full-fledged smile. "You know I'm going to wear you down."

"You're right." He held up his cup in salute. "Welcome to the workshop."

"And just so you know, I have another reason, although it's related to the first."

His sigh was one of acquiescence. "Lay it on me."

"I have a girl in my tutoring group who's been having a hard time in math class. I saw that she signed up and thought this would be a good way to show her how math works in real life."

Reid seemed to consider her words. "That's a great idea."

"See, it's not only about me bugging you and getting under your skin."

He grinned. "You do have that effect on me."

Pleased by his words, and the warm regard in his eyes, she tried to control the full body shiver, but failed. Hoping her voice sounded steady, she said, "I can't help with your dating dilemma, but this class will equip me for the responsibility of homeownership."

Reid nodded, his brow wrinkled in concentration. "You know, the timing will be great."

"Why's that?"

"I have wood being delivered to the Hanover house today. I'm building a deck."

"Oh, my gosh, that'll be amazing." Heidi could already envision the dinner parties she'd hold, or the evenings she'd nestle into a lounge chair, watching the sun set behind the mountains.

If Reid sold her the house, that is.

"It's going to take most of the week to cement the posts into the ground and then start the floor since my guys are spread thin between the two projects. If you take the class, you could learn how to help me finish the job."

"And you thought having an intern would be a bad idea."

He sent her a grim smile. "The jury is still out."

She laughed. "I know it's open to the public, but you honestly don't mind me taking the workshop?"

"I should be used to your go-for-it attitude." He held up a finger. "Just promise not to hammer any fingers or puncture any skin with a nail."

"I'll be careful. I certainly don't want to hurt myself."

"I was talking about me."

She tried to get angry at his teasing, but the smile on his face took away the heat. They'd been working together for just about two weeks now, and the serious man who'd let her join his crew frowned less and smiled more often. She knew things with his father continued to be awkward, but it was good to see him loosening up a bit.

He tilted his cup to drain the coffee in one swallow, then rose. "I have to get going." He pushed his chair in. "Any other surprises I should be aware of?"

"Like the single, age-appropriate interior decorator your grandmother is sending to the new project?"

He went still.

She burst out laughing. "You are so easy."

"That's not funny. She mentioned introducing me to a designer she's met."

Heidi's smile faded. "Really, I was just teasing."

"You should know better, Heidi. This is getting out of control."

She felt bad for teasing him now. "I'm sorry."

Now it was his turn to laugh.

"What was that for?"

"Gotcha. There is no designer."

And the competitive streak between them continued.

"See you tomorrow," he said. He tossed his cup in the trash can and made his way down the sidewalk.

It should be against the law for a man to look so good. His broad shoulders moved with the easy sway of his stride. The man was much too hot for his own good.

She rose. "Be careful, Mr. Smarty-pants. One conversation with your grandmother and it'll be raining interior decorators on you."

Except she really didn't want that.

THE HOW-TO SEMINAR went smoothly, despite Heidi's clumsy attempt at using tools. Reid had to admit, this brilliant woman was finally getting the hang of things. She'd gotten the four sides of her tea caddy together without any disasters. He still had the use of all his fingers to show for it, so all in all, a good day.

She looked so cute, her hair pulled back, dressed in a bright red T-shirt and jeans, biting her lower lip as she concentrated. She fit in like one of the kids, except she was all woman.

They'd started the morning by measuring and cutting pieces of wood, then smoothing the rough edges. Reid had chuckled as he listened to Heidi's running commentary about using math in daily applications. Mia, the young girl who had jumped to team up with Todd, rolled her eyes every time Heidi pointed out another facet of math use. He finally separated them just to keep the peace.

They'd taken a break for lunch, then returned to assembling their projects. Right now, Heidi was figuring out how to screw the hinges for the lid of the caddy. She was engrossed in her task, which made him smile. Once she put her mind to something, there was no stopping her. It made him kind of sad, thinking that once the house on Hanover was done, they wouldn't see each other on a regular basis anymore.

The afternoon flew by, with all the attendees working hard.

"What's next?" she asked.

"You stain the wood."

She looked around. "Where's the can?"

"Not here. You take it home to finish."

"Oh, no. You promised me a complete product."

"Heidi, I don't have any stain here."

She grabbed her purse. "Let's go get some."

It wasn't like he had plans, so why not?

Eventually, the seminar wound down and they made a quick trip to the local home improvement store. Heidi talked him into a bite to eat, then they returned to the community center with stain, brushes and cleanup cloths. Josh was just signing off on the last project.

"You guys hanging around?" he asked as he packed up his tools.

"For a while," Reid said.

"Mac comes in at about eight to clean. He can lock up after you guys."

"Thanks."

Grabbing the handle of his toolbox, Josh left them alone.

After the near kiss at Masterson House, Reid thought things would be awkward between himself and Heidi, especially after her reminder that they were friends. But he was pleasantly surprised. No tension ruined the workshop. He was enjoying his time with Heidi.

A pungent aroma filled the room as soon as he pried open the can of stain. After picking out a brush, Heidi started swiping the stain along the grain of the wood. The warm pecan, her choice, had been the correct color for her caddy.

"You're right," he complimented. "You do okay with a brush in your hands."

"At least now you have proof that I won't mess up the walls at the remodel when we start to paint."

"Sometime this week."

She looked up. "Have you picked out the color palette yet?"

"I'm going pretty neutral."

She bit her lip, then said, "Can I make a suggestion?"

He should have known. "Why not?"

"I was thinking a sunny yellow in the living room. The windows are so big and beautiful. With all the natural light, the color will be very welcoming."

"Usually I leave the choices up to the future homeowner."

"Since that future homeowner will be me, try to picture the room in my color."

He closed his eyes. It worked. He pictured the yellow walls, but also Heidi, fussing with the furnishings in the room as she made the house a home.

"As for the kitchen," she said, evidently not noticing his silence, "I was thinking a soft gray to really showcase the white cabinets."

"Not bad."

She wiped her fingers on a cloth. "Interns rock."

He chuckled.

"On a completely different topic, you're really good with kids," she said.

"Thanks. I get a kick out of their enthusiasm. Reminds me of the hours I spent with Pops."

Heidi used the cloth and worked the stain into the wood. "Mind if I ask you a question?"

"Does it have anything to do with sassy interns?"

She grinned. "No. It's more personal."

"Why not? We seem to be having a moment."

She hesitated, as if debating the wisdom of asking her question, but clearly curiosity got the better of her. "Why did you leave Masterson Enterprises? I thought you loved it there."

He froze. The one topic he hated discussing. "I did." He picked up a towel he'd tossed aside and folded it. "My father and I couldn't see eye to eye."

"But you guys always had issues. What was different this time?"

He picked up one of the clean brushes from the package, studying it while deciding how much to reveal. "Have you ever been pushed to the edge?"

She continued wiping the stain. "I have. Not a great feeling."

"No. Especially when I had a lot of ideas to make the company more successful."

"Let me guess. Your ideas were ignored?"

He shot her a surprised glance, then turned

his attention to the brush. "More like Dad didn't appreciate that I had more to offer our clients. It was a sticking point between us."

"But instead of fixing it, you just pretend life goes on?"

"It's exhausting, trying to be relevant when you only get crumbs."

Sure, Reid could hold his own in the business world. It was his father's growing worry that Reid would shove him aside that had become the issue. Reid would never do that to his dad, but his father would do anything to remain in control of Masterson Enterprises, so his treatment of Reid hurt.

"So, that's why you're flipping houses."

"I know I'm good at it and I can make money until…"

She met his gaze, compassion swimming in her amber eyes. "Until?"

He lifted a shoulder. "I'm not really sure." He still toyed with the idea of leaving Golden, but hadn't made a firm decision yet. Was he waiting to see if his father would realize that he only wanted the best for the family business? If so, a change of heart from his father might be a long time coming.

Silence filled the room, broken only by the sound of a steady brush over wood as Heidi worked. There really wasn't any more to say.

"Flipping houses is good," she finally said.

He chuckled. "Thanks for the vote of confidence."

Her hand stopped as she looked at him. "Reid, you're doing something you like and that's productive. You haven't checked out completely. That counts for something."

Did it though? His grandmother hinted that he was needed at the office. His mother didn't push, but the sorrow in her eyes said it all. She hated that her husband and son were at odds. Even Logan questioned Reid's decisions.

Yeah, leaving town was becoming more appealing all the time.

Until he met Heidi's gaze. The concern for him, how she had his best interests at heart, seemed to be the only thing keeping him here. Until her house was finished, that is.

His chest grew tight. "Maybe."

A door slammed down the hallway, followed by the jingle of keys growing closer. An older man stuck his head in the open doorway. "Hey, Reid. Here to clean."

"We should be out of here soon."

Mac nodded and went about his business.

"We should probably clean up," Heidi said. She gathered the used cloths covered in stain and stuffed them in the plastic store bag.

"Not a good idea."

"Why not?"

"Didn't you read the warning label?"

"On what?"

"The stain can."

She shook her head.

"Not safe," he told her. "By keeping the materials separate, we can avoid hazards. Working with chemicals can be tricky. And sometimes dangerous if not stored properly."

Instead of arguing, she nodded and took the used cloths from the bag to carry to the sink in the corner of the room. She rinsed the brush and cloths while Reid stored all the unused supplies in the bag.

It wasn't long before they had everything tidy. Heidi looked over at her caddy. "Can I keep this here until it dries?"

"Sure. You can pick it up Monday when the center opens."

"I can't wait to show it off. Serena, Carrie and the others will be so jealous of my awesome skills." She snapped her fingers. "Hey, maybe we could schedule this workshop for a girls' night out."

Girls' night? And give his grandmother an edge? He could imagine the wily woman sending more of her candidates his way. Reid groaned. "No chance."

"Okay, only serious woodworkers. I get it."

"Thanks." He joined Heidi at the table to appreciate her fine effort. "I'm impressed."

"You should be."

He glanced at the wall clock. "It's nearly nine."

"Really? Wow." She smiled at him. "I had fun today. Thanks."

His gaze fell to her lips. His heartbeat kicked up and he found himself wanting to kiss her. But that couldn't happen. "You're wel—"

His words trailed off as the lights went off and a door slammed somewhere in the distance.

"What the..."

Moving through the darkness, and bumping into a table or two, it took Reid a minute to locate the light switch. When it didn't work, he stepped into the hallway. "Hey, Mac," he yelled. "We're still here."

He heard keys in the distance, then, "Sorry, Reid. I thought you'd left."

"Just turn the lights back on and we'll split."

Long seconds later, the overhead lighting flipped on. As his eyes adjusted to the sudden flare of light, Reid said, "Mac turns off the main panel at night."

He turned to face Heidi and froze. She had one hand on the table as if to balance herself, trying desperately to breathe. Her chest hitched, her eyes were not focused and she made funny noises in her throat.

"Heidi?"

He inched closer. When she didn't respond, he began to softly stroke her arm.

"Hey, it's okay. I'm here."

She blinked. Her gaze became clearer as she dragged in air. In her hand, the brush she'd been holding, shook. Reid gently took it from her. "Heidi?"

He watched her throat move as she swallowed. "I'm okay," came her hoarse reply.

"What happened?"

"The dark. I…don't do good in the dark."

He frowned, then remembered the times she'd begged off going anywhere at night unless it was well lit. He thought she was just being prickly, the new kid in town, but now…

"How long has this been going on?"

Her words stuttered. "S-since I was a kid."

"I'm sorry. I didn't know."

She pushed away from the table, tucking strands of hair that stuck to her damp neck into the ponytail. "Nobody knows." She shot him a terrified look. "And you are not going to tell anyone. Swear to me."

"No, I won't. I promise."

She nodded and continued drawing gulps of air.

Reid grabbed their belongings, handing Heidi's purse to her, then he gently steered her from the room.

"Where are we going?"

"Outside. You need fresh air."

Remarkably, she didn't put up a fuss. When his hand slid down her arm to her hand, he laced their fingers tightly together. Once in the parking lot, he led Heidi to her car, the heel of her boot catching in a crack in the asphalt. When she stumbled, he caught her, pulling her close. Their gazes locked and after a static moment, Heidi eased away.

Reid ran a hand over his head, shaken at seeing Heidi so distressed. She leaned against the car hood, her gaze pinpointed on a lamppost located in the distance on Main Street. Reid didn't want to rush her, so he moved next to her, their shoulders brushing, and he waited.

When she finally spoke, she kept her gaze on the beacon of light. "I told you my mom and I moved around a lot when I was a kid. We never stayed in one place for very long, unless she was into some guy, and even then, that never lasted. But during those brief periods, she would mostly forget I was alive."

Reid remained quiet. She wouldn't meet his gaze.

"I'm not sure what, exactly, happened to make her that way. She never said. Once I was older and on my own, I tried to understand why we were always moving and why she didn't form close relationships with anyone. I guessed there was maybe some kind of trauma in her childhood. Once I studied the topic, I realized the signs were there, but as a kid, I was oblivious to the dynamics of her behavior."

How should he respond to that? He wasn't sure. He kept listening.

"When I was real little, the places where we bunked weren't too bad. Usually these were friends with decent homes." She cleared her throat. "Though, as I got older, the places we stayed in weren't very nice, or clean. Lots of times there was no electricity. People coming in and out." She stared at the night, sounding monotone like she was reciting this story as if someone else had lived it. "This one afternoon, my mom said she was going to the store. We were rooming at an old run-down motel. She told me to lock the door and she'd be back later. I waited and waited. Eventually, it got dark and the lights didn't work. I was scared, so I crawled under the covers, unable to sleep until she got home."

"But she didn't?"

He felt her nod. Hot anger flooded Reid over her mother's neglect. How could a mother, any person for that matter, do that to a child?

"The next day she still hadn't returned. I stayed at the window, watching for her, worried, but nothing. Later, lots of people started arriving. It got dark again and still my mom didn't show. I crawled into bed, but there was lots of noise outside. Loud laughs and yells, bottles clinking. Even at that age I knew there was a party going on."

"How old were you?"

"Fourteen."

He closed his eyes.

"I was doing okay until people pounded on the door. Tapped on the window. I froze. Couldn't move. Then the knob jiggled like someone was trying to get inside. I ran into the bathroom, slammed and locked the door, straining to hear if anyone managed to break in. They must have moved on, but I was a wreck. The next day I left."

No wonder she acted strange when the lights went out or were too dim. She relived that night every time. And he, her so-called friend, had never understood why.

"Then you came to Golden."

She finally looked at him, her eyes sparkling with unshed tears. "We'd been in Golden the summer before. I met Alveda outside Sit A Spell when my mom begged for change." She paused. A slight smile touched her lips. "My mom went in for coffee and Alveda started up a conversation with me. I could tell right away she saw how it was. As usual, my mom took her time, so Alveda went to Frieda's Bakery to get me a sandwich and juice." She laughed, without a shred of humor. "I ate it like I hadn't eaten in weeks."

He saw red. "Had you?"

She dipped her head. "Yes, but our meals were, um, limited."

He nodded, his fury at the news hard to accept.

"Just before she left, Alveda slipped me a bag with more goodies and a piece of paper. Told me if I ever needed anything, night or day, to let her know. Later, when we'd left Golden, I looked at the paper. It had a phone number and address. I couldn't call her—we never had a phone—but at least I could find her. After that night in the hotel, I hitched my way here." She met his gaze. "You know the rest."

"But I don't. How did you end up permanently with Alveda?"

"We worked something out."

Which didn't tell him much, but after the emotional journey she'd just confided, he wasn't going to press. "So, your mom just gave you up?"

"Pretty much."

Shocked to the core, he tried to find the right words, but there were none. "Heidi, I don't know what to say."

"Don't say anything, Reid. In fact, forget I said anything."

"I can't do that."

"Fine, but at least don't look at me with pity." She pushed away from the car and turned to him. "I'm not that little girl anymore. Okay, the dark still freaks me out, especially when it's so thick I can't see my hand in front of my face, but what happened doesn't own me."

"I didn't think it did." He brushed an errant curl from her forehead, pleased when she relaxed. "You're amazing, you know that?"

"Hardly. There are kids out there who've had it a lot worse than me."

"Maybe, but you were able to grab the lifeline that Alveda offered. You changed your future. You did that."

"Yeah. I did." She shook her head. "I can't believe you saw me like this."

"It's nothing to be ashamed of, Heidi. Besides, we go way back. I'll never let you go through anything that terrifying by yourself again." He paused. "But I gotta ask, how did you hide your fear all this time?"

"I'm a pro. I knew when to remove myself from a situation that would make me… relive that night…before I got upset or anyone caught on."

"But then you had to go through those times alone, when you were scared."

She sent him a wobbly smile. "Well, usually I don't find myself in a community center when the building lights suddenly go out."

His heart squeezed at her attempt to lighten the mood. "Which makes me a lousy friend. I should have noticed before now."

She placed her hand on his arm. The heat went straight to his heart. "No, Reid. How could you? I never told you. Never let on. There's no way you could have known."

"Thanks." His throat was thick with emotion. "For telling me about that night."

"I don't know what else I could have done."

"You could have told me to mind my own business."

"I suppose."

A car zoomed by, a fume of gas exhaust left in its wake. Reid suspected Mac had finished for the night.

"Heidi, I—"

"I think I'm going to head home, Reid. It's been a long day and I'm tired."

He agreed because what else could he do? Especially after she'd bared her soul to him?

All he could picture was the brave little girl who'd grown up to be this incredible woman and friend. Scratch that. After how his heart had cracked as he'd listened to her story, she'd become even more important to him than a friend.

Now he just had to figure out what to do about it.

CHAPTER EIGHT

"GRANDMOTHER, WE HAVE to call a truce."

Seated in the formal living room at Masterson House on Sunday afternoon, Reid stared at his grandmother calmly.

"Why, Reid, whatever do you mean?"

"Don't pull the innocent act with me."

Her hand covered her heart. "Me?"

Rising, he shoved his hands into his pants pockets and stalked to the window. Sunlight streamed in through the clear glass. Outside, life teemed; from the spring blossoms opening wide to welcome the warm sun, to bees buzzing from flower to flower searching for pollen. A rabbit darted across the front lawn.

He grinned. He was sure Heidi would have a comment about the animal as it scurried away. She had lots of opinions. When they were younger, they'd had a great time debating issues, but now, he wanted her outlook on everything. Wanted to listen to her for hours as she pointed out the good things in this world.

And yet Heidi hid her traumatic childhood from everyone.

He still couldn't wrap his mind around her story. It explained so much. So many little things he'd overlooked when they were growing up. Yet she'd become a strong woman, maybe because of the trials she'd endured, working diligently to move past the things that would have broken another person. Perhaps that was why, whether she knew it or not, Heidi viewed life with hope.

His grandmother's voice cut into the thoughts that had been running through his head ever since Heidi had shared her secret. "Reid, please tell me what you mean."

Reining in his frustration on all fronts, he turned. His grandmother sat in her favorite chair, regal as a queen. Despite her meddling, he loved her to his core.

"Grandmother, your interference in my life has to end."

"What interference, dear?"

Tamping down his aggravation, he began to pace the old wood floor covered by a large tapestry rug. "The women who accidentally show up when I'm eating lunch or stopping for a cup of coffee."

"Perhaps the women were running errands."

"Really? You're going with that?"

"I will admit, I do see lots of different people in my travels about town." She gave an effortless shrug. "If I mention to one or two of them what you're up to, I can't control their actions."

He sank down at the end of the couch, his arms resting on his thighs as he faced her. "I don't need you finding me a girlfriend."

"You haven't been doing a very good job on your own."

"Maybe there's a reason."

"Like what? Making me happy in knowing you have someone to share your life with? Denying me great-grandbabies?"

He kept from rolling his eyes, the eternal question *why?* echoing in his head. "When I find the right woman, things will be different."

"But Reid, you're not even trying."

He began pacing again. "I have a lot going on. There are two renovations happening and there's another house I'm interested in buying."

"You're truly never going back to the family business?"

He met her gaze, needing her to understand. "Not right now."

She nodded, not without sorrow lining her face.

"All right then." She clasped her hands in her lap. "These houses of yours. Do they make you happy?"

"Sure," he said, looking out the window so she couldn't read the reservation on his face.

"You don't sound very convinced."

"It's different than Masterson Enterprises, but as fulfilling."

"You sound like your grandfather."

Reid turned to see his grandmother's smile.

"He tolerated the office but loved working with his hands. I think you tolerate flipping houses but love the thrill of making deals in the office."

He couldn't deny her analysis. It was true. His grandfather had tolerated the business world. Pops's brother had left Golden, never to return, which necessitated Pops remaining involved due to family loyalty.

Reid's father had eventually taken the helm and built the company and because of that, didn't intend to give Reid any amount of control. It wasn't like Reid wanted to run the company alone, in spite of what his father thought. He had good ideas to offer clients, which his father saw as competition.

Reid was at a crossroads but hadn't yet decided which fork in the road to follow. "You know I can't work with Father."

"I do."

But the truth was, his father wasn't getting any younger. Someone would take over whether his father liked it or not. It wouldn't be Logan. As things stood, maybe not even Reid. Would his father want to sell? The idea made Reid cringe.

"He hasn't made any plans for retirement yet, has he?"

"Not that I'm aware of."

If only he and his father could talk, a real conversation, not his father *telling* him how to do his job or which clients he could handle, then they might have a chance. Unfortunately, run-ins with his dad always pulled them further apart instead of solving their problems.

Maybe his idea of leaving Golden was smart. Yes, he loved his hometown, but despite that, he wasn't sure if he and his dad could ever find common ground.

Both he and Grandmother were silent, lost in their thoughts until his mother came into view.

She glimpsed Reid and a big smile crossed her face. "It's my busy son who's finally come to visit his mother."

Reid chuckled. Bonnie Masterson, with sparkling green eyes a similar shade to his, was dressed smartly, as usual. Her heart-shaped face framed by blond hair held a familiar expression of love. "I thought I'd have to hire Logan to find you."

"I've hired Logan in the past," his grandmother piled on. "He's a very good PI."

"What's with you two ganging up on me?" Reid asked, returning his mother's greeting of a kiss.

Bonnie glanced at his grandmother. "What is Gayle Ann going on about now?"

"Grandbabies," his grandmother said.

"She does bring up a good point." His mother's smile grew.

Reid ran a hand over his chin. "Why don't you two have this conversation with Logan? He's the one getting married."

"We have," came the chorus from both women.

"Look, I'm far from that stage in my life, so let's move on to a different topic."

His mother took a seat on the couch, smoothing her skirt as she crossed one leg over the other. His mother's clothing choices, her hairstyle and subdued makeup reflected a woman who had an innate elegance no amount of money could buy. His grandmother looked the same, but wore a floral dress, a change from the power suits she loved.

The expression on his mother's face turned serious. "Reid, I'm glad you stopped by. I wanted to talk to you."

He sank down beside her. "Is something wrong?"

"I'm not sure." She exchanged a glance with his grandmother, then slipped one of her hands in his. The gesture usually came before conversations Reid dreaded. "Your father hasn't been himself lately."

A prickling sense of unease ran over him. "What does that mean?"

"He's quiet. Not sleeping well."

"He spends long hours alone at the office," Grandmother added.

"It may be that he's just pushing himself too much, but I've scheduled a doctor's appointment for week after next. Stubborn man refused anything sooner."

Guilt pressed against Reid's chest. Because he'd walked away, his father was taking too much of the load? Granted, his dad liked it that way, but he was getting older. Running the company by himself had possibly become too much for him. If anything happened to him, it could be Reid's doing by his leaving Masterson Enterprises.

"I'm not telling you this so you'll set foot in the office," his mother continued.

Yes, he knew her better than that.

"But you and Logan should be aware."

"I…" He glanced down the hallway toward his father's study. "Is he home?"

"No. It's a lovely day so I insisted that he take some downtime. He's on the golf course."

Reid couldn't remember the last time his father had played a round. He swallowed hard. "If he needs—"

His mother cut him off. "Reid, I know your father can be unyielding. I've been married to him for a very long time." Her expression softened. "The business can run as it is for now. Both of you were wise to hire good employees." She let out a deep breath. "I don't mean that to be harsh, but despite what you think of your father, he has set up Masterson Enterprises to continue smoothly and successfully."

He couldn't deny that fact. Arthur Masterson was hands-on, but also looked to the future and made plans accordingly. It was dealing with his son he had a problem with.

"If there is anything to be concerned about, I'll let you and Logan know right away," his mother finished.

He nodded. Bonnie Masterson had the situation in her capable hands.

She patted his hand. Conversation over. "So, tell me, how are your renovations going?"

"Good. We're on schedule," he said, trying

to instill enthusiasm in his voice while digesting his mother's bombshell.

"Heidi is helping him with that cute little house on Hanover Lane," Grandmother said.

His mother looked surprised. "Really? I thought she was an accountant."

"She is, but she wants to buy the house once I'm finished, so she's involved."

"That's very sweet of you, Reid."

He thought of how Heidi had bulldozed her way onto the project and controlled a grimace. Sweetness on his part had nothing to do with it. It was simply Heidi fighting for what she wanted.

Seemed she had to do that a lot in her life.

His mother was still speaking but he'd missed what she had said. "Wait. Can you go back?"

She shot him a stern look. "I asked what she's doing at the house."

"She helped me take down a wall for an open floor plan. This week she'll be painting the living room."

One of his mother's shaped eyebrows rose. "A wall?"

"Part of the reno." He glimpsed the curious expressions on both faces. Felt his face heat. "She insisted."

Grandmother chuckled. "She does know her own mind."

"I suppose it's wonderful that the two of you are collaborating on a project." His mother tilted her head. "How long has it been since you spent time together?"

"A while." He thought back. "We haven't kept up like when we were in high school. After college, I started at the business, she was getting her accounting firm up and running. Our paths have crossed from time to time at Smitty's and we worked the last Oktoberfest together."

"What a shame you've grown apart." His mother grinned and sent a veiled look at Grandmother. "Remember the time those two decided to hike all the way up to Bailey's Point? Heidi turned her ankle and Reid wouldn't leave her alone to go get help. Then it started raining and they were stranded up there until Arthur and Logan went searching for them."

Oh, he remembered. It had been a good day—if you overlooked the sprained ankle and torrential rain, that is—one of the last before they started college and headed in different directions.

Heidi had turned her ankle as they stepped around an exposed tree root, embarrassed since they'd hiked that particular trail many times without any mishaps. When the rain started, they'd huddled together under his rain slicker, leaning against the backpacks, their wet clothes practically stuck together. Since there was no cell phone signal up there, she insisted he go down the trail for help, but he refused to leave her alone. Good thing too, because it was dark by the time his family located them. She would have hated waiting alone, keeping the fear bottled up inside. How had she hidden her phobia all these years without letting on? He added courage to the many traits he marveled over when it came to Heidi.

His mother frowned. "It's a shame you two lost track of each other."

"We're making up for lost time now." Which made him think not only about her strength, but also how attractive she'd become. How more and more he wanted to taste her lips. Was it a bad idea?

It had been a gradual thing, he realized, this awareness of each other. He wasn't blind; he saw that she felt the same way. She might be tough, but she wore her emotions on her sleeve. And when he did almost kiss her, he felt sure she'd have kissed him back if the heat in her eyes was any indication.

But all roads led back to it being a bad idea.

They were friends. Did he want that to change? Did she? He supposed the wisest move would be to ask, but how did he start that conversation? *So, Heidi, I noticed you didn't turn down my almost kissing you. Think there's something to explore here? Also, are you aware of how important you've become to me?*

That would go over like gangbusters.

"And Heidi," Grandmother prodded. "Is she a good intern?"

He mentally shook off the vision of Heidi's lips. "Hardest worker I've ever had."

Pride crossed his grandmother's face. "I've always had a special place in my heart for that girl."

"We all do," his mother agreed.

He didn't say it out loud, but with each day they spent together at the house reno, Heidi was more and more vital to his life. Different from when they were kids. More like he wanted to spend every hour with her, learning what made her tick. What she wanted for her future. If they could reach their goals as one.

She'd always been there for him. Would he ruin the tried-and-true camaraderie they had by asking for more?

At the noticeable silence in the room, Reid eyed both women. He recognized determination when he saw it. Using his best authoritative voice, he warned, "Grandmother."

"Don't Grandmother me, young man."

"Then please don't get any ideas because Heidi and I are friends. That's all."

"Which we all know, dear."

"What are we talking about?" his mother asked.

"Grandmother is on the matchmaking bandwagon again."

"Really, Gayle Ann. We have one wedding we're preparing for. Give Reid a break."

"You want him happily settled as much as I do."

"That's true," Bonnie said, "but he'll follow his own path to love."

Reid wanted to hug her.

She sent him a pointed look. "But after Logan and Serena's wedding, all bets are off."

"Ganging up," he muttered under his breath.

His mother rose and patted his cheek. "It's because we love you."

He knew that, but it didn't make it any less annoying.

"Now I have calls to make. The Ladies Guild spring fundraiser is coming up and I'm head of the committee this year." His mom smiled at him. "I'll call you when I have details."

Reid swallowed a groan. Last fall Grandmother had tricked him and Logan into attending a high tea charity event to support the Guild. It should have been an excruciating afternoon, but Heidi had been there and thanks to her he'd actually had fun.

She had a way of doing that. Taking experiences he'd rather miss and making them worthwhile. Even demo day had been more interesting with her around.

Once his mother left, Reid focused on the reason he'd come here. He rose, hoping to gain some advantage over his grandmother, which didn't happen often. "Can we agree on a truce?"

She released a long-suffering sigh. "I suppose we can both try. But Reid, if you won't look toward your future, I can't make any promises."

"Grandmother, that defeats the purpose of a truce."

She shrugged. "I'm too old to change, so that doesn't bode well for either of us."

"Fair enough, but give me a little more time."

She huffed out a breath. "Fine."

"Thank you." He leaned down to kiss her cheek.

She grinned. "You never did make things easy."

"Where's the fun in that?"

Leaving his grandmother chuckling, Reid got to his truck, his mind already gearing up for the week ahead. His crew would be focused on the new project, prepping electrical and plumbing jobs. Meanwhile, he had the deck to get started on at the Hanover house. Heidi had picked out the wall colors for the interior and he'd placed the order, so painting would begin, as well. It meant he'd be bumping into her all week. He was looking forward to seeing how she turned painting into a fun activity, because, let's face it, she did everything with gusto.

With his grandmother off the matchmaking hunt for the time being, he could have one singular focus—spending time with his friend Heidi. Strictly business. No machinations disrupting their time together. His week was looking up.

GAYLE ANN PUSHED open the door to the kitchen. Her cohorts sat around the table, empty coffee cups and pie plates in front of them. A fresh pot was brewing, gurgling in the machine. The pie sat in the center of the round table, the juicy fruit still fragrant after they cut into the flaky center.

"Well?" Alveda asked. "How did it go?"

Gayle Ann rubbed her hands together. "Our plan is working."

Besides Alveda and the judge, Gayle Ann had invited two other women to join the group. Bunny Wright, whose nephews owned and operated Deep North Adventures, along with Wanda Sue Harper, owner of Put Your Feet Up vacation tours and rentals, which she ran with her children. The assembled group were of varying ages, but old enough to want to see their loved ones happy and in love.

"Reid hasn't caught on?" Bunny asked.

"He's too worried about my sending eligible women in his direction to figure out we planned those chance meetings with Heidi." Gayle Ann hooked air quotes around the words *chance meetings*. "Alveda, you finding out that Heidi would be around during those times really aided our scheme."

"And neither Reid nor Heidi has figured out you're trying to match them together?" Wanda Sue asked, clearly not convinced.

"I must admit," Harry said, "Gayle Ann seems to have the situation well thought-out."

"Like that should be a surprise," Gayle Ann quipped.

"Heidi did mention that she was surprised not every eligible woman in town had been pointed at Reid." Alveda grinned. "She might be a bit jealous that no one has asked her to catch Reid's eye."

"Between our plans for them and their working together on that house, they'll see how right they are for each other," Gayle Ann said. "This plan was in motion the minute Reid bought the Hanover house. We knew Heidi wanted it, so Alveda played up her immediate interest in making a deal with the listing agent. Heidi insisting on joining the renovation was icing on the cake."

"Like you said all along—" Alveda nodded at Gayle Ann "—they're meant to be."

Wanda Sue frowned. "I thought those two were just friends?"

Gayle Ann clasped her hands over her heart. "Sometimes friendship can blossom into the best kind of love."

Alveda nodded her head. "Spoken like a true romantic."

"Nothing wrong with that," Harry replied, his dark gaze catching Gayle Ann's. She blinked, then focused on the conversation.

Gayle Ann pulled out a chair and sat. "Once Reid and Heidi are a couple, we'll take recommendations for our next match. We'll then come up with a plan of action. Decide who would be good with whom." She looked between Bunny and Wanda Sue. "Although I imagine you two already have ideas."

"It's been on my mind," Wanda Sue allowed.

"Each case will be different," Gayle Ann went on. "We have to be willing to think outside the box. Get creative. Make it look like the couples involved are figuring their relationships out all on their own when we're the ones actually pulling the strings."

"You would have made a mighty fine lawyer," Harry complimented Gayle Ann.

She preened. "I always thought so."

Bunny rolled her eyes.

"The key is not getting caught," Harry added as he cut himself another slice of pie. He nodded at Alveda. "Hats off to the baker."

Alveda beamed.

Oh, that rascal was a charmer.

"See, that's the part I'm stuck on," Bunny said. "Our young 'uns may be terrible at love, but they're not dumb."

Alveda got up to fetch the coffeepot and refilled their cups. "That's where the sneaky comes in."

Wanda Sue grinned. "I do like that part."

"Our objective is to be one step ahead." Gayle Ann nodded at Harry. "And this man is an expert."

"Why thank you."

A little flutter caught in Gayle Ann's stomach when he smiled.

"They are smart," Harry conceded, "but the secret is letting them think they have one over on us. Pride always comes before the fall."

Gayle Ann agreed. "And in this case, the fall results in love."

"Makes sense," Wanda Sue said as she poured creamer into her cup.

Gayle Ann glanced at the newcomers. "Convinced we know what we're doing?"

"I had my doubts," Bunny said, "but so far, so good. Anyone looking at Reid and Heidi can see those two are falling fast."

Alveda cut more pieces of pie to place on the empty plates.

"You're going to make me have to walk more this week," Bunny grumbled, but took another bite. "Mmm. Well worth the effort."

They're hooked, Gayle Ann thought, happy with her new, dedicated recruits.

"You're truly turning this into a club?" Wanda Sue asked after they'd all tasted the pie.

"We say we want to turn Golden into a premier vacation destination," Gayle Ann reminded them. "To make that happen, we need people—the next generation—to see all the good they've got here and stay. We've done all we can to highlight the town. It's time to pass the torch. Matching our beloveds with their true loves will make sure Golden grows and prospers."

"But there are only five of us," Wanda Sue pointed out. "And there are more young couples out there we won't have direct contact with."

"In time we'll grow," Gayle Ann said. "We work the bugs out now and polish our craft."

Alveda snorted. "Oh, you're crafty all right."

Gayle Ann shot her partner in crime a perturbed glance, then held her hand out over the table. "Let's make a pact."

Everyone stared at her.

"C'mon. We're in this together."

Harry placed his warm hand over hers. "I'm in."

Alveda followed suit. "I'm already in, but reckon we should make it official."

Bunny glanced at Wanda Sue and shrugged. "My nephews aren't getting any younger." She added her hand.

Wanda Sue shook her head. "This is a little odd, but Faith just got a divorce." She placed her hand on top. "Count me in."

"It's official," Gayle Ann said. She lifted

her hand, which made all the others go up in the air, then they broke off. "I welcome you to the Golden Matchmakers Club."

CHAPTER NINE

SATURDAY MORNING REID stopped by Sit A Spell for his daily dose of caffeine. He was headed to the Hanover house, but after noticing Heidi's car parked on the street, he made a detour to Blue Ridge Cottage.

They'd only run into each other here and there in the course of the week. Her schedule was full, so she hadn't been able to help him with the deck or to start painting the interior of the house until today. He'd seen her briefly at the community center, but she was too busy to talk. The end of the school year was fast approaching and the students needed her attention. It had been late when she finally left, after working with Mia. He'd hung out in his room until she was finished, waiting to make sure she got to her car without incident, like the lights in the building suddenly shutting off. She'd been surprised, but pleased, over his concern. He'd hoped they might spend time together under the stars—maybe he'd actually steal a kiss this time. But she had an early meeting the next morning and had to take off, promising they'd meet up for coffee.

Which hadn't happened, so he looked forward to today, hoping to find a way to bring up this unexpected attraction between them.

He entered Blue Ridge Cottage, the scent of lavender reaching his nose. He stopped short at the group of chattering women surrounding a table on the sales floor. Serena circled the women, making observations about their works in progress. He craned his neck, trying to get a glimpse of what caused them to be in such high spirits.

"Personal greeting cards," came a voice to his right.

He jerked, then turned his head to find Heidi smiling at him. Today she'd pulled her hair up into a high ponytail, which gave him the opportunity to view her lovely face. Her amber eyes sparkled, her high cheekbones lent character to her features. It was like seeing her for the first time and his heart seized. How could that be? They'd known each other for what seemed like forever and he'd never been undone by her. Why was today different? Like, earth-shattering special? He fought the urge to run a hand over his heart in response to this new awareness of his friend.

"Reid?"

Get your act together.

He shook his head. "Sorry. Got distracted by all the excitement."

She regarded the group with warmth. "These ladies do love their classes." She glanced at Reid with a sly grin and he had to remind himself to breathe. "Or an excuse to get together and gossip."

He cleared his throat. "I'll go with the second. This is Golden, after all."

"I still don't get the appeal." Her forehead wrinkled. "I suppose you had to grow up here to understand."

"You did pretty much grow up here."

She shot him a quick glance.

"And you've escaped being the target of gossip, so be thankful," he hurried to say, hoping it didn't bother her to reference the past.

But instead of troubled, her gaze turned perceptive. "People still speculating why you left Masterson Enterprises?"

Yeah, she saw right down to the core of the matter.

"Probably. Although no one has come right out and asked."

"Hey, folks might love to talk, but they also know when to be polite if necessary."

Meaning the fallout with his dad. He took a sip of coffee, not wanting to get into this conversation. Instead, he asked, "You're coming to the house, right?"

"As soon as Serena's class is over." She nodded toward the sales counter. "I'm finishing up some bookkeeping and then we'll be there."

"We?"

"Yes. I invited Serena. Hope you don't mind."

He tried to ignore the jab of disappointment, but it didn't work. He wouldn't have Heidi to himself all day like he'd imagined. "Who's going to watch the store?"

"Carrie. Serena wanted to help and to be honest, it'll make the job go faster with more hands."

Which meant the renovation would be finishing up soon, as well. If everything went as planned, Heidi would have her dream house within weeks, ready to move on to the next phase of her life. They'd carry on as friends, even though he'd discovered lately that he wanted to be more.

And when they went their separate ways? What would he have then? Empty houses to flip while still being separated from the family business. He didn't want to dwell on that depressing thought.

When he didn't respond, Heidi playfully batted at his arm. "You know wherever Serena is, Logan will be. He can work on the deck with you."

His gaze met hers. "You were supposed to help me finish up."

She chuckled. "Weren't you saying that you didn't want me within thirty yards of a hammer? Or nails?"

"I…" He shook his head.

"I am getting the hang of using tools, if I do say so myself, but today I'm donning my painter's hat."

"The more the merrier," came his dull reply.

"You don't sound very excited." Heidi tilted her head, examining him as if she could read the irritation bubbling up inside him. That wasn't possible, was it? "Are you okay?"

"Sure." He had to figure out how to deal with this interest in Heidi before he got himself into deep trouble. "I'm gonna get going. See you soon?"

She frowned. "In about an hour."

He nodded and strode from the store. What was wrong with him? He was acting like a five-year-old who didn't get his way. So, there would be additional people at the house today. Maybe he should consider that a good thing, before he did something dumb like kiss her— man, he wanted to kiss her—and ruin the one sure thing he could rely on, their friendship.

Once at the house, he got right to work. He slipped on sunglasses against the glare invading the backyard. The sun had risen above the tree line, warming his shoulders as his muscles flexed from hammering and cutting. It was quiet, except for the occasional songbird. The flutelike melody of a wood thrush caught his attention, along with squirrels jumping from tree branch to tree branch, interspersed with the shouts of kids down the road. He measured and cut, the buzz from the saw spoiling the natural symphony. By the time he heard voices coming through the front door, he'd completed the last of the planks for the deck floor. Now came the railing.

Wiping sawdust from his face, he ventured inside. Two large paint buckets sat in the middle of the empty living room. Logan was in the process of opening one of them to pour paint into a pan. Heidi rifled through a bag, pulling out brushes, rollers and paint rags, while Serena carried in the extension poles to attach to the rollers. They were all dressed in work clothes, just like he was. He took in the scene, his chest tight. Heidi. His family. His most favorite people in the world.

"Hey, bro," Logan said, finally noticing him. "I brought the troops."

Heidi placed a hand on her hip. "Okay, first,

I asked Serena, which means you're my troop. And second, what else were you going to do today?"

"Take a break from wedding stuff?"

Serena came to Heidi's side and frowned at her fiancé. "Care to rephrase that?"

"Spend the day with my fiancée."

"Better." Serena went over to place a kiss on Logan's cheek.

"Oh, no." Logan tapped his lips with one finger. "You can do better than that."

Serena rolled her eyes, but gave him the desired kiss.

Reid noticed Heidi send him a quick glance, then suddenly become very busy. He wondered if she was thinking about the night they'd almost kissed. About the tug of attraction that seemed to be growing daily. Wondered if she wished they'd given in to the spontaneous impulse instead of running away.

Logan rubbed his hands together. "Reid, give me a few minutes to get the paint poured and I'll join you."

"That is, if you trust us to get the job done," Heidi teased.

Reid met her gaze. "I trust you."

She blinked, then got busy.

Walking outside, Reid readied the two-by-fours for the next step on the deck. Logan came out just as the measuring tape zipped back into its cover and Reid used a pencil to record the mark where he needed to cut.

"They're painting up a storm in there," his brother informed him.

Reid slipped the pencil behind his ear. "I'm sure they are. You and Serena sure seem to be on the same page."

"We are. It's all good, brother."

Grabbing a strip of wood, Reid snorted.

"When you find the love of your life, you'll understand."

What if he already had and was screwing it up? Okay, things with Heidi hadn't gone far enough to mess up yet, but he wasn't doing a stellar job aligning his feelings to his actions.

"So, what're we doing?" Logan asked.

"Cutting wood for the railing." Reid pointed to the other end of the deck, needing to get to work so he could sort out his thoughts. "Let's secure them around the periphery."

The two worked well as a team, cutting and nailing. It reminded Reid of growing up with Logan. All the good times they'd shared. In between the buzz of the saw, he heard female laughter drifting from the house. He really wanted to be in there with Heidi, but he understood that she wanted to get this job done under her own steam. He got it, this house was important to her. More important, was he?

When half the posts were up, Logan stopped to wipe his forehead.

"It's getting hot out here."

Reid strolled over to a cooler located on the grass and chose two water bottles, tossing one to Logan. They moved to the shade of a leafy oak tree and took a few moments to cool down.

"Thanks for coming," Reid said, wiping the cool water from his lips.

"Even though you don't need my help?"

"I always want you around—you know that."

Logan took another chug and nodded. Waited a beat. "I spoke to Grandmother."

Please, not about his dating life again.

"About?"

"Dad."

A hard knot tightened in Reid's gut.

"She's concerned about his health. So is Mother."

"I had the same conversation with them."

"She mentioned that he's seeing a doctor on Wednesday."

Reid nodded.

"I ran into him, as well."

Reid met his brother's gaze, his stomach clenching at his worried expression.

"He doesn't look good."

Reid closed his eyes. Guilt washed over him.

"What are you going to do if Masterson Enterprises needs you to come back?"

"I've thought about that ever since Mother gave me the news." He paused, then spoke in a low voice. "Do the right thing, of course."

"Even if you don't want to?"

Oh, he wanted to, but would rather it wasn't at the expense of his father's health. "I'm not going to let the family down."

"You mean Dad?"

He did, because through it all, his father's opinion still mattered to him.

"This isn't going away," Logan said. "Dad will be retiring soon, and one way or another, this conversation will come up again."

"Since when are you invested in what happens with Masterson Enterprises? You've made it clear you don't want to be involved."

"I never did. But you, my brother, are a different story."

Could that be why his dad wanted Logan involved with the company? Logan had no interest, which would mean he wouldn't give his father any static, unlike Reid.

"Let's wait until after he sees the doctor before we dig all this up."

The women came around the side of the house to join them. *Saved.* He took two more bottles out of the cooler and handed them out. Serena took hers and went to stand beside Logan.

"Thanks," Heidi said. "We have the wall around the French doors to complete, then we'll move into the kitchen."

"That was fast."

"Mad painting skills. Serena cuts in and I roll."

He chuckled, noticing a big smudge of cheery yellow paint on her cheek. Without thinking, he reached over to wipe it off. His finger lingered over her satiny skin, and for the life of him, he couldn't move away. She shivered. The gentle breeze lifted a few strands of hair that had escaped her ponytail, but she didn't brush them away. Their eyes met, Heidi's filled with questions. His heart pounded. Here in the dazzling sunlight, he wanted nothing more than to lower his head and kiss her. Have her return that kiss.

She moved aside, breaking the intense contact, her motion signaling her reservations loud and clear.

He shoved his hands in his front pockets.

She held up the bottle. "Break's over."

"Don't let me keep you from your master-piece," he said.

She looked around him. "C'mon, Serena. Let's switch jobs this time."

Serena sent them both an odd look.

"The sooner we finish, the sooner I can plan on moving in," Heidi said with a wave of her hand.

It was then that Reid realized he had to keep his longing for Heidi to a minimum. His brother and Serena were much too observant for his comfort.

"Oh, sure," Serena crabbed. "I get half a wall to cut in and you do the easy part."

"And I have to be careful not to make a mess around the doors, so we're even."

The two playfully argued as they headed back inside. Trying to ignore his reaction to Heidi, he watched until she was gone, then turned to join Logan.

"So, you and Heidi are a thing?"

Reid couldn't ignore his brother's assess-ing gaze.

"I saw that move. Classic."

"She had paint on her face." His voice had taken on a defensive edge.

"And you had an excuse to touch her." He shrugged. "I get it."

There was no point in fighting the obvious. Right now he needed his big brother's advice. "What do I do?"

"Find out how she feels."

Okay, Reid knew that. But still… "What if she only wants to be friends?"

Logan chuckled. "I saw her face, bro. Her look was anything but friendly."

He tried not to let his brother's observation give him hope, because he still had to get the truth from Heidi herself.

"What if changing our relationship at this point in our lives ruins everything?"

Logan moved close and slapped him on the back. "Looks like you have more than one decision to make."

LATER THAT EVENING, the sun began to sink behind the mountaintops, so the lights were blazing in the house when Heidi parked behind Reid's truck. After a long day's effort, the painting was done. Next, she'd have to tackle the trim, but she was several steps closer to her goal. Come Monday, the floors were being restored to their original luster. Then the bathroom and kitchen cabinets would be installed, and the exterior painted by professionals. Once they were there, Reid could sign off.

The Hanover house would be hers.

So, why the melancholy?

Because her interaction with Reid would return to pre-house days when they only saw each other at town events or weddings and funerals. She wouldn't be able to surprise him with dinner, like tonight. They'd leave without important things being said.

If she were only brave enough to speak them.

With a firm resolve fueling her, Heidi tamped down the internal debate and hurried up the walk and into the house. The smell of fresh paint still lingered in the air. Everything was silent except for the music coming from the backyard. Large bag in hand, she strode outside to the completed deck. Reid was on the grass, packing up the table saw. A shiver ran over her. Just like the one she'd tried to cover when he'd touched her cheek earlier.

She'd been speechless. Didn't know what to do. While she'd wanted to lean in and let his palm cup her face, she was afraid of rushing things. Yes, their mutual interest was off the charts, but they hadn't spoken about it. Nothing could happen until they did.

"You finished," she said, catching him off guard.

"Heidi, what are you doing here? I thought you left for the night."

"I stopped at Smitty's for dinner. It smelled so good, I got takeout."

Reid sniffed the air. "Barbecue ribs?"

"With coleslaw and freshly baked rolls. A jug of sweet tea."

He stomped up the stairs. "What did I do to deserve dinner?"

She turned to admire the house. "This."

He took the bag from her hand and opened it, the tantalizing smell escaping into the night. "Well worth it."

"How about a picnic?"

"Sounds good to me."

She'd made sure Jamey added plates, utensils and plenty of napkins before leaving the pub. Taking a seat on the steps, feet dangling over the grass, they unpacked the feast and dug in.

"I don't know about you, but I was starving," she said, taking a bite from a meaty rib.

"I could eat this meal every night for the rest of my life," he said.

"Don't you dare let Alveda hear that."

"I'm not dumb. Those words would never leave my lips if she was around."

Heidi grinned, picturing Alveda's affronted expression if she ever learned the truth.

She took a breath, loving the earthy perfume surrounding them. The wildflowers edging the trees before disappearing into the woods were bright spots of life. White trilliums, with a few rose-pink blossoms scattered into the mix. Orange azaleas with a few flowers still on the stems. Yellow trout lilies. If things went according to plan, all of this would be hers.

"It's so beautiful here." She tried to keep her emotions in check, but it was hard.

"I suppose after moving around so much, you enjoy staying in one place."

"I do. That's why this house is so important to me."

He nodded, taking another bite from a rib.

She nodded over her shoulder at the iPod hooked to an outdoor speaker. "You remembered my favorites."

"You made me listen whether I wanted to or not."

"The only decent memory I have growing up is my mom introducing me to her favorite tunes. She was a big fan of '70s and '80s music. I guess that's why I like it so much."

"The connection."

Reid smiled, just like he had in high school, but now he was older. More mature. The setting sun cast shadows around him and she fell for him a little bit more.

"We rocked to a lot of this music in high

school." He puffed out his chest. "We were the cool kids."

She let out a laugh. "You were. I was a nerd."

"You always did manage to beat me in school."

"I felt like I had a lot to prove. The poor homeless girl who had to be sure she was worthy of all the help Alveda and others had given me."

While her early schooling had been spotty when she lived with her mother, Heidi'd had an innate curiosity and intellect. She read anything she could get her hands on. It may not have been a formal education, but it had worked for her.

Reid lowered the rib in his hands. "Is that how you saw yourself?"

"Yes."

"Wow. I don't think anyone else did."

"How can you say that?"

"You were quiet in school, but everyone liked you. Trust me, whenever we butted heads, you had more people rallying around you than I did."

"Reid, you were a star baseball player."

"Until I had the first of my big arguments with my dad."

Oh, no, she'd stepped in it now. "Reid. I shouldn't have brought that up."

"Hey, you told me your deep secret."

And she'd survived. Was glad she'd told him. Did he need to do the same? "If I can handle talking about the dark, how about you tell me your worst moment in life."

He glanced at her and then away. "You don't want to hear it."

"Try me."

He placed the rib on a plate, took his time wiping his fingers with a napkin. This was so like Reid, thinking before speaking. Making sure he got it right. "When I joined the family business after college, I had a lot to learn. My dad was happy to show me the ropes. For the first time in forever, we were a team. I couldn't believe all it took to bring us together was working at the office with him." His eyes went dark. "But as years went by, I didn't need his advice, having carved out a place for myself, yet he continued to tell me what to do."

"Maybe he was trying to be a good dad?"

He lifted one shoulder in a shrug. "At first, sure. But I had different approaches to building portfolios for our clients. Different opinions on where to invest money or which real estate projects looked promising. Suggestions to make the commercial construction more efficient. I'm not saying Dad's old-school strategies were wrong, but he started putting up resistance any time I mentioned a more efficient strategy to increase profits. It was his way or no way."

He shook his head, his eyes taking on a faraway glaze. She wanted to reach out, reassure him, but he seemed closed off. She clasped her hands tightly together to keep from breaking the moment.

"Some of his clients asked me to handle their accounts. I was surprised, excited that they'd noticed my fresh insight, but feeling bad at the same time." He shook his head. "Dad never made it easy. The night I left the business, it was an argument over a client."

"Someone else who wanted your expertise?"

"Yes. A long-standing client Dad first brought to the company when he started out. But as with most businesses, this one was growing and changing with the times and the CEO wasn't happy that Dad wasn't looking for new avenues to expand their business. They asked to transfer their account to me and he flipped."

Heidi bit her lip. She remembered the night in high school when his father had upset Reid enough that she'd had to stop him from getting into trouble. By the look on his face, this clash must have been even worse than that.

"We'd already had arguments about other clients moving to me. That's when he got on the kick to talk Logan into joining us, no matter how many times Logan expressed disinterest or his lack of expertise in the business. But when Mr. Jacobs, the CEO of the company Dad personally looked after, asked for the switch, Dad blew up."

Reid jumped up. His footsteps back and forth echoed against the wood as he paced. Slowly, Heidi rose as well, keeping out of his path.

"It was late one evening. He called me to his office. You could cut the tension with a knife as soon as I entered. It didn't take long for him to tell me what had happened, for him to accuse me of stealing his clients. I told him we could work together, but he railed. Suggested I wanted to push him out, take over the company, which was never my intention."

He walked to the newly installed railing. Gripped the edge and stared into the darkness. She moved beside him, wishing to ease his pain.

"He told me that when push came to shove, I'd blow all the accounts, just like I had when I struck out in the championship baseball game.

Then all the work the company had done over the years would be gone for good. Because of me."

Heidi gasped. She slipped her hand into the crook of his arm. Rested her head on his shoulder. "He's wrong."

"See, that's the thing. I know he's wrong. I'm good at what I do. All I ever wanted was for us to work together. I thought he wanted it too. But him never believing in me…saying I made him look bad…" The words seemed to catch in his throat. "That was the last straw."

She hugged him tighter and whispered, "I believe in you."

He went still for a long moment. His gaze moved around the deck, not meeting hers. She lowered her head, trying to ignore the disappointment that he hadn't responded to her heartfelt declaration.

"Mother told me that he hasn't been feeling well. He's got a doctor's appointment this week. Depending on the results, I might be needed at Masterson Enterprises."

She lifted her head and studied his profile. "Would that be so terrible?"

"To be honest, I don't really know."

What a two-edged sword. To want to return to the business he loved, but not because his father wanted him there.

"Did your mom say what's wrong?"

"She didn't know, only said he hadn't been feeling good."

"Stress?"

"Most likely."

They were quiet. Music still streamed from the iPod. It should have been a beautiful end to the evening, but instead Reid was worried about his father. Since she hadn't talked to her own mother for years now, a deep sadness filled her. Reid didn't know how lucky he was, despite the rift with his dad.

"You're a good man, Reid. I know you'll help your family if needed."

"I just wish my father appreciated what I gave up. He thinks I'm acting childish. Like how he treats me isn't a big deal." He scoffed. "Maybe I should just leave Golden."

"What?" She reared back. "Seriously?"

"What's here for me?"

She tried not to take that personally—she knew he was venting. "Your grandmother, parents, brother, future sister-in-law, possible nieces and nephews, the chance to flip another house and, if you're lucky, me as your permanent intern."

He turned to look at her. The moon was rising, casting light on his handsome face.

"I'd miss the chance of seeing you in action again."

She infused passion into her voice. "Then it's settled. No leaving Golden."

"Well, if you say so. Then it must be the law."

"Correct."

He chuckled. The song changed to an upbeat tempo. "Remember this tune? We practiced our dancing technique in the barn when we were younger." He held out a hand. "The lights are on inside, so we won't be dancing in the dark."

She rolled her eyes as his words matched the lyrics of the song. Although she appreciated his acknowledging her feelings. Really, when she was around him, she felt safe. It had grown darker since they'd eaten, the perfect time to let loose and shake off a little of the tension brought on by the serious conversation.

"Why not," she said, giving them both room to move. By the time the dance was over, they were breathless and laughing.

"Still got it," he said, his face so much more relaxed than minutes earlier.

"You always were lighter on your feet than me."

The tempo slowed, this time to a romantic ballad about discovering new love. As if by magic, they moved into each other arms, swaying to the lilting vocal and haunting instrumental. Heidi rested her hand on Reid's chest, against his heartbeat. Feeling home, like she always had with him. At first it had been because of their friendship. Now it felt deeper.

"Why did you move away when I touched you earlier?" he asked, so close his breath tickled her ear.

"I don't know."

"I think you do."

She shivered. "Because I've wanted your attention for a while now, Reid, but I'm not sure how you feel."

His head moved a fraction. Their gazes met. "My attention, as your friend?"

Summoning her courage, she answered, "No. More than that."

He rested his forehead against hers. "So, it's not one-sided."

Just as she'd hoped. "Not one-sided?"

"Heidi, I've been feeling this…attraction to you for a while. I wasn't sure if it was mutual, but then when we almost kissed at the engagement party, I've been wondering what's going on."

"Same here. I was too afraid to ask."

He tugged her close. She could feel his smile against her temple. "Me too. With so many years of friendship between us, I wasn't sure if this was possible."

She turned her head. "There's only one way to find out."

His expression turned serious. "You're sure."

"More than sure," she whispered.

He lowered his head and after what felt like an eternity later, he finally brushed his lips over hers. Fleetingly at first, as if one of them might come to their senses and run for the hills. But soon the kiss became more intense. Her heart pounded. Her blood raced. This was what she'd been waiting for, even when she hadn't known she needed it.

The kiss went on with the moon's light blanketing them. When the music changed to a raucous number, the spell was broken.

She ended the kiss, but didn't want to leave the safety of his arms. To her delight, he didn't seem to be in any hurry to let her go.

"So, now what?" She asked the obvious question.

His eyes were troubled. "I honestly don't know."

It seemed to be the prevailing sentiment. She had no clue either.

A beat passed before she said, "Reid, you have to promise me something."

He met her gaze and the intensity took her breath away. "Anything."

"No matter what happens, we'll always be friends."

"That's an easy promise to make."

Was it? Her qualms were silenced when he swooped in and kissed her again. Her stomach tilted like she was on a roller-coaster ride and her head swam, but she circled her arms around his neck, holding on to Reid with every fiber of her being.

Could she have everything she wanted? The house? Reid? It was almost too much to hope for.

CHAPTER TEN

THE NEXT FEW days flew by in a whirl. Still stunned by their unforgettable kiss on the deck, Heidi and Reid decided to keep their being a couple from friends and family, to give the two of them more time to figure out what was happening between them.

Honestly, she wasn't sure if that was a smart idea. Someone was bound to see them acting like more than friends—yes, she was hoping for a lot of kisses—and keeping secrets wasn't the best way to start this new chapter in their lives. But they were both cautious by nature, so she agreed to the secret, hoping time would sort out the rest.

On Wednesday morning, the door of Blue Ridge Cottage opened with a merry ring of the bell. It was inching closer to May. Where had the time gone? The temperate weather had brought increased foot traffic down Main Street, and before long summer tourists would arrive, hopefully in full force. Heidi looked up from the counter to glimpse Mrs. M., her purse hooked over her arm, marching briskly in Heidi's direction. She couldn't help but smile in greeting.

"Mrs. M. To what do we owe this visit?"

"Just making the rounds. Checking on my favorite tenants."

Mrs. M. owned a sizable amount of property in Golden, this store included, so she was a fixture around town. "All your tenants are your favorite."

"Unless they don't pay their rent. Then we have words."

Heidi chuckled. She would not want to go up against Mrs. M.'s impressive negotiating skills.

"Where is Serena?"

"In the storeroom. A shipment came in so she's opening boxes."

"I'll be right there," came her boss's voice from the back.

"Another Golden scene gracing her merchandise?" Mrs. M. asked.

"Of course. Serena wouldn't dare draw any other location."

Mrs. M. harrumphed in agreement. Then her expression went all sketchy and she asked, "So, tell me, Heidi, what's new?"

She felt her face flush. Did she know about Reid? That they were…together? Not that they were seeing each other, not yet, anyway. They hadn't gone out on a date, but they intended to. And then everyone would know.

Good grief. Pull it together.

The older woman tilted her head, waiting for an answer.

"Not much," Heidi replied. "You know how it goes."

Mrs. M. sent her a long look. "And the Hanover house. Are you nearly finished?"

Her heart tugged at the idea. She wanted to move in, but she also wanted an excuse to keep working with Reid. They'd had so much fun, teasing and putting in the effort to make the house a future home. She'd discovered that he was very good at renovating, as well as being very generous with his time to interns, and found herself falling deeply for her friend.

Mrs. M. still watched her.

"The project should be complete in the next week or so. Once the house passes the final inspection, we can move toward the closing."

"Homeownership is wonderful, my dear. You'll enjoy every moment."

She thought so too, but now when she pictured the house in her mind, she was sad that Reid wouldn't be there. He'd be off on another job. Sure, if they did start dating, he'd come over for dinner or to sit on the deck with her at sunset, but she was almost afraid to admit she wanted forever.

Serena appeared with arms loaded down with boxes.

"How did they come out?" Heidi asked, taking one package from the stack. The scene Serena had captured was a view from Pine Tree Lookout overlooking Golden Lake. Her boss had sketched the series when she and Logan had gone up to the popular spot as they were falling in love. Heidi gazed at the scene, knowing the backstory behind the drawing, and could feel the love Serena felt for Logan.

Would Reid come to feel the same about her?

She nearly sighed. When had she turned into such a romantic?

"The printer did an exceptional job," Serena said, a satisfied smile on her face.

"May I?" Mrs. M. held out her hand and was handed a box. "Oh, my, Serena, this is absolutely lovely."

Serena placed the boxes on the main display table, in the direct path of shoppers as they entered the store. Heidi took a new-product sign from behind the counter and placed it beside the merchandise. They all took a step back to observe the collection, then Heidi moved a few boxes around so the drawing was facing out, to catch a customer's gaze. Serena hurried to the storeroom and returned with other matching stationery items in the series.

Once they'd rearranged the products for maximum attraction, Mrs. M. cornered Serena. "Have you decided about your bridal shower? I can reserve the historic mansion in Gold Dust Park if you like that location."

"I'll be honest, I'm torn between there or your home. The engagement party was so lovely and special since it was in the house where Logan grew up, but…"

"What is it, dear?"

A pained grimace crossed Serena's face. "I don't want to make extra work for you or Alveda."

"Are you kidding? Alveda will be thrilled," Heidi had to say. "As much as she enjoyed the catered menu at the engagement party, she'd be honored to prepare food for your shower."

"I know all that, but I want it to be easy and let everyone have fun."

Heidi didn't understand the fuss. "Alveda told me she'd like to do it. Anyone who knows her will tell you so, as well."

"I must agree," Mrs. M. said. "She puts her heart in her cooking."

"And she is fabulous," Serena said, sounding like she was leaning toward the shower at

Masterson House. "Could you give me a little more time to decide?"

"Most certainly. In the meantime, there are other decisions to make. Like where to hold the ceremony."

Serena groaned. "Logan and I haven't decided on that location either."

"I thought you couldn't wait to get married?" Heidi teased.

"I can't." She frowned. "All the details though, they're difficult. Plus, I have the Florida contingent to think about, so I have to take them into account too."

Serena's father lived in Florida and had gotten remarried in the winter. Serena had suddenly gained four brothers and their significant others.

"You do have a bunch of logistics to figure out."

Mrs. M. patted Serena's arm. "Not to worry. I've spoken to Jasmine on the phone. We don't want this to turn into too much pressure."

Serena blinked. "You've spoken to my stepmother? I don't know whether to be thrilled or terrified."

"Terrified," Heidi blurted.

"Jasmine is a force of nature. She reminds me of someone," Mrs. M. said with an approving smile.

Mrs. M. and Jasmine were cut from the same cloth. They both knew how to get things done by gently pushing the people they cared about. The unsuspecting person never knew they were being pushed until it was too late. Heidi silently chuckled before a thought hit her. Was Mrs. M. pulling strings? Casting a sideways glance at the woman, she couldn't be sure. Mrs. M. was a sly one, to say the least.

"And speaking of the wedding," Mrs. M. said, turning her sights on Heidi. "Will you be bringing a date or should we start looking for a nice eligible bachelor for you?"

Oh, no. She recognized that tone. Just a bit too casual for Heidi's liking. What if Mrs. M. tried to fix her up?

Her stomach dropped. What did she say? Should she tell Mrs. M. that she and Reid had started a relationship? Well, hadn't really started, more like talked about it. She didn't want to be too premature and complicate things.

Mrs. M. waved her hand. "We have plenty of time. Between you and Reid, I'll find the perfect dates for both of you." She turned to Serena. "Now, about the date for the ceremony?"

"Logan is checking a few things and then we'll announce it."

A disgruntled expression darkened Mrs. M.'s face. "This year, I hope."

Serena chuckled. "Definitely this year."

"Very good. I was hoping—" A ringing came from the direction of Mrs. M.'s purse. She paused midsentence and pulled out her phone to read the screen. "It's Bonnie. I must take the call."

Heidi leaned over to Serena and whispered, "I wouldn't want to be in your shoes. You've got a lot on your plate."

"Tell me about it. Between the store and vetting wedding options, I'm running out of hours in the day."

"You could ask for help. I'm—"

Mrs. M.'s gasp stopped her thought. Heidi looked over to see the woman's face turn pale as she reached out a hand to steady herself against the display table.

"I'll be right there."

"Mrs. M., what's wrong?" Heidi asked, concerned by her agitated state.

"It's my son, Arthur. He went to a doctor's appointment this morning and complained of chest pain. Apparently, it got worse as the visit went on so they're taking him now to the hospital for tests."

Serena ran over to put her arm around Mrs. M.

"What can we do?" Heidi asked as she joined the women.

"I should meet them there." Mrs. M. started hunting for her keys with shaky hands. When she found the ring, Serena took them away.

"I'll drive us there. And I'll call Logan on the way."

"Do you want me to get a hold of Reid?" Heidi asked.

"Please," Mrs. M. said, distracted by the turn of events. "Arthur's sons should be there."

Heidi hurried to the counter to find her phone then hit the contact for Reid. No answer. She remembered him saying something about cutting bathroom tile in a new house this morning. Perhaps he couldn't hear his phone ring.

Before leaving, Serena called over her shoulder, "If you want to come to the hospital, call Carrie to fill in."

"Okay. See you soon."

She quickly called Carrie, who promised to be downstairs in a few minutes. She called Reid again, but it went right to voice mail. She had her keys ready when Carrie opened the back door and ran into the showroom.

"Go, go," she said, waving Heidi out the door.

Not wasting a minute, Heidi rushed to the car and was quickly on the road, headed up the turning mountain road to the house where Reid was working. She pulled up to find trucks in the driveway, so she parked at the end and ran toward the house.

She found Phil first, who was sitting on the open tailgate of a truck, immersed in his phone. He glanced up, face flushing as he was caught goofing off. He jumped down and quickly shoved his phone in his pants pocket.

"Where's Reid?"

The kid shrugged.

She ran past him, through the garage and into the kitchen. Reid's crew stopped working when she burst into the room.

"Reid?"

Joe pointed down a hallway. Just as she hurried in that direction, a loud buzz started up. She rounded a corner and found Reid busy cutting tile, water running over the blade, droplets flying. When he noticed her, he turned off the saw and removed his safety goggles. Sent her a wide smile.

"Heidi. Were we supposed to meet today?"

"Reid," she said, catching her breath. "It's your dad. He's gone to the hospital."

He dropped the goggles on the table supporting the saw. "What's wrong?"

"They're not sure. Heart, I think. He needs tests." She explained the call his grandmother received and how she'd raced over when she couldn't reach him. "You should go."

He froze for a moment, like he was unsure what to do, then snapped to attention. He grabbed her hand as he passed and they hustled down the hallway. He called out a brief explanation to his crew, then they were outside, where he stopped short.

"My truck is blocked in."

"My car isn't. C'mon." She squeezed his hand and they ran to her sedan. Once inside, she fired up the engine and sped off, making record time to the hospital.

All the while Reid was silent, staring straight ahead, his hands balled on his thighs. Heidi didn't know what to say, so she just concentrated on getting Reid there in one piece. She pulled up to the emergency room entrance and told him, "Go. I'll park and then find you."

Still silent, he jumped out and strode to the door. It took a few minutes before she finally found a spot and called Alveda to fill her in and promise her updates. Then she was inside the building, searching for the Masterson family. Thankfully, she found them in no time.

In the private waiting room, Reid was embracing his mother, while Logan and Serena stood with their arms wrapped around each other, matching worried expressions on their drawn faces. Mrs. M. sat near a window, fidgeting with the clasp on her purse. Heidi hurried over to take a seat beside her.

The older woman's smile fell flat. "Thank you for finding Reid."

Heidi nodded, then looked over at him. His face was expressionless and she worried about his state of mind.

"Do you know anything yet?" she asked Mrs. M.

"They took him off somewhere."

Just then a man in surgical scrubs strode into the room, and they all faced him. Bonnie moved forward for the news.

"I'm Dr. Patel. Your husband needs a heart catheterization to better diagnose the extent of his cardiovascular condition. They're prepping him now, if you'd like to see him."

"Yes," Bonnie said, following the doctor.

"Do you want to go, as well?" Heidi asked Mrs. M.

"No. Bonnie can handle whatever decisions need to be made."

Heidi's heart broke. This was her son. Certainly Mrs. M. wanted to be in the know, but deferred to Bonnie. The rest of the group rallied around Mrs. M.

"Can I get you anything, Grandmother?" Logan asked.

"You can't rush the doctor, so no."

Reid sank down into the chair on the other side of his grandmother, briefly meeting Heidi's gaze before gently taking Mrs. M.'s hand. "He'll be okay."

Was Reid trying to assure himself as well as his grandmother? Probably, but Heidi knew this was a lot more complicated for Reid, especially when she noticed the guilt reflected in his eyes.

They sat quietly, voices on the overhead speakers breaking the silence from time to time. Heidi hadn't spent much time in places like this. The stringent antiseptic smell and hurried pace of the nurses and doctors made her uneasy.

Finally, after what seemed like forever, Bonnie returned. "Arthur is undergoing the procedure now," she reported. "After they inject the dye, and if there is a blockage in the artery as they suspect, they'll do an angioplasty and place a stent to keep the artery open."

"Is he okay?" Logan asked.

"You know your father. Complaining the entire time, but I think this has opened his eyes. He needs to start putting his health first."

Reid rose and went to stand by the window, his hands shoved deep in his jeans pockets. His T-shirt was still wet from the tile work, his boots dusty and hair mussed, as if he'd run his hand through it a dozen times. He'd never looked more handsome. Or more lost.

Heidi wanted to go over and give him comfort, but the leave-me-alone vibe was strong. That she understood, since she'd given off the same warning many times in her life. She'd just have to wait him out.

An hour and a half later, the doctor came back. Everyone jumped up to hear the news.

"How is my husband?" Bonnie asked.

"He's in recovery now. The procedure went well." The doctor informed them, "We did have to insert a stent, but he will be fine. Once he sees a cardiologist, he might need medication and surely several lifestyle changes, but I believe we were able to keep this condition from getting worse."

Relieved, Heidi blew out a long breath. She imagined everyone else doing the same as they heard the prognosis.

"We want to make sure the recovery process goes well, so we're keeping him overnight and will likely release him tomorrow morning."

Bonnie's hand flew to her throat. "I didn't expect... I'm not prepared."

The doctor smiled at her. "He will be in recovery for a few hours. If you need to go home and collect some things, he'll be fine until you return." He nodded, then left the room.

Logan spoke first. "Serena, why don't you drive Grandmother and Mother home. I'll get Mother's car and meet you there."

"Certainly."

He looked at his brother, but Reid remained silent.

"Um, I drove Reid here," Heidi piped up. "We can go to the store and get Mrs. M.'s car."

"Does that plan work for you?" Logan asked Reid.

"Yes."

Heidi grabbed her purse and keys, waiting for Reid to move as the others filed out of the room.

She walked over to him. "Hey, are you okay?"

"I'm not sure. This is surreal."

"I suppose no one wants to deal with their parent's mortality." Not that she'd ever have that problem, since she had no idea where her mother was. But Alveda? She was getting up there in years and worried Heidi when she refused to slow down.

He ran a hand over the back of his neck.

"Reid, this isn't your fault."

"Isn't it? I left the family business. Mother

said he was doing too much. Why did I have to be so stubborn?"

"I'm going to repeat myself—this isn't your fault. Your mother finally got him to go to the doctor and he'll be fine. You heard Dr. Patel."

"It should have never gotten this far."

"And if you were still part of Masterson Enterprises? Would that mean his heart wouldn't have issues?"

He glanced at her and for a long moment he was silent. "You're right," he eventually conceded.

"Of course, I am."

"And annoying."

"That too."

She took his hand, laced her fingers with his. To her relief, he didn't pull away. Once they were at her car, he stopped her.

"What do I say to him?"

Heidi heard the uncertainty in his voice and ached for him. "Tell him that you love him, no matter what's gone on between you two."

"That simple?"

"Reid, I may not come from a big, messy family, but I've observed enough of them to know that the only thing that matters in the end is loving each other. I'm not saying it'll be easy, but it's the right thing."

"Right." Except he didn't look convinced.

She drove him to Mrs. M.'s car, wishing he'd open up more, but knew he wouldn't say a word until he was ready. Before he got out, he met her gaze. "You're coming to the house, right?"

"I don't know. This seems like a family thing, Reid."

He took her hand. "You are family. And I'd really like you to be there."

She paused, the fear on his face making her decision. "Okay."

He leaned over the console and lightly brushed his lips over hers. "Thanks for being here for me."

He got out of the car and strode away, shoulders straight. Heidi could tell something had shifted in Reid, something deep inside. Would he draw her in or push her aside?

She couldn't help but speculate what would happen going forward.

As soon as Reid stepped inside Masterson House, the scent of fresh coffee reached him. Alveda had clearly started getting ready for those who would gather soon. It felt strange to be here, knowing his dad was in the hospital rather than busy in his office, but his family needed him.

They needed you before this and where had you been?

He cast off the silent question as he stood in the foyer. It was quiet, eerie almost, except for low voices coming from the direction of the kitchen. Not wanting to see anyone yet, he detoured down the hallway to his father's study.

The scent of wood polish, and the mints his dad always kept handy in a crystal bowl, greeted him. His father's sanctuary. How many times had Reid played in here as a child while his father conducted business? Countless. What he wouldn't give to relive those times now.

The dark mahogany desk was cluttered with papers, the matching dark shelves held books that had been read and reread over the years. Off to the side was a credenza with various framed pictures. Reid had always thought it strange that his father kept family photos within reach, especially since he'd had a troubled relationship with both Reid and Logan in years past.

In the silence he walked over and stared at each frame.

His parents' wedding photo. Logan in full military uniform from his time in the service. Reid's high school graduation picture. Behind it, a snapshot from one of his baseball games.

With a start, he picked it up. He recalled that game. The entire family had shown up to cheer him on. After, they'd gathered for a family pose, smiling because Reid had steered the team to victory. On the outskirts of the group was Heidi, Reid's baseball hat perched on her head. He remembered dropping it on her after his team had won.

As he took in her features, his chest grew tight. She'd always been there when it was important. Why had he never noticed her steady presence until recently? How her sunny smile always gave him hope? But what of the future? They'd just agreed to see where their feelings would take them, but now this.

"Your father always did like shutting himself up in here."

He jerked, setting the frame down, and turned to find his grandmother hovering in the open doorway.

"He probably wouldn't like me trespassing now."

"I don't think he'd mind."

She came inside, ran her hand over the sturdy bookshelves. So much like the well-built house itself. Taking a circuit of the room, she stopped in front of Reid.

"Your father can't be at work for a while. He needs rest after this procedure. Your mother has already decided that they are going away for a few weeks."

He nodded, his heart pounding. He thought he was ready, but... *Please don't say it.*

"I know this is difficult for all of us, but out of everyone in the family, you have the knowledge to keep the company running during his longer absence."

He closed his eyes, waiting for the inevitable.

"I wouldn't ask, but we're in a bind here, Reid. We need you to go back to Masterson Enterprises."

She'd said it.

"We need you to fill in for your father. I suppose he'll have to make some personal decisions while they're away." She reached up to lay a hand on his cheek. "I'd say this is your destiny, but I don't want you to think I'm being melodramatic."

He puffed out a breath that almost sounded like a laugh.

"I can certainly support you, but you will have to make the big decisions going forward."

"And if Father doesn't like them?"

"It can't be helped."

He had a hard time pulling air into his lungs.

"Besides, I have faith in you."

If only his father did.

"You know, Reid, you and Arthur are a lot alike. That's why you two bang heads all the time."

Yes, Reid was aware. The more time he'd spent with the man, he could see how much he was starting to act like his father. He hadn't wanted to admit it, but could his leaving the firm have been a subconscious move? When Reid looked in the mirror, he even saw his father and realized he didn't want to walk down that same path. Bitterness and disappointment were things he could live without.

It was quite an eye-opener. He thought he'd have more time to figure out his next moves, but that didn't seem possible any longer.

Grandmother broke into his thoughts. "Can you get your house renovation projects covered?"

He inhaled. "Yes. My crew is the best and they know what to do."

"Then it's settled."

He raised one eyebrow. "I haven't said yes."

She stared at him.

He wasn't ready to give in just yet. "Can you give me a couple minutes?"

"I can, but in the end, you'll do the right thing."

Yes. He would. They all knew it.

His grandmother left and Reid stood in the

middle of the room. This was his shot to return to the family business. He should embrace it, but until he and his father talked, he couldn't see a future there. But he wanted this. Badly.

There was a knock on the door. Heidi. She stood still, as if unsure if she should enter. He waved her inside.

"I brought you some iced tea," she said, holding out a glass tumbler.

He took it, staring at the brown liquid as if it contained all of life's answers.

"At the risk of being annoying, how are you holding up?"

He shot her a grimace and got right to the matter at hand. "Grandmother asked me to fill in for Dad."

"And you're surprised?"

"No. I…" He raked a hand through his hair. "I'm not sure what to do."

She walked right in front of him. Took the glass from his hand and placed it on the desk, then stared him square in the eye. "Pros?"

"I get to work for the family company. Make decisions. Feel involved again."

She nodded. "Cons?"

"Eventually my father will return. Will he retire? Let me take the helm? Or will we argue and go back to square one?"

"You've laid out all the facts. Can you not make a decision?"

He closed his eyes. Swallowed the hurt rising there. "What if he doesn't want me there?"

She waited until he met her gaze again. "Don't give him a reason to push you out."

"You make it sound so easy."

She placed her hands on his shoulders. Her touch steadied him. "Nothing is easy, Reid. But you want this, don't you?"

"I do. But for Dad to be gone for health reasons? Not a win here."

"But your family will stand beside you no matter what." Her eyes sparkled. Did he read faith there? "So will I."

He rested his forehead against hers. Drank in the floral fragrance that always accompanied her. He needed her encouragement as much as he needed air. How had he missed this essential bond between them?

"What do you want, Reid?" she whispered.

"A second chance."

"Then take it."

At her words he leaned in. Swept his lips over hers. He circled his arms around her waist, thankful she was here. In his arms. The woman he'd never realized he'd needed so much, the woman who'd been at his side whenever it counted.

After long minutes, he pulled away, but kept her close. "Promise you'll stick around?"

"Haven't I always?"

He couldn't stop himself. He kissed her again, the promise ringing in his ears.

Voices filtered from the foyer. Had the news gotten out? Were there folks stopping by, concerned about his father? He'd have to face them.

"Everything will be okay," she said.

"You don't know that."

She opened her mouth to argue, but he placed a finger against her warm lips.

"What I do know is that you are the one sure thing in my life." He took in her precious features. Let out a ragged breath. "You've always been a good friend, Heidi."

Reid hugged her and left the room.

In his wake, Heidi's heart seized in her chest. Reid had just said the most wonderful words to her but framed them in the context of being friends. Confusion overwhelmed her. What about the kiss? The longing she felt between them? Was this all she was going to get?

The question was too disheartening to examine.

Tamping down her trepidation, she joined the others in the formal living room. The Masterson family rallied around each other and the visitors who were beginning to stop by as news about Mr. Masterson's condition became known. It was a stark reminder that the only family she had was Alveda, and even she, as Gayle Ann's confidant, was more connected to these folks than Heidi would ever be.

As more concerned friends arrived, Heidi distanced herself from the group, marveling at how Reid could engage in small talk while masking his worry over his father. He had that indefinable likeability factor that made him a successful businessman. No wonder he missed working at the office. Masterson Enterprises, and these people, were his world.

She placed a hand over her swirling stomach, wondering if she'd ever fit in, or if she'd only ever be comfortable viewing their lives from the sidelines.

CHAPTER ELEVEN

"YOU LOOK LIKE you've got the weight of the world on your shoulders."

Seated at the kitchen table in Masterson House four days after Arthur's emergency procedure, Gayle Ann tried to compose her features. Clearly, she wasn't successful at it. Alveda was observant and knew Gayle Ann much too well for her to hide anything.

"It's Reid," she said, voicing her concern out loud for the first time since her grandson had returned to Masterson Enterprises.

"Reid is where he wants to be," Alveda assured her, pouring another cup of coffee for them both.

"That's the problem," Gayle Ann answered. "I'm not sure Reid being at the office is good for his relationship with Heidi." She picked up a spoon and set it in the cup, moving it around in small circles.

"Are you afraid he'll put the job first?" Alveda asked, taking a seat at the table. The just-out-of-the-oven pie cooling on the counter smelled heavenly, but went untouched. Neither had much of an appetite since they'd returned home from Sunday services and barely touched their lunch.

"I do. Reid doesn't see it, but he's a lot like his father. I don't want the business to consume him like it has Arthur."

"Would the spark between Heidi and Reid fizzle out?"

"Yes, or something like that. I'm afraid I put him on the spot." She frowned. "From what I've heard, Reid went into the office the day after Arthur's test, just like I asked. He worked late both Thursday and Friday night, and then went back late Saturday for a few hours. Knowing him, he's there right now. He should have been out with Heidi over the weekend having fun, not buried under paperwork."

Alveda lifted her cup, holding it between both hands mere inches from her mouth, seemingly lost in thought. After a moment, she lowered her cup.

"Heidi did mention that she hasn't seen Reid in the last few days. I assumed it was because they were both busy."

"They are busy, but because of how Reid left things, I'm sure he's going to put in overtime to prove himself to his father."

"Heidi must have noticed too. When I spoke to her, she didn't sound happy. I asked her point-blank what was troubling her, but she brushed me off."

Gayle Ann looked at her friend, anticipating the answer to her question, but asked it anyway. "They haven't been to the Hanover renovation since the emergency call about Arthur, have they?"

"No. Heidi said it's on hold until things at Masterson Enterprises are settled."

"Which could mean anything."

What was her grandson thinking? Happiness was within arm's reach, but he refused to grab on tight.

Alveda cut into her thoughts. "I wouldn't worry too much. Heidi will chase him down to finish if he really gets behind. She still has her sights set on that place."

"And what if she gets the house and Reid resumes his place permanently at Masterson? What will happen to the romance they've just begun to acknowledge?"

"It was your crazy idea to get them together." Alveda's voice rose. "You brought the house to Reid's attention after I told you Heidi wanted to buy it. I sent her in his direction when he first started to make plans for that place. I told you we never should have interfered."

"But we did. With good intentions."

"Still think your matchmaking club is a smart idea?" Alveda huffed. "We pushed them together and now they might get hurt."

Gayle Ann shook her head. "I disagree. They were meant to be together."

"You always were stubborn," Alveda muttered, picking up her cup again.

"And you agreed to give matching them a chance. Look how far we've come."

"You're still worried. You can't hide it from me." Alveda's brows knitted together. "Doesn't bode well for their future. If that young man breaks Heidi's heart…"

"I know. You'll never forgive me." Gayle Ann stared into her cup. "Trust me, I won't forgive myself either."

"Then what do we do?"

At Alveda's challenge, Gayle Ann felt a new infusion of hope. She wouldn't give up. Not when they were so close.

She squared her shoulders and proclaimed, "Exactly what we've been doing. Keep working behind the scenes."

Alveda's jaw dropped. "Won't that just make matters worse?"

"Not if our timing is right."

Alveda shook her head, a strand of hair escaping her bun. "I almost hate to ask, but do you have a plan B?"

"I'm the leader of a matchmaking club. Of course, I have a plan."

Alveda snorted.

Gayle Ann sent her friend a weary glance. "Okay, I'm working on one."

"That does not inspire confidence."

Gayle Ann refused to lose. There was too much at stake. Heidi was the future for her grandson. She could also offer him a life not consumed by business deals and spreadsheets. They were a good team. Hadn't they learned that from the house renovation? If Reid would spend more time away from the office…

Then it hit her. She sent Alveda a sly smile.

"Not sure I like the looks of that grin."

"Not to worry," Gayle Ann assured her. "I have a solution and the person to help me pull it off."

MONDAY MORNING, Reid took a short break to stretch the muscles in his lower back. He'd been at the Masterson offices since seven, getting up to speed on the status of projects, including who was working with whom and analyzing their financial bottom line. He was energized as he hadn't been in a long time, in spite of the long hours he'd already put in.

After his father came home from the hospital, he'd spent the day resting at home. Thankfully the procedure had gone well, and amazingly, his father was feeling better almost immediately. Taking advantage of this, Reid's mother whisked the senior Masterson off on Friday morning for a getaway to their cabin on the far side of the lake. Reid hadn't had to run into his father at all, which made the transition easier, but knew that day was coming, so he'd get in as much work as possible while he could.

Ernie was handling the current renovations at the three homes. Phil was tasked with staining the deck at the Hanover house. Reid didn't want to question Ernie about his grandson's assignment after he'd left the older man in charge, but Reid didn't have great expectations. Phil hadn't proven to be all that motivated or conscientious. He was Ernie's family so Reid would hope for the best.

The remodel was nearly complete with the final inspection scheduled for the end of this week. Then Heidi would be able to purchase her dream home.

Thinking of Heidi, he wandered over to the window and gazed down at Main Street.

From here he could see most of the stores up and down the thoroughfare, doors opening to begin the day. Mrs. Albert was on the sidewalk, broom in hand, sweeping the concrete around her shop. Buck stood in front of the Jerky Shack, cleaning the large glass window. He supposed Heidi would be arriving at Blue Ridge Cottage soon, or perhaps she'd be dealing with a client, going over a bookkeeping account.

He missed her, her ready smile and how she always challenged him to prove a point. He'd been grateful for her steady presence when he'd gotten the news about his dad, that she remained at the hospital until they were sure the procedure was a success. His solid friend, yet not his friend. He found himself thinking about her at different points during the day, wanting to share a funny incident or an idea he'd come up with. This was definitely more than friendship, although he wasn't sure what word to use, because wanting to be with Heidi had become as essential as breathing for him. On the other hand, being day in and day out at the busy office was a chance he couldn't refuse.

He was torn.

When he'd called to reschedule their first date on Saturday, he could hear the disappointment in her voice, but she understood that he'd wanted to stop by the office. They'd have plenty of time for dates, he promised her. It made sense that he should get caught up on the family business, then his life would return to normal. Then they would pursue the next step.

At least, that was the plan.

Maybe he should call her to ask about having lunch today? A few hours together was something, right? He went to his desk to search for his cell, noticing a note from his assistant reminding him about a 1:00 p.m. meeting. Okay, he'd shoot for lunch tomorrow if nothing came up.

He'd just settled in his chair with another file when he heard his grandmother's voice.

"Don't worry, Darlene, Reid will see me."

His desk phone lit up just as Grandmother walked into the room. He lifted the receiver and pressed the interoffice button. "It's okay, Darlene. She's already here."

"If the she you mean is me," his grandmother said as she dropped her purse in an empty chair, "then perhaps you could be a little more respectful of your elder."

Reid rose and skirted the desk to give his grandmother a kiss.

"You certainly don't need an introduction."

She gave a curt nod, then looked up at him, reading his face. "You're doing okay with all this?"

"Of course. You asked me to step in and to be honest, I've been enjoying the change of pace."

"You don't miss manual labor?"

"Not right now. I'm giving my mind a long overdue workout."

"Hmm."

His grandmother thinking too long on any one topic never went well for him. "What does that mean?"

"I don't like you logging such long hours. You're too young to be cooped up in this office."

"Well, I can't very well do this job from a reno site." He waved a hand in front of him to show off his office attire of button-down shirt, slacks and dress shoes. "I'm not even dressed for it."

"Reid, you have a life. Make sure you use your days wisely. I don't—"

The desk phone buzzed again. As Reid reached over to answer, his grandmother said, "Aren't you the popular one this morning."

Reid chuckled. "Yes, Darlene?"

Just then Judge Carmichael walked into the office.

"Yes, I see he's here," Reid commented in a dry tone.

"Hope you don't mind me dropping in," the judge said, his silver hair perfectly combed, his conservative clothing adding an air of authority, but most of all, his smile conveying his nonchalance about barging in.

"I don't recall us having an appointment," Reid said, already suspicious of the dual surprise visits.

"I asked him to stop by," Grandmother informed him.

That explained nothing.

"To what do I owe the pleasure of both of you here in my office?" Reid asked.

"You know the judge and I are on the town council."

"How could I forget?" The council had delayed a few construction jobs Reid had arranged in the past. Didn't matter that they were family, if his grandmother didn't like an aspect of a proposal, she'd hold it up until modifications were made.

"With all that has gone on with your father, Harry had to remind me about the upcoming council meeting."

Reid crossed his arms over his chest. "That doesn't explain why you're here."

The judge chuckled.

"Don't be a smart aleck," Grandmother scolded. "I'm getting to that part."

Reid glanced at his desk, longing to read reports that most people might find boring but he thrived on.

"To continue," his grandmother said, slipping into her haughty voice. "Since you've been busy with your remodeling projects, I haven't seen you very much…"

He got the hint.

"But I have a special idea for the town and I need your help before presenting it to the council."

"It's quite admirable," the judge added.

The two older folks smiled at each other. Two peas in a pod, if you asked Reid. Nothing but trouble.

He cleared his throat. "And this idea?"

"Oh, right." Grandmother got back to business. "I've long wanted a large sign at the south end of the business district, welcoming visitors to Golden. We never replaced the ones that came down years ago. Your father and I discussed it at length and decided Masterson Enterprises would sponsor a new sign, so we don't need to dip into the public coffers. I know the council will approve it because they don't have to pay the bill, but you know how busy your father gets, so it was put on the back burner, so to speak."

"If you've discussed it with Dad, why are you here now?"

"The upcoming meeting. Keep up, Reid." She tsk-tsked. "I need a spec to present to the members. Measurements, materials, design. You know the drill."

He smothered the chuckle rising in his chest. Grandmother was on a roll.

"Since your father is gone and you are so very handy with those kinds of details, I want you to come to the location with me. Let me present my vision so you can draw up a plan."

Reid tapped a few keys on his laptop to pull up his daily calendar. "When did you have in mind?"

"Now."

He looked up. "Right now?"

"No better time than the present."

"Grandmother, I'm busy."

Her hand moved in a dismissive wave. "You're never too busy for your grandmother."

He bit back a retort because he knew she was not leaving until her mission was complete.

"Fine. Let's head to this…location."

"Excellent. Grab some paper and your measuring tape and we'll be on our way."

Judge Carmichael swept his arm toward the door in a grand gesture. "After you," he said to Grandmother.

"Aren't you a gentleman," she preened.

Reid rolled his eyes as he snatched up his cell phone and other items before following the two work disrupters.

His grandmother's phone rang and she fished it from her purse. "Yes?" She nodded briskly. "Thank you."

Once on the sidewalk outside the building, Reid turned to head south, but Grandmother headed north.

"Grandmother, wait," he said, jogging to catch up with her. "You said you wanted the sign on south Main. You're going in the wrong direction."

She regarded the two men. "Coffee first. I haven't had a cup yet."

"I find that hard to believe. Alveda has a fresh pot going before you get up in the morning."

"Today she was busy," his grandmother replied, her pace picking up speed as the three headed to Sit A Spell.

Reid counted to ten in his head while reluctantly following his grandmother.

"Well, I wouldn't mind another cup," the judge announced.

Reid followed, scrolling through his phone to read over his prepared notes for the day. This little outing would push his schedule back an hour at least.

"Here we are," Grandmother said as if Reid had never been to the coffee shop before. "The usual, Reid?"

"What?" He looked up. "Sure."

"Stay off that thing," his grandmother ordered before she and the judge disappeared inside.

Shaking his head, Reid typed in a few ideas that had been percolating in his mind. He vaguely registered the cars moving up and down Main Street, barely acknowledged the conversation around him as people went about their daily routines. Until he heard one particular voice that made his senses come alive.

"Reid? What are you doing here?"

He glanced up, surprised and pleased to see Heidi. "Hey, stranger."

She sent him a furtive glance. "You've been the busy one, not me."

Right. "Looks like not too busy for a coffee break."

"With your grandmother?" Heidi motioned her head over her shoulder. "Ran into her inside."

"She's got a project she wants me to handle."

Heidi laughed. "She does know you're running a large company, doesn't she?"

"Apparently that doesn't matter."

"She does get her way."

He drank Heidi in, taking pleasure in the way her soft hair curled over her shoulders. The sunlight highlighted the brown strands, her amber eyes sparkled, eyes only for him. She wore a striped blouse and navy skirt with matching shoes, the picture of professionalism.

But most of all, he liked that she made him feel like he could do anything. That he was more than just his father's son. His own man. More than a placeholder, until his father realized Reid was on his side, not out to take his place. Heidi had always had faith in him, no matter if it was a school event or a family issue. He couldn't imagine her not being a part of his life. He needed to make time to be with her.

"So, what is your grandmother's grand plan?" she asked.

"A Golden welcome sign."

Her eyebrows arched high. "A what?"

"There's a town council meeting and she wanted me to come up with specs to present a new sign to the members."

"I'm surprised we don't already have a sign."

"There was one at each end of the business district years ago, but they were old and weathered, so someone tore them down. Grandmother's decided it's time to replace at least one of them."

"Knowing Mrs. M., she'll get it done."

"But in the process, she's cutting into my time at Masterson Enterprises."

Heidi frowned. "I'm sure you can make it up later, whatever needs to be done."

"I already have two meetings I can't miss." And an important call to a bank that he should have already made, plus checking in with the contractors handling various jobs in progress.

"Reid."

His mind had jumped ahead. If he returned to his desk in thirty minutes, he could still make the call. Catching the others would be a bit more tricky...

"Reid!"

He blinked. Focused on her. "Yeah?"

An annoyed expression crossed her face. "Chill."

He blew out a breath.

"You can spare some time for your grandmother. The other things will be there when you get back."

He knew that. Tucking the work details away, he refocused. "Thanks for reminding me."

"I wouldn't think you'd need reminding."

She sounded ticked.

"You know how caught up I can get."

A shadow passed over her eyes. "I do."

Before he could apologize for the little time they'd had together lately, his grandmother and the judge returned.

"Oh, good, Heidi." She handed Reid his coffee. "Reid told you about the sign?"

"Yes. I think it's a great idea, Mrs. M."

"Good, because we could use your input, as well."

Heidi's eyes went wide. "I'm not really the creative person here. You should ask Serena."

Grandmother's lips pursed. The universal sign that whether you liked it or not, Gayle Ann Masterson's agenda came first.

"Um…I'm early for my shift so I suppose I can spare a few minutes."

Reid had to hide a grin when Heidi gave in.

"Wonderful. Let's make our way to the location."

Reid waited until Heidi fell into step behind his grandmother and strode along beside her.

"Sorry about this."

"Don't be. I'm glad your grandmother included me. Makes me feel like a true part of the town."

"You are a true part of Golden."

She shrugged before taking a sip from her cup.

Over the last few weeks, he'd gotten used to the chatty Heidi. Where was the plucky woman who'd insisted she be Reid's intern? When she didn't respond to the conversation, he grew concerned.

He nudged her arm with his elbow. "You okay?"

"Sure. I have a busy day myself. I'm meeting with a new client."

"That's great."

"It is. So, I could really use a new home office to work out of."

The house. The one he personally hadn't been working on since returning to Masterson Enterprises. Guilt made his face hot.

"One of the guys will be there for the final inspection," he told her.

"And then?"

"We move on to the sale."

"Which you'll be a part of, right?" she pressed.

"Lisa is handling the paperwork. Other than signing off, I'm not really needed."

She sent him a side glance. "You're going to let me finish up on my own?"

"No," he backpedaled. "I can do whatever you need."

"I need you to walk through this process with me," she said in a voice of steel.

"Heidi, it's not a big deal. You'll be fine."

"It is a big deal, Reid." She puffed out a breath. "I've never done this before. It's a huge step and I thought…no, I'd hoped, we'd do this together."

He ran a hand through his hair. "You're right."

Her gaze turned pleading. "So, you'll be there for me?"

How could he refuse her? He took hold of her hand and laced her fingers in his. "Yes. I will."

He felt her relax.

"Here we are," Grandmother announced a few blocks from the coffee shop. From here, the businesses ran north; family homes spread out in the blocks south and farther into the hills and valleys beyond.

He sent Heidi a reassuring glance, then dropped her hand. Withdrawing a pencil from his shirt pocket, he asked, "What did you have in mind, Grandmother?"

"I want it to be on this original spot." His

grandmother pointed to an overgrown lot that had been vacant for years. "I'll need the vote from the council, but this is a perfect location."

Reid agreed. He found a better view, visualizing how to best display the sign.

"It doesn't need to be very large," she went on, "but I do want visitors to know that they've entered our town."

On paper, Reid drew a rectangular shape and posts that would lift it off the ground.

"Although I'm not sure about the design."

"Why not make it a contest, Mrs. M.?" Heidi suggested. "Ask the folks in town to come up with ideas."

Grandmother turned and grinned. "I love that. The more we involve our townspeople in the decisions, the more excited they'll be."

"From the Chamber of Commerce reports, business has been growing," Heidi added. "A lot of my clients have seen an increase in sales."

Grandmother clasped her hands over her heart. "I'm so pleased to hear that." Her eyes twinkled. "And since you're so good with numbers, why don't you and Reid team up? Between the two of you, we'll have a firm estimate in place that will make the council happy."

Reid frowned. "I thought you were paying for it?"

"Well, let's see," his grandmother said, switching her attention to the judge. "Do you foresee any legal troubles?"

"I'll do a record search on the lot. See if there are any obstacles to placing it there."

"Not to worry. I know the owner."

Reid narrowed his eyes. "Grandmother?"

"Yes, it's me, okay?" She continued the discussion as if the admission was not important. "We'll clean up this area, erect the sign and add lovely landscaping. The first thing anyone entering the town will see is a pretty welcome to Golden."

Heidi sidled over to Reid. "You didn't know?"

"My grandmother owns more property that I'm aware of. Besides, she doesn't run her business through Masterson Enterprises, so I can't keep up with her."

"I like her style."

Reid met Heidi's amused gaze. "I like your style too."

Her eyes widened, then she looked away.

Why did she seem so unsure about them? "Well, I do."

She pointed discreetly to where his grandmother and the judge were deep in conversation. "You don't want Mrs. M. to hear."

"What if I don't care?"

A frown creased her forehead. "Are you sure? Because you and I were just starting to figure this thing out and then you went AWOL."

Guilt made his breath catch. She was right. "I'm sorry, Heidi. You have every reason to be upset with me."

Her angry expression eased.

"Just because I promised to fill in doesn't mean you aren't important to me." He had to work hard to not be a carbon copy of his dad, chained to the office all hours of the day. Reid liked where things were going with Heidi. Liked that he could enjoy a warm spring day with a beautiful woman who got him. "Let's take our time, but along the way I'm going to compliment you if I feel like it."

A half smile appeared, and his heartbeat took off.

"Is this a new, improved Reid?"

"What can I say? Working at the office has been good for me."

"I can see that." Her smile grew more confident. "I was hoping we might get together one night this week. I want to walk through the house one more time, see if I missed any last upgrades before the final inspection."

"We could do that."

The excitement gleaming in her eyes was contagious. "What works for you?"

"I have a meeting tonight."

"And tomorrow night we're with the kids at the community center."

"I'll have to check my schedule. I know I have some other things going on."

"But we can meet before the inspector comes out, right?"

"I'll have to call you. Set up a time when I can get away from the office."

Her smile slipped. "You just said you'd be there for me."

"I will. We can work around my schedule."

A car honked behind him. Reid turned to see his brother behind the wheel. He waved and when he turned around, Heidi's smile had disappeared.

"I don't think that works for me," she informed him.

What had happened? One moment she was happy, and now? He wasn't sure. "Why not?"

"You seem more interested in your family business than the fact that time is running out on my house."

"Heidi, it's a house. It'll be there."

She drew in a breath and he realized his mistake.

"I forgot. You flip properties and then you get out."

"Heidi…"

"I get it." She glanced up the street. "Serena's waiting for me. I'll call your office and set up an appointment." She turned on her heel and started to walk away.

"Heidi, wait."

She spun around, her face blank of emotion, and walked backward a few steps. "I get it, Reid. You have important things to do." Then she rotated, making her way to the store.

As he watched her cross the street, his heart pounded. Why did the family business and time with Heidi have to be at odds? Couldn't he have both?

CHAPTER TWELVE

"Where is Heidi going?" Gayle Ann asked her grandson. By the dazed expression on his face, he wasn't happy about her leaving so suddenly.

"She had to get to work." He stared at Heidi's retreating form, then focused on her. "I need to leave too."

"Not until you get those measurements."

With a scowl, Reid handed the pad and pencil to the judge, took out the tape measure to check the distance and asked, "Is this about the size you want?"

"Yes. It'll be visible, but not pretentious."

He called out some numbers, which Harry jotted down, then the tape measure zipped into its case. "Is that it for now?"

They'd finished town business, yes, but what about the dark cloud hovering over her grandson? Had she miscalculated by insisting Reid return to Masterson Enterprises? Thrown a permanent wrench in the relationship between Reid and Heidi? "Reid, what happened to Heidi? Why did she—"

Harry reached over to touch her arm. "I think your grandson has all the information he needs to get started."

Gayle Ann searched his gaze, then turned to Reid. "You will get the specs to me before the meeting, won't you, Reid?"

"Yes. I'll go get started." He gathered his things, clearly distracted. "Anything else?"

"No. Go on."

With a nod, Reid strode away in the same direction as Heidi, but not with Heidi. Oh, dear. This wasn't good.

Gayle Ann stood next to Harry, watching the angry steps of her grandson.

"I don't like this. Not one little bit."

"Obviously something happened there between them."

"I thought suggesting they work together again would help them see they're going to lose each other if they don't focus on their relationship. Maybe I can do more…"

"May I say something, Gayle Ann?"

She glanced at the judge, hoping he had an idea. "Please."

"I think you've done enough."

"What? Not nearly."

He took one of her hands and squeezed it in his. "You've done what you can. It's up to them now."

"But the matchmaking… They aren't together."

"I'm not an expert at this matchmaking business, but I do know how to read people. It's up to Heidi and Reid to determine if their relationship will work. You can throw them together all you want, find ways to keep them in each other's path, but unless they work at this, it won't happen."

Gayle Ann pursed her lips in frustration. "They belong together."

"I agree. After watching them, I believe they know this too."

She sent him an imploring look. "So, I just give up?"

"You continue to be the wonderful grandmother you are, but let Reid figure out how he feels about Heidi and what to do about it."

Her heart sank at the idea of the two young people missing their chance. "I don't want him to lose Heidi because he puts the family business first. His success won't mean anything if he doesn't have the love of his life by his side."

"He needs to come to that conclusion on his own."

Deep down she recognized the wisdom in Harry's words. She just didn't like it much. "I suppose you're right."

"I am. Now how about we head back to

town and get something to eat. You look like you need to regroup."

He placed her hand in the crook of his arm and they began to stroll down Main Street. Her mind whirled, coming up with scenarios to prove to the young couple they had a future together. But Harry was correct in his observation. Unless Heidi and Reid were convinced beyond a shadow of a doubt that they were the love of each other's lives, nothing Gayle Ann said or did would matter.

All she could do now was hope the events she had set into motion would come to the desired conclusion.

"AM I BEING too clingy?" Heidi frowned. "I am being too clingy."

She sat on one end of the couch in her small living room later that night while Alveda sat on the other, scratching Mr. Whiskers's head. The older woman had stopped by to drop off another batch of homemade cat food.

"You are the least clingy person I know," Alveda insisted.

"And I don't like feeling this way, but ever since Reid went back to the office, it's like everything else takes second place."

"You know that boy thinks he has to prove something."

"I do, and that makes me feel like a small person for feeling left out."

She rose to pace the tight area between the living room and table where she'd spread out her accounting projects.

"I don't expect him to drop everything for me, but we were going to start da—ah, spending more time together and so far, nothing." Thankfully she caught herself. She hadn't revealed to Alveda that she and Reid had talked about dating. It was still too soon. "He's already pushing back about the party for the teens at the community center. Worse, I wanted him to go with me to the house inspection and he's backtracking."

Alveda was silent for a long moment, then said, "Are you upset about his time constraints or is it something else?"

Heidi flopped back down onto the couch. Mr. Whiskers let out a plaintive meow.

"It's silly."

Alveda reached over and patted her hand. "Nothing you tell me is silly."

"It's just…" Tears burned the backs of her eyes. "What if I'm not enough?"

"You stop that train of thought right now," Alveda ordered. "That boy is lucky to have you."

She brushed away a lone tear. "You've always been my biggest cheerleader."

"It's been my honor and pleasure."

"But?"

Alveda placed the cat by her feet and scooted closer.

"You've always shied away from love, although, if you ask me, you've got the biggest heart of anyone I know. You've also turned into an amazing young woman. If there is a special bond growing between you and Reid, then trust that things will work out the way they're supposed to."

Heidi rubbed her temples as she considered Alveda's advice.

"So, you're saying I expect too much?"

"No. I'm saying you go out there and make it happen. You're not the only woman who's ever had to fight for love. Give Reid a reason to see that this can work between you both, no matter your individual hopes and dreams."

"But I want us to be in this together."

"Then make sure you tell him that too. He won't know otherwise."

Could it be that simple? Yes, she wanted to see where the change in their relationship would take them. Was ready for them to officially start dating. Alveda was right, he wouldn't know if she kept silent.

"Ooooh, look at this sharply dressed man," Heidi said as she waltzed into Reid's office the next morning. Heidi had needed space to cool down after her conversation with Reid. After her heart-to-heart with Alveda, the time had also allowed her to examine her feelings about them becoming a couple.

This was Reid, the one constant friend in her life, so how could she stay mad? Now that Reid had settled at the office, she hoped he'd gotten his confidence back and could focus on them now.

"I have an image to maintain," he said, his face lighting up as she gave him the once-over.

She had to admit, she was impressed by the professional clothing of crisp blue shirt, striped tie, paired with navy suit pants and shined shoes. He'd gotten his hair trimmed and had shaved, a world away from the slightly scruffy construction foreman look Heidi was getting used to, and, to be honest, liked.

She tilted her head. "I kinda miss the tool belt."

He laughed. "Don't worry, I'll be wearing it this weekend."

"Working two jobs?"

"For a while."

"Welcome to my world." She moved some

papers aside and placed a bag from Frieda's Bakery on his cluttered desk.

"You're feeding me again?"

"It's the only way to see you at this point."

He'd been holed up in the Masterson Enterprises office long enough. She'd decided she was tired of waiting for him to make their relationship a priority and surprised him with a midmorning snack.

"Sorry. It's taken me longer than I thought to get up to speed with the current projects. Then I saw a couple of new opportunities, so I've put in a lot of late nights." He opened the bag. "A chocolate doughnut? You know me well."

She did. He was clearly in his element. So, why did a sense of sadness creep over her?

"Making progress?"

"I am." He smiled and the shadows that had been so prevalent in his eyes were gone. He looked...happy.

"When is your dad due back?"

"Next week, I think. I haven't spoken to Mother since they went away."

Heidi leaned against the desk. "Think you'll stick around?"

"I'm going to sit down with Dad. Clear the air once and for all."

This was a positive and important step, facing his father to decide the future of the company. What did that mean moving forward? Of course, he wouldn't have an answer until the conversation took place. But until then… "What about your current renovations?"

"I'll still be involved to a degree. But Ernie can lead the crew."

"And the final inspection on the Hanover house?"

He met her gaze head-on. "I haven't pushed it off, Heidi. We had to reschedule because Phil didn't finish the final staining and cleanup like I asked."

She supposed she was glad it wasn't held up because his work here took precedence, but she was disappointed in the delay.

"I had to ask." She paused. Took a breath. "I want us to be open now, Reid. About everything."

"I agree, Heidi."

The conviction in his voice put her at ease. She sent him a relieved smile.

"And it'll get done, I promise." He pointed to the cluttered desktop. "I have enough to keep me busy until then."

Which meant this was where he wanted to be. She supposed she shouldn't fight the inevitable. He'd made no secret of the fact that if things worked out, he'd return to the family business in a heartbeat. Did his insistence to prove himself to his father cancel out a personal life permanently?

"Do you have lots to catch up on?" she asked, fiddling with the tie of her wraparound denim dress.

"Yes, but nothing I haven't done before. One project in particular has really taken up the majority of my attention." He pulled a file out of a stack. "Mind if I run something by you?"

He had that intense gleam in his eyes, the one that made her heart skip a beat. Would it always be like this? Heidi affected by a mere look? She hoped so.

"It's a project I'm reviewing."

He was sharing his work problems with her? That was huge. She reined in her excitement. "Sure."

Reid handed her the file.

"What am I looking at?"

"My dad started projections for a new affordable housing complex about thirty minutes south of here. It's a pretty ambitious project."

She read the concern on his face. "You guys have never done anything like this before?"

"Not on this scale." He frowned. "I've been reading the proposal, which at first seemed doable."

"But?"

"I started crunching the numbers. I can do the job for a lot less than Dad has laid out, with subcontractors who I feel do a better quality job." He pointed at the file. "Would you compare his numbers against mine?"

Surprised, but pleased, she said, "Reid, I don't advise on construction jobs."

"No, but you do know how to read a financial report, and that's what I need here. A neutral opinion."

She pulled out the papers, laying them on the desk, side by side. Her mind whirled as she calculated the figures. Reid was right, his father's analysis was much more expensive.

"I agree. Your dad's numbers are high, especially if you want the end product to be affordable for buyers. You seem to have a better handle on the bottom line."

He ran a hand through his hair. "That's what I'm afraid of. He won't like me second-guessing his work, but in order for this project to stay on budget, we have to start with lower numbers."

"What will you do?"

"I've already made calls to contractors I've worked with in the past and who I trust. If I can get estimates from them, I'll have a better plan to approach my father with."

Instead of putting the matter aside, his forehead furrowed in thought.

"Is there more?"

He rubbed the wrinkles away. "I don't know. Just a hunch that he's gotten himself in too deep."

She placed the papers back in the file and handed it to him. "If anyone can figure it out, it's you."

He sent her a distracted smile. "Thanks."

"Look at us, being all couplely," she said, hoping to take his mind off the upcoming conversation with his father and move it back to them. They hadn't been out once since deciding to date. Did that make them a couple? She wasn't sure. "Is that even a word?"

He chuckled as he tossed the file on the desk. "It is now."

He rounded the desk and looped his arms around her waist. Pulled her close. She inhaled his tangy cologne. Placed her fingers against the soft fabric of his shirt, feeling his body heat beneath.

"I'm sorry I've been so preoccupied," he whispered against her lips. "I've missed you." Then he proceeded to kiss the breath out of her.

She twined her arms around his neck and returned the gesture one hundred percent. While their first kiss had been breathtaking and exciting, this kiss felt more lasting. Like she'd found her way home. To Reid.

Breaking away, she smiled shyly at him. "I might make these morning visits a regular part of my day."

"I wouldn't mind." He moved in to kiss her again when his desk phone rang. He blew out a breath. "Sorry. I have to take this."

When he dropped his arms, she missed his warmth. Was she being silly? Good grief, he was only steps away from her. She turned to look at him, the light pouring in from the window framing him, and her heart melted. Oh, she had it bad.

He was in his element here. He'd taken command, just like he had with the house renovations, but there was something different today. A purpose that seemed to glow from within. He carried on his business, totally professional, unaware that she was watching him.

Soon, he hung up and began writing on a legal pad.

"Are you going to be at the community center tonight?" Heidi asked, another reason why she'd stopped by his office.

"Hmm?"

"You missed last week." Josh had filled in for him. Heidi had been surprised he hadn't told her, but chalked it up to his busy week at the Masterson office. "This will be our last get-together. School is out soon."

He looked up. "I forgot."

"We're having a pizza party for all the kids." She reined in her disappointment. "How could you forget? We planned this weeks ago."

"I should be able to make it," he said, searching for something on his computer.

She wasn't convinced.

"The kids are looking forward to the end-of-school bash," she reminded him.

"So you said."

"Reid." She couldn't keep the annoyance from her tone.

He found what he was looking for and gave her his attention. "Sorry. My mind was elsewhere."

"Reid, I know what being here means to you. I'm glad you have this opportunity to be part of the family business you've missed so much. But at what cost?"

The air in the room suddenly grew thick. "What do you mean? I have a chance to prove to my father that I'm needed here."

"That's true, but are you going to completely put aside the rest of your life? You've started a good business flipping houses. You've made a mark in the community by renovating older homes. Can't you do both? And what about carving out time away from work?"

His lips thinned into a hard line. He walked to the window, shoving his hands in his pockets as he stared outside for what seemed like forever. Finally, he turned to her.

"We've discussed it, Heidi. Flipping houses has been good, but you know I want this. I have a different attitude now. I'm willing to do whatever I need to in order to stay." He shot her an imploring look. "This is where I'm meant to be, just like you know the house on Hanover Lane is your forever home."

Her heart sank. She'd dreamed of nothing else but owning that house since the first moment she saw it, well before her relationship with Reid had changed. As they grew to be more than friends, she realized now she couldn't live without him. She'd never imagined she'd be in this place.

One glance at his unyielding stance and Heidi knew she needed to voice her opinion before she chickened out. It might ruin things between them, but she was his friend first and would always tell him the truth.

"Isn't your whole argument for feeling left out that your father puts the business before you? That he never takes your suggestions seriously? I don't want to see you lose out on a life beyond his impossible expectations." She paused. Tried to form the right argument to get him to see reason.

"I don't want to see—" she waved her hand between them "—whatever this is happening between us flicker out because you need to prove your worth to your father. You are worthy, Reid. To me, anyway." She waited a beat. "Doesn't that count?"

He looked shocked and she wondered if she'd gone too far.

"I'm sorry if I overstepped."

"You sure know how to get to the root of the problem," he said in a hoarse voice.

"I want the best for you."

He nodded. "Yeah, I know you do."

She decided to take things down a notch. She'd made her point. He would have to take the next step. "Do you think you can slow down for one night?"

"I can." He met her gaze, his solemn. "I promise."

Relief poured through her. She'd take him at his word. If he said he'd be at the community center, he'd be there.

"I need to get going." She looped her purse strap over her shoulder. "Call me later? Maybe we can get lunch."

"Not this afternoon. I have a meeting."

"Tomorrow then." She hoped he didn't hear the fear in her voice. She didn't want to sound needy.

His expression was carefully blank when he said, "We'll talk after the party tonight."

"About the house?" Or them? She was almost afraid to ask.

"That and more."

She puffed out a breath. "Could you be any more vague?"

"It'll be worth it." His phone rang again. "I really need to answer this."

She started to leave. "Get it." But he didn't hear her since he was already speaking to the person on the call, as if she'd been dismissed.

She left the office and tried to ignore the growing ache in her stomach. Did her distress come from simply missing Reid or was there more to it? Could this be why she was feeling…off-kilter? He promised to be at the community center later. With news. She should be excited, right?

Still, the worry wouldn't leave her. Once at Blue Ridge Cottage, it didn't take Serena long to notice Heidi was not herself.

"What's up?" her boss asked, sitting on the other side of the counter, her colored pencils and sketch pad out as she shaded another Golden nature scene.

Heidi looked up from a quarterly report she was trying to study. "Up?"

"You've been unusually quiet since you started your shift."

"It's nothing. Just some things on my mind."

Serena pointed a green pencil at her. "Try again."

As much as Heidi was grateful to have good friends, she didn't like the fifth degree or having her emotions read so easily.

"I…" Where did she start?

"It's about Reid, isn't it?"

She frowned at Serena. "Like you don't already know?"

"It's been pretty obvious since you became his *intern*."

Heidi's cheeks grew warm. She never really thought she and Reid were going to fool others by easing into this relationship. Turns out they'd been obvious all along.

"What gave me away?"

"Your little smiles whenever you talk about him. How you two look at each other when you're together like there's no one else in the room. I'm surprised you didn't notice the growing attraction sooner."

One eyebrow kicked up. "Sooner than when?"

"Last fall. At Oktoberfest."

And here she thought they'd only ever been friends like always. Seems she was the last one to know. "Yikes. Talk about being slow on the uptake."

"That, and you've mentioned his tool belt a dozen times."

She lifted one shoulder. "It's a nice belt."

Serena laughed as she took a blue pencil to add color to the drawing.

Heidi scowled at her friend. "Stop."

"I'm not surprised. You two are good together. He makes you happy and you ground him."

"You figured all that out just by a few tells?"

"I always thought you and Reid would be a good match, but Logan advised me to stay out of your love life."

"Love life?" she scoffed.

Serena's eyes took on a serious glint. "Exactly."

Heidi froze. *Love?*

Hearing Serena's words echo in her head, she wondered if it could be true. Yes, she'd fallen in love with Reid. Heart and soul. There was no going back for her, and that was saying a lot since she didn't give her heart away easily. Love completely. Heidi had doubted she'd ever be family material.

But she and Alveda had become a family

of sorts. It seemed possible, the family dream. And if she was honest with herself, she wanted a relationship with Reid more than a house. Question was, would he be willing to give up things for her if he felt the same way? Now that he had the chance to prove himself again?

He'd already slipped into the groove of being in the office. Had forgotten about the party for the kids. And the way he was so focused on the task at hand? It had made Heidi feel like she was a second thought. She'd been there once, not being enough. Didn't know if she could live through it again.

Her mother had never put Heidi first, no matter how much Heidi had loved her. Would the same thing happen with Reid? If he had to choose between his place at Masterson Enterprises or her, would her love for him be enough? Just entertaining the thought made her chest ache. Was she secure enough in herself to love him, even if his focus might always be the company?

Dropping her pencil, Serena said, "There's a lot of thinking going on over there."

"Sorry." Heidi shook her head. "You're right. I...um..."

"Just put two and two together?"

Reality sank in. "I think I've known for a

while now. Just never put words to the feelings."

"So, this is exciting, right?"

"I don't know. We've always been friends only."

"But now you have a chance to go deeper." Serena took a charcoal pencil and started sketching. "Figure out why you're attracted to each other. How to make it work."

Could it be that simple? "Reid and I just recently admitted that we want to be together. We've never spoken about love."

"But you're working toward it."

Were they?

"Serena, he has the opportunity to do his dream job. Granted, it'll mean figuring things out with his dad, but what will that mean for us?"

Serena frowned, like she didn't understand the question. "That you'll be happy."

If only Heidi could be that sure.

"Or," Heidi countered, "Reid will focus on his real true love, the business."

"Oh, I don't think—"

Heidi cut her off. "You haven't seen him there. He fits in. He's a vital part of what is going on."

"So, you share the experience." Serena laid down the pencil. "I'm not a private investigator like Logan, but I'm interested in what he does. And he asks about the store all the time."

Frustrated, Heidi gripped the counter. "This is different."

Serena's smile dimmed. "Spell it out for me."

Taking a breath, she admitted her worst fear. "Why would he want to love me? I'm not that special."

Serena seemed stunned. "What are you talking about?"

"I know I've never spoken about my childhood, but trust me, I wasn't really wanted."

"Oh, Heidi, that can't be right."

"My mom never took having a child seriously. I grew up moving from place to place. Haven't you ever wondered why I ended up with Alveda?"

"Sure, but I didn't want to make you uncomfortable by asking. And besides, when I first got to Golden, I was hiding my past, so I respected your silence on the subject."

Okay, so her friend had been respectful. But she'd also been wanted by her parents. Never had to wonder why her love wasn't enough.

"Your dad always loved you. I can't ever be sure about my mother."

An unpleasant silence took over the empty store. Heidi was so glad there were no shoppers browsing and eavesdropping on this excruciatingly terrible conversation.

"What has all this got to do with Reid?" Serena asked.

"I'm worried that I'm not that important to him."

"I'm confused. You two are together, right?"

"Yes. But look how long it's taken us. This romantic stuff just caught us both by surprise. And now he spends long hours at the office. What if our relationship isn't strong enough to make a lasting future?"

"Then you keep fighting."

Heidi drew into herself, her voice small and unsure when she spoke, sounding like the little girl who was afraid of the dark. "What if he doesn't want to?"

Serena slipped from her stool and pulled Heidi into an embrace. For once, she didn't shrug away. The warmth and concern coming from her friend had tears forming in Heidi's eyes. Her throat clogged. How could she have gone from so happy to be with Reid to this unsure of herself?

She pulled away, wiping her eyes. This was why she'd always been alone. Nothing hurt you that way. Miffed at herself, she decided she wasn't about to let her insecurities, or the past she'd worked so hard to overcome, set her back now.

"This was dumb. I've made a big production out of nothing. I should just talk to Reid instead of thinking worst-case scenario."

"Now you're making sense."

Was she? Heidi wasn't sure. After all, she'd allowed the conversation at Reid's office to put foolish ideas in her head. Let the wounds of the past color her future. No more.

Serena volleyed a dare her way. "Heidi Welch, you are not going to throw in the towel. Pull yourself together and convince Reid that he can't live without you."

Serena was right. As long as she believed in her own worth, she'd never have to feel unloved again.

Not one to back down from a good challenge, Heidi decided she'd tell Reid exactly how she felt tonight. If she could get over her fear of the dark, she could also get over the fear of giving her heart away.

CHAPTER THIRTEEN

REID WAS STILL in the office. He had one final meeting before he could head to the community center to join Heidi and the kids. After the long day he'd had, he was looking forward to a distraction, mainly watching Heidi interact with the teens. She engaged with the students, made them think and react. Funny how she did the same for him.

He'd been thinking about a lot of things lately, Heidi at the top of the list. But there was also the family issue. Did he stay at Masterson Enterprises? He supposed only time, and his father's health, would tell.

A mental picture of Heidi had him smiling. She also laughed a lot, which made him more at ease than he'd been for a long time. He didn't care where they were as long as they were together. Was it possible that falling for her had been inevitable? Once he'd gotten out of his own way, he was surprised he hadn't noticed how much he needed to be with her. Tonight, he'd tell her how he felt, take a chance on a future with her. He wouldn't worry about—

"Earth to Reid."

Shaking his head, Reid looked across the desk.

"Where were you?" asked Sam, the contractor Reid was meeting with about the town sign.

"Sorry."

"Looks like you've checked out for the night."

Reid shrugged. "I've got plans."

He glanced at his watch. Six thirty. He still had to run by the Hanover remodel. Phil had called to tell Reid he'd finished staining the deck, but knowing Phil, Reid needed to check the kid's work. So much for making it to the party on time.

Sam sent him a knowing smile. "I recognize that look. It has to be a woman."

Not just any woman. Heidi. She needed to know the depths of his feelings.

"So, you'll get back to me with the proposal?" Reid asked as he stood to reach out and give Sam a handshake.

"You got it. Shouldn't take long."

Reid walked him to the door. "Great. Give me a call when you're ready to submit the plans."

Before Sam could leave, Arthur Masterson walked through the door. Reid nodded at Sam as he exited, trying to ignore the bad feeling that had suddenly charged the air by his father's unexpected presence.

"Dad, what are you doing here? Aren't you supposed to be taking it easy?"

His father shot him an amused glance. "It's my office."

"Yes, I mean, I thought you were away with Mother."

"A man can only rest so long before getting stir crazy." His father shrugged, as if his showing up here was no big deal. "I decided to stop in and see what you're up to."

The uneasy sensation landed squarely on Reid's shoulders and pressed down hard.

"What kind of proposal is Sam putting together for you?"

Reid shot his dad a curious look.

"I overheard you two talking," Arthur said as he strolled to the desk and started thumbing through the paperwork Reid had divided into neat piles.

"A job for Grandmother."

"Not the town sign." His father shook his head.

Not liking the way he seemed to reject the idea, Reid championed his grandmother. "It's important to her."

His father nodded, distracted by the papers.

"How did you talk Mother into letting you come here tonight?"

"She doesn't know I'm gone." A smug grin curved his father's lips. "Snuck out while she was unpacking."

Reid came to the side of the desk. "You should have told her."

"She knows I need to keep busy with work."

The mounting tension grew with each tick of the clock.

Reid reached for his phone. "I'll call her. She'll be worried when she finds you missing." He'd just pulled up her contact when his father spoke in a harsh tone.

"What's this?"

Reid glanced at the folder his father was holding and his chest grew tight. The construction job his dad had overbid on.

"I was reading up on your development," Reid said.

His father pulled out a page that had Reid's estimations written on it. The older man's eyes went wide. "And this?"

Reid squared his shoulders, which were still heavy. "I was reworking your numbers."

Disbelief crossed his father's face. "Why? I've been on this deal for quite some time and things are almost in motion."

Might as well dive in headfirst. "When I studied the deal, I realized the numbers seemed a bit high for this type of project. There are methods of spending less and doing a quality job."

His father tossed the file onto the desk with a flick of his wrist. "Really? Because you're so experienced in large-scale developments?"

Biting back an angry retort, Reid said, "I know good contractors. It's not that hard to figure out. Besides, I still work in the field. I have contacts."

"Because flipping houses is just like building an entire housing complex," his father scoffed.

"Bad business is bad business no matter the scope of the project."

His father's eyes went dark. "Are you questioning my decisions?"

Reid stuttered a frustrated breath. "No. Grandmother asked me to take over here at the office after your procedure at the hospital. I was making sure everyone's interests are being taken care of."

"By interfering with my plans?"

Reid held his tongue. There was no use arguing with his father. Been there and it never turned out well.

"Does this mean you've returned?" his father asked.

"That depends on you."

His father blinked. "I thought you liked flipping houses."

"I do. As a sideline. But Masterson Enterprises has always been the place for me."

"Then it's amazing how quickly you departed."

Reid really didn't want to have this conversation, but deep down he'd known that once his father came back, they'd have to face the past in order to secure the future. For both of them.

"We're family. I was happy to help."

His father pointed to the folder. "By making decisions that aren't yours to make."

"Don't you want what is best for the company?" Reid hated his pleading tone but kept on going. "That's all I'm doing. All I've ever done."

His father regarded him for a long moment, then opened the folder again and flipped through the pages. "You have an entirely different list of subcontractors."

"As I said, we can get a better price with these guys."

"And what about loyalty to the ones I've hired throughout the years?"

"There's nothing wrong with that, but the bottom line is that you're going to spend more in the long run. That defeats the entire purpose of building affordable housing if you have to pass the cost on to the people buying the units."

"So, I'm just supposed to tell the companies I've worked with for years that my son found better subcontractors?"

"I'd hoped we could figure this out together."

"I won't have you second-guessing the decisions I've made." His father's face slowly turned red. "You cannot come in and take over this project."

This was worse than Reid had anticipated.

"Have you spoken to any of your contacts?" his father asked.

"A few. Just to get competitive rates for the job."

"And you don't think that bit of news will reach the firms I normally hire?"

"Dad, this isn't a competition between us."

"Maybe, but I won't have you undermining my decision. Stealing projects. Or making me look bad."

Making me look bad.

With a slash of pain, Reid's mind flashed to that night during senior year. Hours after the disaster that was the championship baseball game.

His father had been waiting when he came home, ordering Reid to his office. "What were you thinking?" his father had yelled, pacing the room.

"I messed up. You don't have to remind me."

"It's about our family image, Reid. Your actions reflect on this entire family."

"It's just a game!"

"It's more than that. You didn't give it your all."

Reid's mouth had fallen open.

"You embarrassed our family. Embarrassed me." His father had spoken the words as if Reid were nothing more than old gum stuck on the bottom of his shoe. Inconvenient and annoying.

From that night on, Reid had been trying to get back into his father's good graces by earning exceptional grades in college. He'd worked hard once he came home and started at the company with ideas to make Masterson Enterprises more successful. And still his father found fault in everything he did.

No more.

"It's not always just about you," Reid said, surprised he kept his voice steady.

His father's face turned to stone. "I built

Masterson Enterprises. Your grandfather was never interested. He'd rather be in his shop, fiddling around with his woodworking projects. His brother took off to who knows where and I took up the slack. I put my heart and soul into this company."

"And you think I haven't?" Reid nearly shouted.

"I made the company what it is today."

Reid tapped his hand against his chest. "And I was the one to bring it into the future."

They stared at each other in a silent stand-off.

Reid broke the painful silence first. "I've always respected you."

"By taking my clients? Are you trying to prove that you're better at business than me?" His father seethed. "My say is final."

"Is that what you think this is about? Who has the most control?"

His father looked at him like he was dense. "What else could it be?"

"I don't know." Reid tried to speak but his throat was tight from the humiliation and something much deeper. The realization that nothing he said to his father was ever going to make Reid important to this man. "Maybe I want my father to be proud of me. Of what I've been able to accomplish for this company.

For this family." Reid ran a hand through his hair. "I never wanted the projects to be about me. I wanted us to work together."

His father stared at him.

"Okay. I realize you don't get it. I don't know why I ever thought you would."

How he wished Heidi was here. Just slipping her hand into his as they stood side by side would have given him the strength he needed to get through the next minutes. Why hadn't he told her how important she was to his life? Why had he allowed work to be everything?

He looked at his father and shivered, seeing his future if he didn't change right now.

Heidi probably thought he'd forgotten to meet her at the community center. He didn't want to contemplate the fallout, how Heidi must think he deserted her. Just like her mother.

Unsure what to do next, Reid looked across the room at his father. Arthur had gone pale, the lines on his face deeper than Reid ever remembered. Suddenly, his father, the man he'd looked up to, the man whose respect he'd always been trying to earn, looked fragile. Guilt from pushing his father made Reid feel small and petty.

"I'm sorry, Dad. This wasn't the best time

for a heated conversation. You just got through a procedure and I…"

His father's expression was unreadable. "You…what?"

He stared at his father. Spoke the truth. "Honestly, I don't know."

Reid moved behind the desk to gather up his jacket and some folders for other projects he'd been working on. He had to get out of here. Away from his father, who had made it very clear that Reid did not have a place in Masterson Enterprises. Away from the fact that he'd let Heidi down.

As he crossed the room, his father asked in a quiet voice, "Where are you going?"

"Anywhere but here."

"You're going to walk away again?" This time there wasn't heat in his father's words, more like bewilderment. Defeat.

Reid spun. "Isn't that what you wanted? Since I'm not the silent partner you expected to control?" He could barely get the words out. "News flash, Dad. I'm good at what I do. I may go about things differently than you, but I still get the job done. I don't need you, or Masterson Enterprises, to make me a success." He stopped to pull in an angry breath. "If you run that project on your estimations, you can say goodbye to all the years you've poured into this company, because it'll clean you out."

"What? Who do you think—" his father sputtered.

"Your son," Reid cut in, leaning in so close his father jerked away. "Who is done with you and this company."

He turned on his heel.

"Reid. Wait," his father called to his back.

He didn't stop walking. Right now, he wanted Golden in his rearview mirror.

HEIDI SHIFTED LEFT to right in front of the full-length mirror hanging on her closet door. The angle helped to get a better look at the dress she'd tried on, but she was still uncertain. Yes, it was a perfect fit, full of color. Was it the appropriate outfit to wear when you were planning to tell your longtime friend that you were in love with him?

"What do you think?" she asked the only other presence in the room, receiving silence in return. She swung around to see Mr. Whiskers licking his paw, patently ignoring her.

"A lot of help you are," she crabbed to the gray-and-white-striped tabby, then turned to study her reflection. Smoothing her hands over her hips, she wondered if she was making too much of her clothing choice. Plus, she was going to the community center to hang out with teenagers. Was a flattering dress overkill?

"This is over-the-top," she muttered, changing from the dress into a peach sleeveless blouse, a pair of dark indigo jeans and flats. She pulled her hair into a ponytail and went to the mirror.

"Not glamorous, but it'll do," she decided as she checked her image with a critical eye. She didn't need a fancy outfit to speak from the heart. Nor did she want to make things weird—more than they already were—between herself and Reid. She needed to be plain old Heidi, the woman she was coming to embrace since she and Reid had started down this unexpected path.

How her life had changed in such a short span of time. She'd uncovered a range of emotions for a man she'd always considered her friend. Yet now she could see the possibilities of Reid being so much more. He'd listened to her embarrassing story about her fear of the dark, encouraging instead of pitying her. He'd let her not just dream about a house, he'd actively included her in making it happen. Sure, he was surprised with the change in their relationship as much as she was, but he wasn't afraid to see where this new turn in their relationship took them. How could she love him any more than she already did?

Shaking off her musing, she went to the bed. Mr. Whiskers stared up at her with keen eyes. "I'll miss you," she said, reaching out to give his head a scratch. His loud purr reached her ears. "Yeah, I know, you'll miss me too."

She stopped in the living room before leaving, looking around the small space she'd called home for years. Her gaze fell on the couch she'd found for a great deal on an internet site. From there she took in the odds and ends of furniture scooped up at garage sales she and Serena frequented, looking for deals.

On the kitchen counter sat the tea caddy she'd constructed under Reid's supervision. She grinned at the memory.

Her dining table, or office, was filled to the brim with files and an open laptop. Soon she'd have a real office, if she was able to buy the house from Reid.

"Not *if*, *when*," she corrected herself. She'd grown here, into a confident woman. And while this had been a good starting place, she'd dreamed of the next steps. Now it was time to move on. She'd never been more ready to purchase a home of her own.

She refused to consider a different outcome. Not only did that house offer her security, it was because of that house that she'd spent time with Reid, only to realize she loved him. It was time to leave the darkness of the past and truly embrace the light of her future.

She grabbed her purse, heading out for the night, filled with nervous anticipation.

WHEN SHE ENTERED the community center, she immediately spotted the kids from both her group and Reid's. They'd all gathered in the main activity room where Josh kept an eye on them. She searched for Reid. The pizza had been delivered, but he was nowhere in sight. Her stomach twisted in knots. Had he forgotten about tonight's party? The idea smarted. Yes, he'd been preoccupied lately, but he'd promised to be here.

From the other side of the room, she heard Mia's voice over the din.

"I did it," she proclaimed to the room. "I got my car keys." The girl triumphantly held said keys high for all to see.

When her gaze met Mia's, the teen beelined right for her. Still a bit unsteady because she was thinking about Reid, Heidi pasted on a smile. The girl stopped before her with a sheepish look on her face. "I passed my final test. Brought my final grade up to a C."

"I told you it was possible."

"Sorry I didn't believe you."

"It's all about believing in yourself." She winked at Mia. It had been a journey, but loving Reid had shown Heidi that by believing in herself, she had more than enough love to give Reid. Which she wanted to tell him, if he'd just show up.

Mia slid a slice of pizza from the box and took a big bite. Oh, to have a teenager's metabolism.

"Aren't you eating?" she asked around a mouthful.

"In a minute," Heidi stalled. Her appetite was iffy at best. Not wanting to let the kids down because of her worries, she took a cup and filled it with iced tea from a jug.

"So, my parents want to give you a medal," Mia said.

A medal? For what, caring about Mia? "Not necessary," Heidi said. She loved tutoring and didn't expect anything in return.

Mia shrugged. "Well, they're happy, so I'm happy."

"You're happy because they gave you the car keys," Heidi said in a dry tone.

"True, so happy all around." Mia glanced at the roomful of kids. "Where's Mr. Masterson?"

"I'm not sure."

"Really? I thought you'd know."

She tried to correct her nervous laugh and only made it more awkward. "Why?"

Mia stared at her. "You're kidding, right?"

"I have no clue."

"Obviously." Mia rolled her eyes. "You have a crush on him."

How on earth had Mia noticed? Heidi shouldn't be surprised. Hadn't Serena come to the same conclusion?

"C'mon. No one could miss the looks you two give each other."

Heidi placed a hand on her hip and tried to look authoritative. "And why were you noticing in the first place?"

"Because it's the same way I look at Todd."

Yep, Heidi had it bad because she hadn't once missed the longing in Mia's eyes for Todd.

"And when you weren't looking," Mia continued in a knowing tone, "Mr. Masterson was checking you out."

"No wonder you didn't get higher than a C as a final grade. You were too busy paying attention to other unrelated things."

Mia sent her a gotcha grin. "But I'm not wrong."

No, she wasn't. Heidi bit her lower lip, unsure how to respond. Somehow this seemed an inappropriate conversation to be having with a teen, but on the other hand, Mia had nailed it. Math might not be Mia's strong suit, but she definitely had other superpowers.

Soon Mia moved on to her group of friends. Heidi glanced at her watch.

"Wondering where Reid is?" Josh asked as he joined her, holding a slice of pizza in his hand.

Since he'd filled in when Reid couldn't make some of the classes, Heidi had made sure to include Josh in tonight's festivities.

"He must be hung up at the office."

"I saw his truck there when I drove by," he said before taking a bite.

Was Reid really putting work before the kids? Before her? And what about the conversation after the party?

"He promised he'd be here," Heidi insisted, infusing confidence in her voice to cover the mounting hurt.

"You know how he gets when he's at the office," Josh gave her a knowing smile and wandered off, leaving Heidi to grapple with her roller coaster of emotions.

Not ready to throw in the towel, she found her phone and called Reid. The call went right to voice mail. Okay, maybe he was driving and couldn't answer. Made sense. She'd go with that explanation.

After an hour, Heidi glanced at her watch for the fifth time since arriving at the community center. Still no Reid.

"Don't panic," she assured herself as she looked at her phone a few minutes later, hoping she'd missed a call. Nothing.

It was at that exact moment she knew for sure that Reid wasn't coming. It was clear. He hadn't made an appearance, nor had he answered her call.

He didn't want her.

With a sinking heart, she kept up sunny conversation while helping Mia and a few other kids clean up, then said goodbye as they hurried off. The end of the school year was a hectic time. As much as Heidi wanted to give in to a pity party, she wouldn't.

Tonight had been an eye-opener. It confirmed what she'd learned from growing up with her mother. That you could love someone with all your being, but it didn't mean a thing if that love wasn't returned. Especially if there were more important things in the other person's life.

She looked around the empty room. Alone again.

To her dismay, tears simmered just below the surface.

How had she thought she'd be immune to getting hurt by another important person in her life yet again?

Everything in life was short-term, from owning a home to love. Hadn't she understood that early on? Why had she thought falling for Reid would be different? He'd obviously chosen his path, and it didn't include her or the beautiful changes in their friendship.

The pain she'd been fighting slowly crept across her heart. With shaking fingers, she flipped the wall switch to turn off the lights. She walked down the lit hallway and made her way out into the quiet spring night. Well, quiet except for the musical call of birds in an overhead tree branch. It made her think of Reid, and she found herself lonelier than ever.

The vast lavender sky held many shades tonight, ranging from a watery pale sheen intensifying to purple, then indigo, as night settled in. Before long, stars would dot the sky. At the thought, she could no longer hold back the tears.

No more sharing kisses with the man she loved. No more laughing and supporting each other. Heidi was grateful that she hadn't made a fool of herself by admitting her love for Reid.

Wouldn't he have gotten a laugh out of that? His old friend falling for him. Why had she ever thought this was a good idea? Because her worst fears about people not reciprocating her love were realized.

She swiped hot tears from her cheeks as she refocused on the most important thing in her life, putting down roots at the Hanover house. She and Mr. Whiskers would be completely content on their own. She had friends and her accounting business was growing. What more did she need?

Reid.

Yeah, well, that wasn't going to happen. It might feel like her heart had been ripped from her chest, but better it happen now before she got in any deeper. Love was not in the cards for Heidi Welch. An image of her mother flashed in her mind.

Fishing for the car keys in her purse, the stark ring of her cell phone startled Heidi. Then filled her with hope. Maybe Reid had a good reason for not showing up tonight. It might be him calling to explain.

Stop.

He'd had his chance and blew it.

She finally pulled out the device and read the screen. Frowned.

"Mrs. M.?" she answered.

"It's Reid," came the older woman's tortured voice.

Heidi went still. Had something happened to him? Oh, no, had Reid been in a car accident? All ability to speak failed her.

"He and his father had a terrible fight," Mrs. M. explained. "We need to find him."

CHAPTER FOURTEEN

AFTER DRIVING AIMLESSLY through Golden, Reid decided he should leave town, just like he'd been thinking about doing for a while now. Clearly, he and his father were never going to see eye to eye. Perhaps with some distance he could figure out what he wanted to do with his life, because being here in Golden wasn't cutting it. Leaving would be best for everyone.

Not everyone.

Shame washed over him. How could he face Heidi now? He'd made a mess of things. He'd broken a promise to her, and worse? He'd made her—both of them really—hope for a future that would never happen. Would she forgive him when she discovered he'd gone? Be glad they hadn't gotten any deeper into their relationship?

Heidi should have been his main focus. He'd ruined their relationship because he was too much like his father instead of being his own man.

The thoughts bombarding his brain were

giving him a headache. Before reaching the town limits, he passed Hanover Lane. Remembering Phil's phone call, he turned the wheel to make a quick visit. The least he could do before leaving once and for all was to make sure Phil had finished the deck job, insuring Heidi's dream home would pass inspection.

Right now, that was all he could gift her. His father's dismissal hurt down to his bones. Until he could overcome the pain and disappointment of not measuring up, what did he have to offer Heidi? He couldn't even carry through on showing up at the community center.

Slowing down as the house came into view, he pulled into the driveway, loose gravel crunching under the tires. After a moment, he turned off the engine and loosened his tie to remove it. Releasing the pent-up frustration simmering inside him, Reid draped his hands over the steering wheel and stared into the shadows of the forest spreading out behind the property line.

The quiet night should have lulled him, but had the opposite effect. He heard shouts and laughter from somewhere down the street. A squirrel raced across the yard and scampered up a tree trunk to hide within the branches.

A slight glimmer of a smile crossed his

lips. Heidi would love living here. The wild-life would keep her amused and on her toes. She'd already planted cheerful flowers along the front walk, putting her personal touch on the place.

Too bad you won't be around to see what else she accomplishes.

That was the catch. Heidi was accomplishing…life. She had a business she loved, volunteered in the community and went after her dreams. If he was truly honest, he'd admit he was jealous. When had Reid last been excited about pursuing his goals? Making his mark on the world? Not in a long time. Instead, he'd been aimless, letting his father's judgment affect his life, to the exclusion of all else. When had he lost the ability to be his own man?

Cool air, carrying the subtle scent of the nearby woods, filled the cab of his truck. Someone must have lit a fire; there was a hint of smoke in the air. Perhaps a family making s'mores on an open pit in the backyard? Lights had started blinking on in nearby houses as the deep shadow of dusk blanketed the area. It was quiet and expected and… What he wanted?

On top of the slight incline sat the empty house, the essence of family life. A home, with large windows—he now understood why this was number one on Heidi's wish list—open rooms painted in bright colors and… A sense of joy. A shimmer of light shone through the windows as dusk descended, as if welcoming people to come inside.

Working on the house with Heidi had given him a boost when he'd pretty much fallen into a boring routine. It was more the woman, not this particular job, that had done that. She'd shown him that there was more to life than just going through the motions. Waiting for the day when his father accepted Reid's place in the business, if that would ever happen. After hearing her childhood story, he'd been horrified and angry at the fear she'd buried deep inside. How could a parent treat a child so shabbily? His father had done something similar to him, only in a different way. Yet Heidi had risen from the ashes of her childhood. Why hadn't Reid?

He stared at the house, his chest tight.

Heidi's house.

Could it be *their* house?

Wasn't Heidi more important than Masterson Enterprises? A resounding yes chorused in his soul. With Heidi, he could take chances, make a difference in the business world, knowing she was home waiting for him, no matter what he did or didn't do. And he would do the same for her. He finally understood what a home represented. Why Heidi wanted it so badly. It wasn't only about the deal or profit, it was about living your best life with those you loved, under one roof. How could he give up a chance of that dream for the meager crumbs he received from his father?

His mind conjured up pictures of Heidi swinging a sledgehammer, a bright smile on her face. Paint on her cheek, giving him an excuse to touch her soft skin as he brushed it away. Kissing her under the stars. Knowing that she returned his kisses with as much enthusiasm as she approached every aspect of her life. The thought of never kissing her, never laughing with her again, caused a stinging pain in his chest.

He sat up, slowly realizing that he wouldn't let his father drive him away from the most important accomplishment of his life—loving Heidi. He'd been a fool not to have seen it sooner. He should have told her he loved her. Was it too late?

There was no way he was leaving town now.

He had to talk to her. Apologize. Tell her he'd probably mess up again, but he wanted a chance with her, if she'd have him. She meant everything to him and he would prove it to her.

As he reached for the key in the ignition, his

gaze moved to the house. He frowned. Wait, had the glowing he thought he saw in the window grown brighter? The sun had nearly sunk behind the trees, effectively enveloping the house in shadows. No one was inside, so there should be no lights on.

He slowly opened his door, stepping out into the night. That's when he noticed the smoke in the air growing stronger. Fueled by instinct, he jogged up the walkway, now noticing a flickering orange tint through the windows. He ran up the steps and quickly unlocked the front door. Once inside, the scent of burning grew heavier. A haze hovered in the air.

He quickly scanned the living room to determine what was going on. His eyes fell on paint cans stacked by the French doors, cleaning rags piled nearby. Concern growing, he strode to the pile, gathering up the rags to safely discard on his way out. That's when his gaze caught sight of the flames licking the rail of the deck.

He went to open the French door, the handle hot to the touch. Jerking back, he then wrapped the rags around his hand for protection. He stuck his head outside, getting a better view. The section of the deck flush against the house was swallowed by a wall of fire. Flames were swiftly moving up the structure, dangerously close to the kitchen window. Below the window, cans of what he assumed were deck stain burned with a fiery vengeance.

Save Heidi's house.

The words echoing in his head, he ran inside, heading straight to the pantry, where he remembered seeing a fire extinguisher. If he could stop the flames from spreading, perhaps he could end this disaster.

To his horror, the crackle from the out-of-control flames had breached the interior. The window cracked and shattered, shards flying across the room. He ducked, but several sharp pieces grazed his skin. He ran his hand over his chin, his fingers damp. No time to worry about cuts right now.

He opened the pantry door, grabbing the extinguisher to point at the unrestrained flames. He pulled the pin and to his dismay, a slight drizzle of white foam dropped to his feet. Great. He tossed the useless equipment down.

Maybe he could use water from the tap? He hurried to the sink, but the fire had now jumped to the wall, fanning out in either direction from the sides of the window. At that moment, Reid realized this was too much for him to handle on his own. He pulled out his phone from his pocket to dial 911, then remembered the cans in the other room. He had to move them, fast, before they blew up.

As he reached the entryway into the living room, an explosion to his left threw him off-balance. He bounced hard against the opposite wall. The phone flew from his fingers as he threw up his arms to protect his face. The acrid scent of chemicals filled his nose while a greasy, dark smoke blurred his vision. Once he straightened himself, he saw that the flames had jumped in from the burning deck, causing the paint cans to explode.

Time to get out of here.

The smoke grew thicker. Reid pulled his shirt collar over his nose, unable to believe how quickly the situation had escalated. The chemicals released into the air were making him light-headed. He doubled over, coughing. If he could get to the door, surely he'd be okay. His vision went fuzzy. Suddenly, his knees gave out and he fell, hands out to steady himself, the heat pressing against him as the intensity of the roaring flames grew.

HEIDI JUMPED INTO her car and zoomed out of the community center parking lot. Her first thought was to drive by the Masterson Enterprises building. Surely Reid would be there, despite an argument with his dad. He had to be there, she reasoned. It was the one place on earth that had the tightest hold on him.

Even more than you.

Yes, the truth pierced her deeply, but it faded in light of the circumstances. She had to find Reid. Later, they'd figure things out.

Even if it means you end up alone?

Yes, because helping Reid was her number one priority right now.

She careened into the parking lot of the office building, then slammed on the brakes. Empty. Not a vehicle in sight. Okay, she wasn't expecting that.

Undeterred, she backed up, driving down Main Street toward the house where Reid was living with Logan. The lights were blazing inside, so she parked in front of the house and ran to the door, alternately banging and pressing on the doorbell.

"Hey, what's all the commotion?" Logan barked, jumping aside when Heidi barged inside.

"I need to talk to Reid."

His eyebrows rose at her tone. "He's not here."

"What? He has to be."

"Sorry." He frowned as he watched her run to check the kitchen and back. "Heidi, is something wrong?"

She quickly explained the call from Mrs. M.

Logan's face instantly showed worry. "That's not good." He stalked to the kitchen and returned with his car keys. "Where have you checked so far?"

"The Masterson office. His truck wasn't there."

"Where else might Reid go?" Logan asked.

Right. She should know since she'd been spending so much time with him lately. She focused, then said, "The new renovation maybe? I'll see if he's there."

Logan nodded and together they rushed for the door.

With an exaggerated nod to Logan, Heidi ran to her vehicle. Once she started the engine, she headed up the twisty mountain road to Reid's latest project, all the while trying not to imagine the worst.

"Please let him be okay," she whispered.

Her mind flashed to that night in high school after the championship baseball game. Reid had been furious after the fight with his dad, determined to do something stupid. Was tonight going to be a repeat of that? Was he off trying to assuage his anger? Let off some steam? Her heart sank. This time she wouldn't be there to stop Reid from doing something he might regret.

She pressed on the gas, finally pulling into the driveway of the vacant house. Set off the main road, the residence was quiet and completely deserted. Not a light illuminating one square inch of the house.

She shivered. The thought of going in there alone spooked her, but not nearly as much as it might have, before she'd admitted her fears to Reid. Just knowing how upset he'd been by her mother's disregard had given Heidi a newfound strength. She went up to the house just to be sure there was no one there. After a quick search around the area, she knew she'd have to try somewhere else. Reid wasn't here.

Where could he have gone? Then she remembered his idle comment about leaving town for good. "No," she whispered, her throat tight. Would he really just take off? Without at least saying goodbye?

Once inside the car, she rested her forehead against the steering wheel, trying to calm her racing thoughts. Maybe he'd gone to see his grandmother. But Mrs. M. hadn't called her to let her know that, so he could be anywhere.

Sitting here was pointless. She fired up the engine and backed out of the driveway, intent on heading toward town. Halfway there, she passed Hanover Lane. On impulse, she turned. Maybe if she returned to the place where she and Reid had worked together, it might help her think more clearly about where he could have gone.

It was worth a try.

TRYING TO BREATHE, Reid fought against the overwhelming urge to cough and failed. His lungs felt like they were being torn apart, his throat rough and scratchy. The heat was so intense, Reid kept to the floor. He knew he had to move, find an exit, but couldn't seem to work up the energy as flames crawled all around him.

Save the house.

The silent scream in his head gave him motivation. If it was the last thing he did, he wouldn't let Heidi's house be destroyed. In what felt like slow motion, Reid rose, his eyes watering as the smoke enveloped him. He coughed again, his chest burning, He blinked, but the tears made his already blurry vision worse.

He couldn't give up. Just a few steps and maybe he could find his phone to call for help. A crashing came from the other room and a wave of hot air whooshed through the house. The fire was getting worse.

He couldn't save the house. If he didn't find the door soon, he might not be able to save himself. He took two steps and the dizziness had him tottering so that he sank to the floor again. He reached out to find something to steady him, his palm landing on the metal lid of a paint can. Scalded, he drew back, his palm sizzling in pain. Exhaustion sapped his strength.

He'd just rest for a moment, then try to escape again.

HEIDI WAS ALMOST to the house when she noticed lights flickering in the windows, as if someone was dancing in the shadows with a frenzy. Was the crew doing last-minute work in order to pass inspection? Reid hadn't mentioned it, but his team could be working late to complete the job.

She pulled into the driveway, her heart nearly bursting with relief when she saw Reid's truck. She ran to his passenger door. Her joy turned to confusion. The cab was empty. Reid was here, somewhere, so everything would be all right.

She was halfway up the walk when she suddenly realized something was wrong. She sniffed the scent of fire, growing stronger the closer she got to the steps. Understanding dawned. The light in the windows came from flames, not normal lighting fixtures. Black smoke curled out of the front door.

Her heart nearly stopped beating. Was Reid inside? She ran up the steps of the house yelling his name.

As she stood in the threshold, the scene was like a fun house gone insane. Flames licked up the walls to race across the ceiling. Through the thick smoke she could make out an orange ball of bright light that was the back deck. She threw her arm over her mouth and nose, afraid to go any farther.

"Reid!" she yelled again, coughing as the thick smoke clogged her throat. Eyes watering, she couldn't see through the heavy haze. Could she have been wrong? Maybe Reid had gone somewhere safe to call for help.

She was just about to turn when she heard a weak moan. The sound piqued her attention. Cautiously making her way toward it, she nearly tripped over a pair of boots. Boots connected to legs that belonged to Reid.

"Oh, my gosh," she said, sinking down beside him. "Are you okay?"

"Can't…catch…my…breath."

"We have to get out of here."

He tried to lift himself up, but collapsed against her. Realizing he was too overcome by the smoke, she positioned herself behind him, pushed up his shoulders and then stuck her hands under his arms.

"You have to help me," she shouted as she began to tug him to a standing position.

He shook his head. "Just…give…boost…"

As he tried to lift his weight, Heidi held on for dear life. He dug in his boot heels and soon had enough traction so that he could stand. She managed to pull him halfway to the front door before he slipped out of her hold.

"Get out," he said, coughing again.

"Not without you."

Sweating now and coughing, she draped his limp arm over her shoulders. On wobbly legs, he moved with her, a lot more quickly than she would have imagined in his current state. Once they were out the door, his arm snaked around her waist and he ran with her across the yard. When they reached the road, he slumped down, the motion taking Heidi with him. He frantically inhaled the fresh air, but it didn't seem to do any good. His breathing was erratic between spasms of coughing. She sat beside him, frantic to help him breathe.

"Lost…my phone." Reid coughed so deeply, the sound startled Heidi. "Need to…call nine…"

"I've got it." Hating to leave Reid, but knowing it was necessary, she jumped up and raced to her car. Her phone was in the console. She grabbed it and dialed 911 as she returned to him. He was covered in soot, there were cuts on his face and his eyes were stark in the light from the fire. Lying on his side, he couldn't stop the coughing.

The next few minutes were the longest of her life. Neighbors came out of their houses, hurrying over to help, but at this point there was nothing to be done for the house. The fire had consumed the entire structure. Someone handed them cold water bottles. Reid managed a few sips, but Heidi was too upset to drink. She watched helplessly as her house was engulfed in shooting flames.

Once she heard sirens in the distance, her pulse slowed marginally. Reid was still having difficulty breathing. She rubbed his shoulders, needing to touch him. Why wasn't the ambulance here yet?

What if she lost him? She shook off the thought, instead focusing on him. She couldn't let her mind go there.

Soon two large fire engines stopped haphazardly in the street, the firefighters dressed in protective gear, getting right to work. Hoses snaked through the yard and before long, water was dousing the flames.

The paramedics arrived and Heidi waved them over to Reid.

"Are you okay?" one of the men asked her as he set his large support bag down beside them.

"Yes. But Reid was inside. There was lots of smoke…"

"We've got it," a second EMT assured her as they focused all their attention on Reid.

She tried not to hover, but her good intentions didn't keep her from his side. Soon the EMTs attached a tight-fitting oxygen mask to Reid's face. They checked his pupils, quietly asked him questions. When one of them gently suggested she give them room, Heidi shot the woman her scariest frown and stayed put. Her heart skipped a beat when she noticed the first paramedic wet a square dressing and place it over Reid's palm, then wrap it with gauze. She was about to ask what he was doing when her phone rang. Reid glanced at her, then at the phone and up again. Right. She needed to answer. Looking at the screen she saw Logan's number and quickly connected.

"He's not at Josh's or back at my folks'," Logan said without waiting for her greeting.

"I found him," she said, her voice shaky. "He's…"

"Heidi?"

Suddenly she couldn't speak. She swallowed multiple times but couldn't utter a sound.

"Heidi! What's all that noise?"

"We're at the Hanover house," she finally barked out. "It's on fire."

Silence. Then she heard him say, "Be right there."

Reassured that family was on the way, Heidi hung up and took a step back, tears filling her eyes as the events of the night finally kicked in. The fire still raged and the chaos around them was a perfect backdrop to complement her inner panic. A window fell in with a loud crash and her spirits sank. All her dreams, literally up in smoke. Where did she go from here?

She jumped when the paramedic gently touched her arm. He nodded toward Reid, as if giving her the okay to join him, then packed up his bag. "The oxygen we administered helped, but I'd suggest you follow up with a visit to your doctor."

Nodding, she tried not to feel overwhelmed. She could do this. Be strong for Reid. Stuff could be replaced; he couldn't. When he reached out for her, she took his good hand, dropping down beside him, grateful that, although his breathing was labored, it was more regular now. The light from the flames created moving shadows across his precious face, highlighting multiple scratches, but he was alive. They both were. Taking a fortifying breath, she sent him a shaky smile.

She'd have plenty of time to break down later.

CHAPTER FIFTEEN

Hours later Reid and Heidi still sat in the damp grass, watching the faint embers glowing in the partially collapsed house. The firefighters were finishing up, having stopped the blaze from spreading beyond the house and into the forest, but not being able to salvage the structure. The scent of damp wood and thick humidity hung in the air. Reid held on to Heidi's hand like he was determined never to let go, which in all actuality was exactly what he intended.

What a nightmare. He still couldn't believe Heidi had shown up. As much as he'd tried to flee the flames, the smoke had disabled him and he thought he was lost. Until one determined woman took matters into her own hands. Not giving up, she'd yelled at him to get moving and, wisely, he listened.

His family had shown up. His grandmother had aged visibly when she took her first look at Reid. His parents had joined her, eyes wide with shock. Logan took over, asking questions, barking orders and basically being the capable older brother. Reid still couldn't talk, which was good, because he didn't know what to say. He'd scared everyone tonight and deserved their anger.

Especially Heidi's. After all was said and done, she might dump him, which was well within her rights to do.

He sneaked a glance in her direction, but her defeated gaze was glued to the remains of the house. He hated to look at the burned-out shell, the awful reminder of his failure, but he forced himself to stare at it. His heart sank at the sight. Would she ever forgive him for not saving her dream home?

The fire trucks finally drove away and a soft silence fell over them. A few neighbors waved goodbye, his family left, after first checking again that he was all right. He assured them he was, and they drove away, leaving him alone with Heidi.

It was now or never to discover what was going on in her mind.

Reid took a sip from a water bottle. Cleared his throat, happy that the burning sensation had subsided.

"What were you doing here?" he asked, his voice croaking.

She shot him a concerned glance. "I could ask you the same question."

He coughed and she took pity on him.

"Your grandmother called," she explained. "She was worried about you after the disagreement with your father."

He grimaced. "*Disagreement* is mild, but yeah, we had words."

"After hearing the news, I had to find you. I didn't want you off doing something foolish like that night years ago."

She hadn't forgotten anything, and yet she'd still come to his rescue. But tonight had been different.

"You mean like leaving town?"

Her head jerked toward him. "Was that the plan?"

Time to be honest. "At first. But it was an impulsive reaction."

"Like you never give in to your impetuous nature," she chided, her tone dry.

He shrugged, embarrassed as he talked it through. "I thought it would be best for everyone if I just took off."

"Not everyone," she said, her voice quiet.

"You're right. And yes, I get that now." He took her hand in his. Rubbed his thumb over her soft palm. How right it felt, sitting with her. There was nowhere else he'd rather be—

cold, wet and glad to be alive. "As I was driving through town, I decided to check out the house before I left. Phil had finished up a job and I wanted to make sure he did it correctly." He stared at the ravaged shell. "For all the good it did."

"What were you thinking running into the fire?"

"It wasn't out of control when I got here. I thought I could put it out. Save it—" his gaze held hers "—for you."

"Oh, Reid." She reached up and gently stroked his cheek.

"I know how much this place means to you."

"Houses can be rebuilt," she said, but he didn't miss the sheen of tears reflected in her eyes.

He grabbed her other hand and held them both tightly in his. "I promise I'll build a new home for you."

"You don't have to."

"I want to." He squeezed her hands as if to make his point. "This time it'll be a promise I keep."

She slipped one hand from his hold and laid it against his chest. "I understand why you weren't at the community center."

"But what if I hadn't stopped by the house? What if I'd just left?" He still couldn't believe he'd nearly walked away from Heidi. "I won't do that to you. Ever. I promise."

She glanced at him. "I believe you. I've always believed in you."

His heart swelled. He could look to all the times they'd shared together, as kids and now as adults, and hear the truth in her words.

"When I saw the flames, I was at a crossroads," he continued. "I could either drive away or save the house." He rested his forehead against hers. "It was easy. I chose you."

A sniffle was her only response.

"We can make this work," he vowed. "But only if you want to."

She shifted, making space between them. "What about the family business? It's been such an integral part of your life."

She didn't say, *more than me*, but he heard the silent accusation nonetheless.

"You are everything to me, Heidi. It took us both a ridiculously long time to figure that out. While I wouldn't trade our friendship for anything in the world, I love you with all my heart." He cupped her face in his hands and gently brushed his lips over hers. He heard her sigh and deepened the kiss. When he finally broke away, he saw the moonlight shimmering in her eyes. "All I want is you." His voice caught. "If you'll have me."

A SOB ESCAPED Heidi's throat.

It was all too much—the fire, worrying over Reid and now, hearing his commitment. This was exactly what she'd wanted, so why was she crying?

"Heidi? You're scaring me."

She swallowed her tears and brushed the moisture from her cheeks. "Sorry. This night…it's been a lot."

He dipped his head so he could catch her gaze. "So, you aren't horrified that I love you?"

She choked out a laugh. "Is that what that declaration was?"

"Yes."

"Then you should know I love you too." She tilted her head as the truth sank in. "I think I always have."

Relief washed over Reid's face. "Funny how we nearly let something like friendship get in the way of being in love."

Her throat went tight at the intensity of the moment. "I was so afraid I'd ruined things between us once I realized I was falling for you. Once I accepted the truth, I was a goner." Her lips quirked up in the corners. "I mean, c'mon, who falls in love with their best friend?"

"Us, apparently."

Her heart soared. How this man got to her. He always had. "I suppose you were right. All the signs were there. We were too caught up in our own past to see a future together."

"I'm glad we finally came to our senses."

Reid managed a soft laugh and wrapped an arm around her, hugging her tight. She rested her head on his shoulder, more at home in his arms than any place she'd ever lived in her life. "This is home," she whispered.

"Not much of one." Regret laced his voice. "I wish I could have done more."

Her head popped up. "Are you kidding? You allowed me to talk my way into your remodel. Gave me hope that I would finally get the security I so desperately wanted." She looked him straight in the eye as she voiced the sentiment in her heart. "The house was a symbol of what I thought I needed. Turns out, my dream was really to experience true love. And you gave that to me."

His smile lit up his face. "Guess I did."

"The fire didn't destroy my dreams, Reid. You are more important to me than any four walls. Being in your arms is home for me."

He kissed her again, the stars shining down on them as they started a new chapter of their lives.

"If you don't mind taking me to Masterson House, we can use the bathrooms there to clean up, then maybe share a slice of Alveda's pie."

"She'd love that." Heidi bumped his shoulder with hers. "I'd love that too."

Despite all the turmoil of the night, Heidi had never been happier.

"You know," she said. "It looks like your grandmother got her way after all."

"True. For all her meddling, she was right about one thing."

"Just one?"

Reid chuckled. "She knew the right woman was out there for me. I just had to open my eyes."

As they strode hand in hand to her car, Reid said, "So, how about a new proposal? One that includes a new house where you can have lots of input—"

"Like there was ever any doubt."

"—and it'll be a joint project. Seems like we make a good team."

She leaned over to give him a quick kiss. "So, we'll be working together a lot more closely in the future?"

His captivating smile thrilled her to her toes. "Sounds like the deal of a lifetime."

THE MEMBERS OF the Golden Matchmakers Club sat in the formal living room at Masterson House, Gayle Ann presiding over the meeting.

Alveda fussed over the members, making sure they had hot coffee and a slice of her peach pie. The judge sat nearby, his gaze occasionally meeting hers with an intensity that made Gayle Ann self-conscious, an unusual reaction for her. Bunny Wright and Wanda Sue Harper sat on the couch, their heads together as they spoke in low tones. What were they up to?

It had been two weeks since the fire. Reid had recovered from the smoke inhalation. But then, why wouldn't he with Heidi taking such good care of him? The two never seemed happier and it was all Gayle Ann could do not to pat herself on the back for a job well done. She'd known deep inside that those two were meant to be together. It had taken the couple long enough to discover the truth for themselves, but it had been worth every minute to watch them fall in love.

The judge interrupted her happy thoughts.

"I heard through the grapevine that the fire inspector completed his report."

"The conclusion?"

"Spontaneous combustion from the stain and oily rags not being disposed of properly. Apparently, Phil didn't separate the materials enough when he was finished staining and the chemicals reacted. It was an accident."

Gayle Ann shivered. "Thank goodness it wasn't any worse."

The judge raised one eyebrow. "The house was destroyed."

"Yes, but no one was hurt or worse, and the event brought Reid and Heidi together for good."

"There is that." The judge chuckled and sipped his coffee.

Footsteps echoed in the foyer. Bonnie and Arthur stopped at the entryway, viewing the guests.

"Sorry to interrupt," Bonnie said. "We wanted to let you know that we're leaving for the airport."

Gayle Ann smiled at her daughter-in-law. "You two have a good time."

Arthur came to her chair, bending over to brush a kiss over Gayle Ann's cheek. "This time, we won't come home until we've made some decisions," he promised.

They said their goodbyes, leaving the group alone again.

"How is Arthur doing after the dustup?" Bunny asked.

"Reid getting caught in that fire scared him," Gayle Ann replied.

Arthur had been inconsolable for days. It wasn't until Reid sat down with him for a frank discussion that Arthur finally broke down and saw the error of his ways.

"Nearly losing Reid caused him to take a good long look at their relationship. I'm pleased to say he finally has his priorities in place. His sons over the business."

"Who's holding down the fort while Arthur and Bonnie are gone?" Wanda Sue asked.

"Reid has agreed to oversee things on a limited basis. He still hasn't decided if he'll stay at Masterson Enterprises full-time. I can't say I blame him." Gayle Ann smiled. "But I know my grandson will figure it all out, especially with Heidi by his side."

"Heard he's got a side deal going on to develop that new vacation resort up the mountain."

Gayle Ann shot the judge a curious look. "You hear a lot of things."

He shrugged. "Someone has to keep their finger on the pulse of this town."

"Which is why you're a welcome addition to this group," she teased.

Again, he sent her a measured stare. What was going on with him?

"Reid is already drawing up plans for that special acre of property he bought," Alveda informed them. "It's a beautiful spot, nestled in the woods with a view of Golden Lake." A satisfied glint lit her eyes. "My girl Heidi has already laid out the house plans just as she wants them. She's picked out paint chips, tile, countertops, you name it. There's no way Reid will get a say."

"That's because she has good taste," Gayle Ann countered.

"More like the boy is crazy for her."

"That works too," Wanda Sue said with a chuckle.

"Perhaps once the house is finished," Bunny said, "there'll be another wedding on the heels of Logan and Serena's big day."

"I should certainly hope so after all the hard work we did." Gayle Ann grinned. "I've already picked out a dress for that ceremony."

Alveda rolled her eyes. "Rushing things?"

"No. Just congratulating myself on a match well done."

Alveda snorted.

"Not without your help," Gayle Ann conceded.

The judge coughed.

Gayle Ann reached over to pat his arm. "And yours too, Harry."

He nodded with satisfaction.

The others in the group laughed.

"So, any further comments on our first successful matchup?" Gayle Ann asked the group as she steered them back to the task. "There should be no doubt going forward that we are quite capable of leading our young ones down the path to love."

"I'll be honest," Bunny said after finishing off her piece of pie. "I had my doubts. But you managed to pull it off."

"Quite effectively," Wanda Sue added.

"We discussed it," Bunny continued as Wanda Sue nodded. "We're in."

"Excellent." Gayle Ann couldn't have been more pleased. "So, ideas for a new couple who needs our unique services?"

Wanda Sue glanced at Bunny. When the other woman winked, Wanda Sue scooted to the end of her seat. "Let me tell you what's going on with my daughter, Faith."

* * * * *

For more romances set in charming Golden, Georgia, from Tara Randel and Harlequin Heartwarming, visit www.Harlequin.com today!